A Flutter in the Dovecote

A Hal Westwood Restoration Mystery

Summer 1660

by Jemima Norton

TUDOR GATE PRESS

LARGE PRINT EDITION

ISBN 0-9740949-0-0

Large Print Edition

For ordering information contact:
www.tudorgatepress.com

This book is dedicated to

Brian

FOR HIS UNFAILING SUPPORT

CHARACTERS

Henry Westwood
   age 59   *Owner of Westwood Hall*

Katherine Westwood
    40   *His wife*

Margery Kingscott
    55   *His sister*

Hal Westwood
    20   *His nephew*

Liberty (Libby) Westwood
    18   *Hal's bride*

Edward (Ned) Westwood
    14   *Hal's step-brother*

Henrietta (Hetta) Westwood
    10   *Hal's step-sister*

Francis Westwood
    57   *Hal's father*

Jacqueline Westwood
    22   *Francis's third wife*

Elizabeth (Bess) Westwood
    16   *Hal's step-sister*

Justice (Justin) Danvers

             19   *Libby's brother*

Constable Dutton

             45   *local constable*

Robert Fenton

             57   *Henry Westwood's friend,*
                   local Justice of the Peace

Sheriff Hughes

             33   *Sheriff of Maucester*

Will Longstaffe

             35   *Henry Westwood's land agent*

Jonas	63	*the blind dovecote keeper*
Tobias	58	*manservant*
Kitty	25	*maidservant*
Marie	31	*Jacqueline's maidservant*
Peterkin	20	*groom*
Sam	13	*stable boy*
Goody Stokes	67	*local wise woman*

Glossary

BD   *Brewer's Dictionary of Phrase & Fable*

OED   *Oxford English Dictionary*

ague   any fit of shaking or shivering *OED 1589*

a shade   the visible, but impalpable, form of a dead person; a ghost or phantom   *OED 1616*

bearded that den   to oppose openly and resolutely; to thwart, affront (partly from the idea of taking a man by his beard   *Middle English   OED 1525*

black-dog   a depression of the spirit   *OED 1724*

bruited   to noise, report rumour, often in conjunction with abroad   *OED 1525*

crowner   coroner

cuirass   a piece of armour for the body, originally leather, reaching to the waist, consisting of a breast plate and a back plate

Devil's tools and his work typical ranting of a Puritan preacher

doublet a close-fitting body garment (with or without sleeves) worn by men from the 14th to 18th century
Middle English OED

dudgeon feeling of anger and resentment;ill humour
OED 1573

ell a measure of length; An English ell is 45 inches.
OED

flagon A large vessel containing a supply of drink for use at the table, especially with a handle and spout.
OED 1512

ingrate an ungrateful person
Middle English Old French   OED 1535

Good Morrow Good Morning

helpmeet a suitable helper; usually a husband or wife

home brewed ale made at home

horse coper a horse dealer

hoyden a rude or ill-bred girl *OED 1593*

Johnny-come-lately   a person who starts later, but suddenly becomes successful

like-minded   in or after the same manner

love locks   particular curls worn in the hair by courtiers

malignancy   a term applied between 1641–1660 by the supporters of Parliament and the Commonwealth to their adversaries

mayhap   perhaps, perchance

minx   a pert girl, a hussy; playfully applied
OED 1542

oil on troubled waters   to appease disturbance; in allusion to the effect of oil poured on water in agitation
BD

parole   word of honour; (especially military) given by prisoners of war that if liberated they will r e f r a i n from taking up arms again for a stated period.
OED 1616

pattern card of all virtue   an example; a model of particular excellence

petty sessions A court held by two or more Justices exercising jurisdiction in minor offences with a particular district.   *Late Middle English   OED*

Robin Goodfellow sportive or capricious elf or goblin believed to haunt English countryside *OED 1531*

sack a type of sherry wine   *OED 1599*

screens passage wooden screen plain or carved erected a few feet into the main hall of house to screen off from view entrances to kitchens, buttery, pantry etc.
Late Medieval

sen'night seven nights (a week)

sleeveless errand ending in, or leading to, nothing; having no adequate result or course;   *OED 1546*

stillroom a room for the distillation of cordials and herbal medicines

tester A canopy over a bed, supported on the posts of the bedstead, or suspended from the ceiling.
Late Middle English   OED

The Bench The judges or magistrates collectively, sitting in the seat of justice.   *OED 1589*

tisane a tea brewed from herbs   *French*

Turkey rug a carpet (or rug) made in or imported from Turkey, or of a style in imitation of it.
OED 1546

Well Met Hello

ENGLISH FEAST DAYS

Corpus Christi	*Mid- June*
May Day	*1st of May*
Lammas	*1st of August*

ENGLISH QUARTER DAYS

THE DAYS WHEN RENTS WERE DUE

Michaelmas

St Michael's Day
29th September

Christmastide

Christmas Day
25th December

Lady Day

Feast of the Annunciation
25th May

Mid- Summer Day

24th June

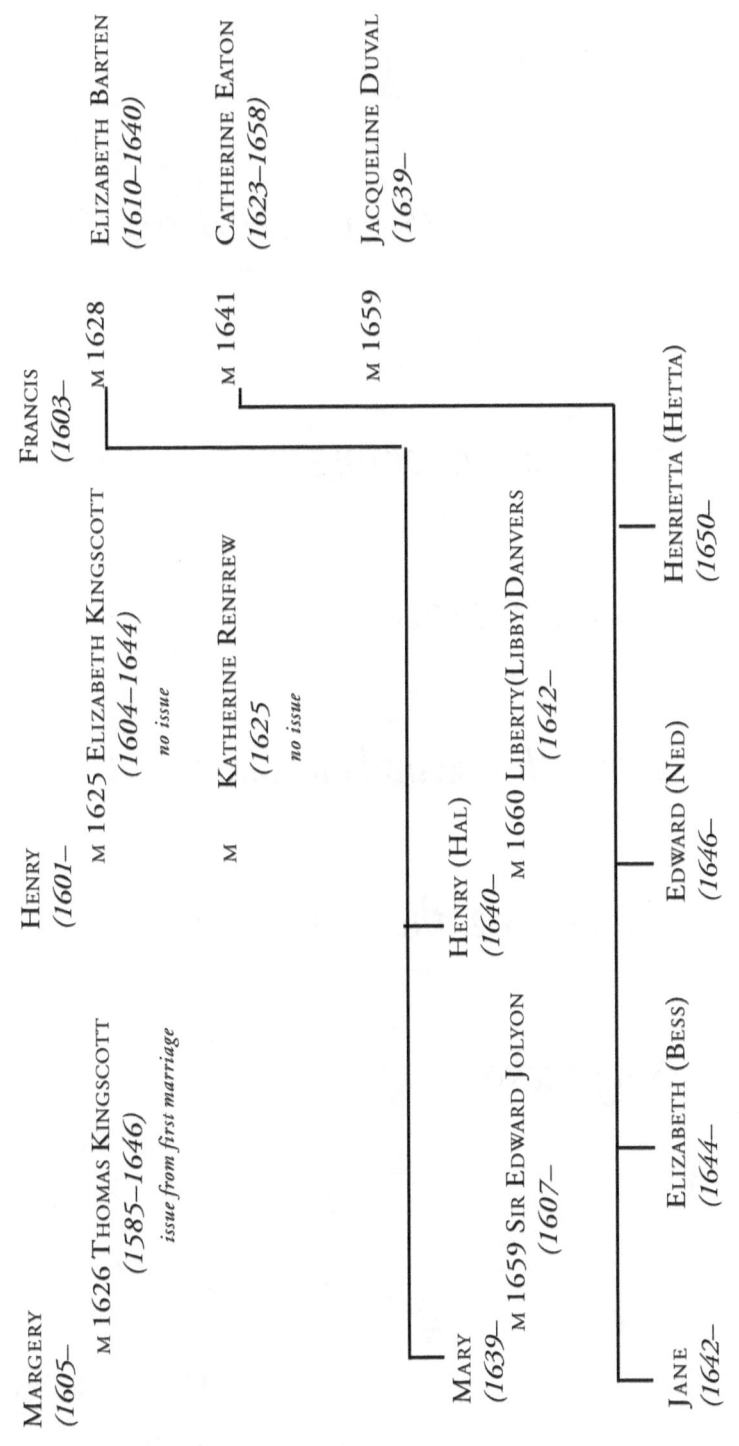

THE WESTWOOD FAMILY TREE
JUNE 1660

FRANCIS
(1603–

HENRY
(1601–

M 1625 ELIZABETH KINGSCOTT
(1604–1644)
no issue

M 1628 ELIZABETH BARTEN
(1610–1640)

M 1641 CATHERINE EATON
(1623–1658)

M 1659 JACQUELINE DUVAL
(1639–

KATHERINE RENFREW
(1625
no issue

M

MARGERY
(1605–

M 1626 THOMAS KINGSCOTT
(1585–1646)
issue from first marriage

HENRY (HAL)
(1640–
M 1660 LIBERTY (LIBBY) DANVERS
(1642–

HENRIETTA (HETTA)
(1650–

EDWARD (NED)
(1646–

ELIZABETH (BESS)
(1644–

MARY
(1639–
M 1659 SIR EDWARD JOLYON
(1607–

JANE
(1642–

"Summer is A-Coming In"

Summer is a coming in,

Loudly sing cuckoo,

Groweth seed and bloweth mead,

And springs the wood anew,

Sing cuckoo

READING ABBEY
1240

Chapter One

"Gone!" said Aunt Margery in a voice of doom. "Completely disappeared!"

"And the rings all ripped off too," remarked her sister-in-law, Aunt Kate.

Liberty allowed her gaze to travel from the faces of her husband's two aunts, who sat ranged opposite, to that of her husband, who uneasily occupied his uncle's chair at the head of the table.

They had been married barely ten days, but already she recognised the harassed expression of his dark handsome face. She knew by the way his mouth twisted into a faint smile of helplessness and his eyes assumed a haunted look that he dreaded the thought of having to take command of the situation.

"Gone?" he repeated blankly.

"Yes, Hal, stolen!" continued Aunt Margery. "And so very valuable a tapestry, too!"

"Presented, so your dear Uncle once informed me

Hal, to your great grandfather by good Queen Bess," said Aunt Kate.

Hal stirred uncomfortably in his seat. Newly arrived, in what was to be their home for the next few months, he felt unequal to dealing with the problem. His eyes swept to the other side of the table, as if seeking help. There sat his younger half-brother and sister. He finally fixed his eye upon fourteen-year-old Ned and asked, "What do you know of this matter?"

Ned looked up from his breakfast, his freckled face conveying all too clearly his opinion of his elder brother. "Me? Why do you ask me?" he demanded truculently.

"You were here," replied Hal, irked as he had been ever since his return to England, by Ned's endless antagonism. Hal's glance wavered uncertainly to the aunts again.

"You are sure in your mind, Ma'am, the tapestry was here before you left for my wedding?"

"It was here last Wednesday sen'night when we left for your wedding, Hal," replied Aunt Kate. "For I told Tobias to see it taken down and the dust beaten out of it against our return."

"Then you'd better ask Tobias the fate of it!" muttered Ned rudely, under his breath.

"He, however, says he knows nothing of it," continued Aunt Kate, her gentle eyes fixed reprovingly upon Ned, who had the grace to look shamefaced. "He says when he came to take it down, it was gone!" She waved her hand behind her toward the end of the hall, which faced Hal and stood reproaching him for its nakedness.

Hal's eyes flickered briefly from the bare wall to the face of his bride, then back to his aunt. "When exactly was this, Ma'am?"

"The very day we arrived home from your wedding, Hal!"

Hal frowned and directed a searching look at his brother and young sister. "Did neither of you notice it's going?" he asked.

Henrietta shook her flaxen head immediately, but Ned, waiting only to swallow a mouthful of bread, declared, with an air of belligerence:

"We did not eat our food in here. Kitty said she had trouble enough seeing to the setting up of all the extra chambers to wait upon children! We took our meals in the kitchen with the servants! Anyhow, we were busy about our own affairs! Just because we weren't wanted at your wedding doesn't mean we were lacking in things to do!"

Irritation showed once again on Hal's face; as if he

found his brother's aggression difficult to deal with.

"Was it a large tapestry, Ma'am?" Libby asked, hoping to keep the peace and addressing the Aunts in general.

"No, Child, not particularly large," replied Margery, her shrewd eyes assessing the girl as she spoke. "Perhaps some two ells square or even a little larger, but it had hung on that wall for as long as I can remember."

"Apart from when it was taken down to be beaten, or have the rings sewn back in," said Aunt Kate. "I remember Margery and I sat and sewed all the rings back into place one year—now just when was that, Margery?"

"It was the September of the Battle of Stow," replied her sister. "Don't you remember? The sound of the cannon fire was making you nervous, so we took it down and made all the rings safe."

"Yes, that's right. It was the summer after dear Anthony was killed." She sighed at the thought of her beloved brother. "And just after Tobias had put it back in place, dear Henry came in with the letters from France, announcing the birth of young Ned there."

"1646," said Hal quickly. "I remember it well, and Ned being born in our lodgings in Paris."

"Strange one so very English should have been born

abroad," mused Aunt Kate, glancing at the stocky boy. "But then he is so like your father, Hal, whereas you favour your dear mother."

Who, thought Libby, as her husband smiled at these recollections, must have been very beautiful. Not that Hal was in any way effeminate, no, not even beside Ned. Tall and slender he might well be, but there was strength in his shoulders and nothing but masculine grace in his every movement. Even his finely drawn features, although easily transferred to a woman's face, had a masculine cast and didn't truly need the moustache he so lovingly cultivated to convince an observer of his manhood.

"I must confess Ma'am, I am not entirely sure what should be done for the best either," Hal was saying slowly. "It strikes me as odd nothing else was taken, no silver or such. Would you like me to speak to the servants again—or would it not be better to wait upon my Uncle's return? Surely he cannot be long delayed now?"

"I most certainly hope not, Hal," replied Aunt Kate, with a troubled smile. "I cannot think what can be keeping him all this time in London when he hates the place so mightily; especially when he almost promised he'd return in time for your wedding." A worried frown crossed her plump, still pretty face. "I must admit I am growing a little uneasy in my mind about him, for there has been no letter either."

"I think I should write to my father in Whitehall and ask him to seek out my uncle," said Hal, as Margery gave her opinion that the post must have gone astray. "As you say, time is passing, although I am sure there is nothing to be concerned about," he added quickly, meeting Aunt Margery's eye.

"I'll also speak about the matter of the tapestry to the servants and try to get to the bottom of it. The complete disappearance of so valuable a tapestry is non-sense. Somebody must know something. I have no doubt, Ma'am, it has been damaged by a piece of care-lessness and hidden for fear of the consequences."

"None of them were here," announced Ned scorn-fully. "It was the feast of Corpus Christi and the fair was held again at Maucester. All went to that."

"What all? Every one?" asked Hal, frowning.

"All save old Jonas, but he sees nothing—being blind!" grinned Ned.

"Where were you and Hetta when there were no ser-vants to tend you?" asked Hal gently.

"We went to the fair too!" he replied, his tone once again truculent. "Why should we not have done so? If we are to be treated little better than servants, why shouldn't we behave as such?"

"I do agree Ned, it is regrettable that your father has not yet found time to engage another woman to tend your little sister," said Aunt Margery, fixing the young boy with her high-nosed stare.

"Indeed, Ma'am, or that Ned should feel so slighted at not receiving an invitation to my wedding," said Hal sharply, finally losing patience with his outspoken brother. "But my father is, as we all know, a very busy man, one who assists the King on matters of state far beyond our understanding. So it is perhaps not so very surprising that neither my sister's nursemaid nor Ned's tutor, who will hopefully knock some manners into his head, along with the Latin and Greek, has not yet arrived."

"I don't need a tutor!" snapped Ned. "Neither do I need to be taught Frenchified manners which will turn me into a copy of you!"

Hal reddened and hastily pressed his lips together. When he did speak, it was to address the table at large.

"I beg you will forgive me if I take my leave of you, Aunts," he said, exhibiting more of the manners Ned found so contemptible. "I have some letters to write and various errands to undertake for my father."

With these words he got up and, bowing politely, went swiftly from the hall, leaving his food half-eaten.

"You may take yourself off, too, Ned!" said Aunt Margery sharply as the door closed behind Hal. "I vow, I am ashamed to see your bad behaviour."

"Pretty words and simpering smiles don't amount to much!" muttered Ned sliding from his stool. "You females are ever taken in by a handsome face! You'll see! He'll do nothing to find the tapestry for all his promises!"

Kate sighed and exchanged a speaking look with Margery as he ran from the chamber. "I fear Francis is correct when he says Ned shows only too well that he has lacked the guiding hand of a father," she remarked, her apologetic glance including Libby.

"Yet it was sensible of Francis to send the younger children to us to be brought up in England," said Margery firmly. "Especially after Catherine's death, and when it meant they were closer to their maternal grandparents, too."

"And in view of the very precarious nature of Francis's existence at the time, indeed Henry thought it was a great pity he didn't send all the children," agreed Kate. "Well, if we are all finished, Hetta, you may say Grace."

The table broke up after Hetta's lisped prayer of

thanks and Libby took the child's offered hand, going with her out into the garden as everyone went about their elected tasks. Whilst the little girl chatted on busily, Libby listened with but half an ear and reflected upon her new life.

As the daughter of a lawyer who had but one cousin in another town, Libby and her brother Justin had not been used to so large a family as Hal had. She had found the acquisition of so many new relations rather daunting in prospect, but not so very bad in reality. There were the two aunts, Kate and Margery, both so different. Aunt Kate was the absent Uncle Henry's wife; a kind and motherly lady. Aunt Margery, the widow of more illustrious kinsfolk, was by contrast, very stern and sharp-tongued. Then, here at Westwood Hall, there were only the younger two of Hal's family, the boy Ned, who seemed to have a grudge against the world and the little girl Henrietta, commonly called Hetta, who was pretty and sweet-natured. It seemed this child was the only one who wanted her company.

Hal's other sisters—and there were three of them—were either married, about to be married or living in London with Hal's father, Francis and his third wife a French woman called Jacqueline. Mary, the eldest, was already married to an elderly knight and lived some miles distant in the neighbouring county. Elizabeth, whom they called Bess, was the next eldest and proving difficult to find a husband for, or so Libby gathered. She and the next sister, Jane, were the daughters of Francis Westwood's second wife, and not so beautiful as Mary was.

Libby had met Francis Westwood himself, on only one occasion, and she hadn't needed her astute father's comment to tell her this was not a man she could admire. Even if Francis hadn't pulled a face on meeting her and muttering something about young Hal buying his future at too heavy a price, she would have instinctively not trusted the loud rather overbearing man. He had filled her father's dusty chamber with his personality, making her feel so unattractive and insignificant. She could only be glad when she was told they were to make their home here at Westwood and not with his father in London.

It seemed strange that a few words said by a minister could have such a profound effect upon her, but it had. That short service had shattered the busy, yet calm and ordered existence of the dutiful daughter of a country lawyer. As she'd left the church, she'd cast the old life aside and been abruptly pitched into the household of her new husband's family.

They were very polite to her and kind, but it had been immediately plain that there was no place for her here. Aunt Kate had been the mistress of the house for many years and Aunt Margery, apart from the few years of her marriage to a widowed kinsman, had lived here all her life. Any help they needed in running this vast house would not be sought from her. That had been plain from the moment she had arrived and the subsequent days had only served to reinforce this truth.

She could make no complaint. The Westwoods, apart from Ned, were all equally polite and kindly firm. Liberty—how she hated that name and in turn hated her timidity, which prevented her from telling them she preferred to be called Libby. Liberty was not to trouble herself Aunt Kate had said with her kind smile; her business was to settle into married life. Aunt Margery had nodded her endorsement, adding the rider that if she truly lacked occupation, she should look to her husband's linen. To Aunt Margery's mind, men as a race needed constant maintenance if they were to show a respectable face to the world.

Libby had immediately gone through Hal's shirts and handkerchiefs, much to his dismay. Most were new, of the finest quality and needed none of her needlework skill, whilst the laundress viewed her interest with such extreme disfavour that she'd been forced to hastily retreat.

So with Hal's linen, indeed all his belongings, in apple pie order, she had to be content with a pile of sewing for the poor of the parish, thoughtfully given to her by Aunt Margery. She couldn't help but think, in spite of it, that there wasn't something really useful she could be doing.

She'd tried to interest herself, as Hal was, in the work going on to restore his father's house, for this was to be their future home. Rushley Manor, a few miles distant, was a casualty of the war, which had divided England until this Spring. Sold by Hal's father Francis Westwood to pay off fines imposed by the government of Oliver Cromwell, it had suffered a chequered career as a farmhouse and then finally been badly gutted by a fire.

Henry Westwood had purchased the ruin and his wedding present to the young couple was to make it habitable for them, but Hal said it would take many months to achieve. It was the progress of these works that absorbed most of his time and left her feeling so lost and alone. She wondered if she should not try again to conquer her fear of horses and become a competent rider to accompany him on his expeditions. Somehow she had to make a pattern of her empty days rather than just follow the little girl about in a forlorn manner. She couldn't help thinking it was very fortunate that this was not to be her permanent home.

"Liberty! Liberty! Ah, there you are, Child!" Aunt Margery, stout and much flushed by hurrying in the unaccustomed heat, appeared before them on the path to the formal garden, holding a small dog on the end of a leash. "Child, if you are not fully occupied, you might walk Kate's pug. Hetta, your Aunt awaits you. It is time you said your Primer, and then when she has done with you, bring your sampler straight to me. We have all those crooked stitches to unpick!"

Libby took the lead from her, anxious to oblige and once again feeling irked at being called Liberty.

In his youth, her father had been a confirmed Puritan and had found himself so much in accord with a group of like-minded brethren, that he left the land of his birth in their company and set sail for the dangers of the New World. There he met his future wife, the daughter of a Puritan of even more exacting standards, and they were soon married. The good, high-minded lady had borne him three children; all named by their grandfather, an elected minister. Liberty, which must come first, followed by Justice and finally Democracy. In giving birth to Democracy, his wife had died and the child, a weakling not fit for the rigours of this world, had soon followed.

Libby's father had been inconsolable. Even his father-in-law and his uncompromising faith had been of little help to him in his grief. He turned his back upon his religion and the New World alike and returned with his small son and daughter to the Old World and the devil. These excesses had been of a relatively short duration and at least they'd finally taught him moderation. He took up his abode in his native town and with experience tempered by sound common sense, settled down to amass a fortune in his chosen field of the law.

Libby, strolling along in the sunshine, with the little dog on the lead, smiled affectionately as she recollected again her father's delight in allying his daughter so well. She could see him now, in her mind's eye, as he'd called her into his chamber where he and Justin, who was on vacation from his university where he was also studying law, sat poring over legal documents. Her father had announced with such gratification, that he'd caught her as big a fish as he ever hoped to see. One such as would have made her maternal grandfather sit up in horror.

To Libby, who had first set eyes on him just over two weeks ago, Hal had been the answer to her prayers.

When her father had informed her of the match he'd made for her with the elder son of a returned Royalist, she'd had a fleeting vision of a dashing Cavalier, all love-locks and lace, one so different to the sober Puritans and Roundheads of her childhood. She'd had to take herself to task for such foolishness, such people only existed in her disordered imagination.

It had been with something akin to foreboding then that she'd met Hal, shortly before her marriage, only to find the substance more perfect than the dream. Inevitably, within a few moments of him bowing over her hand and directing his wistful smile at her, all good sense had flown out of the window. She had fallen headlong in love.

For him it had been different. She knew that, and accepted it with dull resignation. She wasn't a beauty. She'd long had to face the truth. Her mirror told her it daily and no amount of silk or costly lace would ever make her anything but a thin slop of a girl, with a pale face and long, lank hair which stubbornly refused to curl. She had, she frequently told herself, never expected him to love her, and no more he did.

Eunice, her father's second cousin, at whose home the wedding had taken place, had spent some time explaining it to her before the marriage, telling her exactly how she was to accept Hal's kindness and good manners with becoming grace. He too would be tutored on his duty and so she was to be sure to make herself agreeable to him and his family on all occasions. For although they might not be gently bred, Cousin Eunice had said, they too knew how to behave! In any event, she added by way of comfort, Libby could depend upon it, any pill as well gilded as she, would be swallowed, come what may.

She gave a laugh that was half a sob as she realised how much she missed her father and brother. She turned her thoughts resolutely to the task in hand and pulling the dog from a freshly-turned bed of heartsease, continued with the walk.

Chapter Two

Hal returned to Westwood Hall after completing his errand. He cantered through the park, his thoughts on other matters. As he drew close to the stable yard, a cloud of pigeons rose up in a flurry of grey wings and excited cooing. Hal slowed his horse to a walk, observing how the dovecote keeper, old blind Jonas's head came round to mark the coming and going of the household.

"Good morrow, Jonas!" he called, then paused and wondered if he should broach the matter of the feast of Corpus Christi. Then he decided he'd better first seek permission of Will Longstaffe, his uncle's steward.

"Good morrow, Master Hal," he replied promptly. "And a good day it truly be with this balmy breeze!"

"Yes, yes, indeed," said Hal blankly, for being so busy with his thoughts he'd barely noticed the weather.

"Set fair for a spell of fine weather we be, I reckon, young master," continued the old man, lifting his weather-beaten face to the sun and sniffing the air. "Just what's needed for the mowing!"

"Yes," said Hal again, rather at a loss, for he found he could not, as apparently all native-bred Englishmen could, drop into conversation about the weather and crops with any ease.

"Fair weather in July, means full bellies nigh, young master," quoted Jonas with some severity in his tone, then as Hal made no remark, he added, "And where is the Master, thy Uncle, Master Hal, tell me that?"

"I wish I knew, Jonas," said Hal frankly, unconsciously betraying all his nagging anxiety.

"Aye, well never you fret young master!" soothed the old man. "Henry Westwood ain't a man to let us down, not these sixty years past he ain't, no, not since me and him were young 'uns together back at the time the old Queen died! Nay, never you fret, young master, he'll soon be back to settle things!"

It was on the tip of Hal's tongue to tell him sharply he wasn't fretting, but not wanting to hurt the old man's feelings he merely contented himself with a curt: "I'm obliged to you, Jonas!" Hal rode on, leaving the old man to nod his grey head and tell the pigeons settling at his feet that the young man were coming along and would soon be one of them.

As Hal rode on past the massive dovecote and into the main stable yard, he saw the stalwart figure of Will Longstaffe, who stood surveying his domain. Four-square he stood, his hands on his hips, his strong legs planted well apart. The buff leather coat, which had seen service in the last battle of the war, strained across his broad shoulders, as the notes of his favourite tune *Summer is A-Coming In* fell from his lips.

Hal was conscious of a tightening in the pit of his stomach. He dreaded any encounter with the man, for Will had the uncanny knack of making him feel like a foolish schoolboy.

Unconsciously, he straightened his shoulders to be ready for the onslaught of thinly veiled insolence and half pitying, contemptuous solicitude. He found himself defenceless in the face of the agent's ceaseless hostility. It wasn't as overt as Ned's, but was most surely the source of it and had equal power to make him feel miserable.

"Peterkin, give Sam a hand with that new filly! What ails her by heaven?" called Will irritably as the stable lad struggled with a plunging horse.

Sam, a small, slightly-built stable lad clung grimly to the filly's bridle. "Why 'tis the doves, Master Longstaffe, sir!" he explained. "She's allus the same!"

"Nay, 'tis the fault of that fat cat of Mistress Kingscott!" averred Peterkin. He grabbed a handful of the animal's mane and by his superior weight brought the nervous filly back down to the cobbles with a flash of hooves. "It gets amongst them there pigeons and sets 'em all a flutter which makes Maytime here as nervous as a virgin!"

"Drat the creature!" cursed Will, running his eyes over the filly, which was trembling visibly. "Saddle her up, Sam, I'll cure her of that vice. There's only one way with a nervous horse or lass, ride 'em hard!"

Will turned, pretending he'd only just noticed Hal. "Oh, Master Hal, I didn't know you were there, what can I do for you?"

"My Aunts are in some concern over this matter of the missing tapestry. Would you know aught of its fate, Will?" asked Hal with more ease than he felt.

Will swung around fully, annoyance flickering in his deep set eyes and stood before Hal. "I? I?" he cried scornfully. "No, young master, I would not! That be house business. I deal with the land!"

"Yes, I am aware of that," said Hal quickly, catching the grin the stable lad exchanged with the head groom. "I had merely thought that you, as reputedly the best informed man locally, might have heard a whisper."

"I never attend to whispers, young master, and neither will you, if you've a grain o' sense in that pretty
head o' yourn!" he returned promptly. "I don't give my
time to a man who can't talk to me fair and square!
Whispers is for sneaks and cowards!"

"I meant only that in the course of your duties you
might have heard of some odd chance thing," said Hal
stiffly, unable to take issue with his words. "Something
which struck you as amiss, or not right, that's all!"

"Something's amiss that my Master is not come!"
retorted Will, looking him full in the face with such
barely concealed contempt, that Hal knew Will meant
all listening to know he considered it even more amiss
that he had to deal with the likes of Hal.

"It is indeed," agreed Hal coldly. "I have begun to
pursue enquires into it this very day!"

"Better that than fretting about some blamed old bit
o' cloth nobody gives a groat for, like an old tabby,"
replied Will, with a mixture of joviality and ingenu-
ousness, which made it impossible to accuse him of
insult.

"Yes," said Hal distantly. "However, once I've put
those measures in hand, I shall want to talk to any who
may have been involved in the loss of the tapestry. I
assume you can have no objection?"

"You can ask all the damned silly questions you want of the house folk! Just as long as your questions don't get caught up with the men cutting the hay!"

"I shall need to speak to Jonas in some detail." Hal ignored Will's comment, feeling as he had done in the agent's company ever since he had arrived, little more than a fool.

"Ask away!" grinned Will. "I don't reckon as how I'll be asking him to mow hay, not today, leastways! We ain't that short of men, no, nor never were, that we used blind men to mow. Mind, I don't know but that might be the custom in France. There ain't no telling what them Frenchies will do!"

Hal returned no reply to this sally but jumped down from his horse amidst the general laughter, and handed the bridle to the lad. He knew once again Will Longstaffe had worsted him before all the men. Will had reminded him—and them—Hal was next best thing to a Frenchman, being raised as he had in that country for many years.

He strode angrily across the yard and would have entered the house, but he saw Tobias lingering in conversation with the pretty laundry maid. With some relief he summoned the man to his side. Tobias ignored his instructions equally as much as Will, but he didn't openly insult him. Indeed, his manner was obliging in the extreme in anything which didn't involve effort on his part.

"Tobias," Hal said briskly as the manservant joined him, "I want to discuss this missing tapestry with you."

"I never saw the going of it, young master," he interrupted hurriedly, in a manner to disclaim all responsibility for it. "One day it were there a hanging—and the next it were gone!"

"That is hardly so," said Hal sharply. "As I understand the matter, it was last seen the day my aunts left Westwood Hall to attend my wedding."

"Aye, that'll be it, sir. Two days afore Corpus Christi it were," he agreed affably.

"And when my aunts were due back, some four days later, you finally noticed it was missing?" asked Hal, sarcastically.

"There weren't no call to go into the hall, young master! Not with all the other work there was to be done, and me near on my own in this great house. There's no one to help but that Alice, a great lummock she be, and young Molly and Kitty, who are the next best thing to useless. For Sue were down with the quinsies and Dorcas and Marion so busy with the great wash and the linen to do!"

"Not too busy, none of you, nor indeed, so sick, to go fairing in Maucester," said Hal impatiently, interrupting this catalogue of complaints, which was Tobias's usual method of extricating himself from any trouble.

"Why, Will Longstaffe himself gave us the holiday! He said the Master had sent word we were to go fairing on account of your wedding!" cried Tobias indignantly.

"Did it not strike you as strange, knowing of my uncle's views, that he should encourage you to attend a celebration of a Popish feast?" Hal suggested softly.

Tobias looked confounded. "Popish feast? It never ain't, young master! Why, when my grandfather were a lad, they always celebrated Corpus Christi. I mind him telling me of it."

"Your grandfather, Tobias, was most probably harking back to the days of his grandfather, before the split with Rome," said Hal. "However, never mind that now. Tell me instead, was anything else missing, or odd, or unusual about the hall that day?"

At this more straightforward question, Tobias's brow lightened. "Nothing, young master, as I take my oath! Me and Dorcas— aye, and Marion and Alice, too, when they were done—we scoured the house looking for that tapestry. Well, we all knows what store the Master do set by it. Why I don't know, for it ain't nothing but a bit of old cloth, when all's said and done. The colours is that faded now. But there weren't nothing unusual in the hall, nothing at all."

"Nothing? Think now, for even the smallest thing may be important."

Tobias shook his head obstinately. "There were nothing. Nothing at all, just that bit of sand."

"Sand?" asked Hal blankly.

"Aye. Least it felt like sand. In the cracks it were, between the flags. Just as if somebody been cleaning."

Hal frowned. "Is that so very unusual? Perhaps they had?"

"Aye, but I disremember anything being split. Leastways, not there full in front of where the tapestry hung," said Tobias. "Then there were the tag, of course."

"A tag?" asked Hal, wondering if the old man was being deliberately provoking.

"Aye, now where did I put it?" Tobias frowned and scratched at his greying locks before pulling a grimy leather pouch from his belt. He opened the drawstring and tipped the contents into the palm of his hand. "Ah, there it be!" he cried with satisfaction as he extracted a small, metal tag from some greasy coins and held it out to Hal with an air of triumph.

Hal inspected it thoughtfully. "It looks as if it comes

from a doublet lace. Whose is it? Do you know?"

"That be the point, I don't. Master ain't got nothing like it. Too fancy for us simple folk."

Hal turned the tag over in his hand and frowned. "Yes, it would certainly be from the clothes of a gentleman, I would think. Mayhap it fell from one of my uncle's guests and has lain for some time unnoticed?"

Tobias drew himself up. "The hall is swept regular," he announced, in offended tones. "Mistress won't have it any other way. Once a week it is swept clean and scoured by Alice. Mistress Margery watches her most times to see it done well. It were Alice what pointed out the tag of the doublet lace to me. It weren't there the previous week, she said."

"Oh, well, no doubt there is some logical explanation," said Hal peaceably. "Yes, thank you that will be all, Tobias. No, wait! I understand Jonas was the only person to remain here the day you all went to the fair?"

"Aye, he did, but he be purblind. He has been these past ten or more years, blinded by cannon flash in the war he were," returned Tobias.

"Nevertheless, if he were the only one here, he may be able to tell us something."

"I don't see how, but you'll find him by the dovecote, that being his work. All right for some, to spend their days sleeping in the sun. Supposed to watch out for cats and hawks he be. I dunno how many pigeons we lost last year, but Master allus excuses him!"

Hal nodded. He may not have been many weeks at Westwood but he could not fail to know of the enmity between Tobias and Jonas. He had no desire to hear about it all again, so he made good his escape.

In the hallway he hesitated, recollecting that it was hourly becoming imperative for his uncle to return. Instead of going to the yard, he turned aside and made his way to a small chamber not far from the stables. He had seen his uncle keep ledgers in this chamber, attend to his accounts, and when necessary, labour over his correspondence. The letter he had to write to his father was but the work of half-an-hour.

Hal had been lucky in his tutors. Many a well-read Royalist gentleman had been glad to tutor an eager boy during their years of exile in exchange for a pittance and a regular square meal. With the letter signed and sealed, Hal gave the letter to the groom with instructions to see it on its way to London immediately.

Hal considered his thoughts and realised his feelings of disappointment arose because they hadn't returned home and fulfilled the exile's dream.

Coming home hadn't been all he imagined. For him,

born as he was at the outbreak of the war, there had been no stored memories of life in England before the peace was shattered. All Hal's earliest memories were of various lodgings in the Low Countries or in France. His father's reminiscences were most often told over meagre winter fires, in less-than-perfect surroundings. His stories were coloured by the remembered warmth of an English sun, bright in a sky of cloudless blue, perfumed by the scent of fresh-mown hay, peopled by a folk happy and content with their lot. The reality of homecoming had been far from this ideal, yet not so far in essence that Hal couldn't feel the poignancy of something having been lost forever.

Rushley Manor, his father's home, had taken the full impact of the bitter civil war which had rent England asunder. Francis, unlike Henry, had continued to fight for the Royalist cause. He had taken no parole, but paid fines for his malignancy until the small estate was ruined and finally confiscated by Parliament.

It had been Henry's generosity which had saved the day. He had been able to repurchase the house and land and so regain possession of that which was rightfully theirs. But even his warmth of heart had been unable to find the money to restore the ruin.

Francis had been very bitter on his return from exile

in the Spring to see the blackened ruin which was all that was left of his home. For the better part of twenty years he had been fighting for King Charles I, or in exile with his son King Charles II. Was this any reward for a faithful servant of the Crown? Angry and disillusioned like many returning Royalists, Francis saw not a future of ease, but one of ceaseless toil just to return to the affluence he possessed at the outbreak of hostilities in 1642.

Many Royalists all over the country were in the same position. None had any money, least of all the King. Once the first shock was over, Francis's bitterness passed. Henry, the more level-headed brother, waited for the storm to blow itself out and then proposed a compromise. Eventually, after much discussion and rancorous dispute between the brothers, agreement had been reached.

Hal, who had been an unwilling witness to all this noisy wrangling, had been only too happy to make the sacrifice proposed. A few short weeks of negotiation, followed by the signing of a marriage contract and the payment of a large dowry improved their fortunes immensely. Rushley Manor would be reclaimed from decay and lived in again. The sound of human voices would banish the pigeons from the rafters and the crows from the chimney. The exile's dream would come true.

Hal was happy with this thought and clung to it in the confusion that surrounded him, but his anxiety with regard to his Uncle Henry's absence continued to grow. It was so very strange that his uncle had not attended the wedding he was so instrumental in bringing to fruition. The marriage of his nephew, Hal, to Liberty, the daughter of one of his wealthy acquaintances, was the cornerstone of Henry Westwood's plans for the future of his family.

To Hal, pre-occupied with the ordeal of meeting his bride and the actual wedding, the excuses tendered by Aunt Kate and Aunt Margery were acceptable enough. But in the days that followed, he had come to see how uncharacteristic it was of the uncle he had grown so close to.

It seemed that Uncle Henry had stayed away from the wedding so that Hal's father Francis might attend and that Francis had made important business the excuse to remain aloof from the match he didn't truly approve of but could think of no other way of mending their fortunes.

Hal had the uneasy conviction that his role was pre-ordained. He would forever stand between the warring brothers, trying to keep on good terms with both.

Yet none of this explained Henry Westwood's continued absence. He had made it clear that he greatly looked forward to Hal and his new bride's stay at Westwood after the wedding. He had also hinted that if they all suited each other, he, Henry would be happy to make Hal his heir and treat the young couple like the son and daughter-in-law he lacked.

Yet contrary to Hal's expectations, there had been no Uncle Henry to welcome them to Westwood and stranger still, no word of congratulation or explanation since. Hal consciously strove to conceal his disquiet, but was aware, even as he did so, that both aunts, in their separate ways were equally uneasy.

Chapter Three

Lost in thought with his head down, Hal would have passed by his bride without even acknowledging her, but she advanced toward him some way with her hand timidly outstretched.

"Liberty, I beg pardon!" he cried, in consternation as he suddenly recollected who she was. He belatedly remembered his father's excellent advice with regard to taking a wife. "I was so deep in my own thoughts, I fear that I did not notice you. In what way can I be of service to you?"

His manners, so polished and very meticulous, were quelling enough to rob her of coherent speech, so she shook her head dumbly. She could almost long for some of brother Ned's bluntness. At least with Ned one knew where one stood.

"Something is amiss?" he asked in concern, viewing her downcast head. "Has someone, something, disturbed you? Please don't hesitate to confide any problems you may have in me, after all I am your husband."

She raised cornflower-blue eyes to him doubtfully. "It's the little dog," she confessed.

"The little dog?" he repeated blankly, then saw the lead she still held in her hand, "Oh, Aunt Kate's horrid pug, Worsley?"

Libby nodded and thought how horrified her father would be to hear one of the late Lord Protector Oliver Cromwell's Major General's name applied to a pug dog.

"What of him?" he asked patiently.

Too patiently thought Libby, with a flash of anger, as if he were conversing with a feeble-minded child. This foolish behaviour of hers just would not do. The fact that her husband was a handsome young man should be irrelevant. She mustn't allow herself to become a tongue-tied simpleton each time they met. What if her head did spin every time he spoke, and her knees showed a tendency to weakness at the mere hint of a smile? She must make more effort. She was only too well aware she'd never impress him with her charm and beauty. It was now imperative she let him see she wasn't a complete fool too.

"I've lost him," she announced firmly. "I let him loose so that he might run about in the park, but now he won't come back to me when I call. I have chased him all the way to the house, but now he has disappeared into the ruined part of the west wing. I came this way hoping one of the stable lads might help me look for him in there." She met his smiling eyes and felt her knees begin to tremble. "It looks so very dark and frightening in that part of the house!"

His lips curved into a smile, which made her heart miss a beat. "Does it? I must confess I've never set foot in the west wing. That's the part which took all the damage during the war. My uncle held out for the King for three days, you know, hoping that Prince Rupert might come to his aid. He was forced to surrender when they brought up the cannon. I imagine we can think ourselves lucky that we didn't take more damage."

"Yes, I heard all about it. Your Aunt told me when she took me on a tour of the house the day after we arrived," replied Libby woodenly, glancing away.

He saw her face and hastened to amend his error. "Once again I must beg your pardon. I had forgotten our families took different sides in the conflict. How very clumsy of me to even mention it. However we must put all that behind us now. It is past, and is best forgotten by us and all our countrymen. Our marriage is a symbol of the healing of that breach. We should look forward to the future, don't you agree?"

Libby cast him a shrewd glance, still baffled by this veneer of polished manners, which seemed to hold all feeling at bay. "Don't you mean that my money has been allied to your breeding?" she said bluntly.

He opened his eyes wider, and he seemed to draw back from her a little; an action that made her feel instantly as ungracious as Ned himself. She all at once wished her words unsaid.

He ignored her cutting words and replied, with an air of courtesy which made her feel even more ill at ease, "Come, you have no need of a raw stable lad when I am by. I shall escort you to find the erring Worsley; He cannot, in all honesty, have strayed far. We should see the exact state of the damaged wing for ourselves, for we will surely need your money to repair it someday."

This was said in his usual gentle manner, but she had the impression there was just the slightest edge to his tone. She blushed as though slapped and supressed a sigh, then realised that far from convincing him of her wit, he now probably thought her as a sullen ingrate with even less manners than beauty.

Side-by-side, they walked around the rambling house, skirting the garden until they came to the west wing. Unused since the day the besieging Roundheads sent a hail of shells through the roof and ended the determination of his Uncle to hold out for the King. Hal knew that his uncle had lacked the money since, what with the many fines imposed by the Protectorate, trusting to a reversal in his fortunes to rebuild, but as he paused to look up at the crumbling brick and slipping slates he thought they had probably waited too long.

"He went in through there." Libby pointed to a broken windowpane and loose shutter on the far side.

"No doubt he smelt rats," said Hal as he leaned in and called the dog cheerfully. "I always thought Worsley had a miserable existence, tied about with bows of ribbon, washed, brushed and generally petted. Who'd have thought underneath all the bows, there was a real dog, longing to be free? Plainly you freed him, Liberty." He broke off laughing as the aptness of his remark struck him. "Why, one could say you gave him Liberty. Will you do the same for the rest of us? Will you free us all from penury?"

She turned away from his bright, laughing countenance; her heart wrung with love of him, her head filled with doubt. Never make the fatal mistake of falling in love with your husband, her Cousin Eunice had advised. Libby, with no closer female kin, had listened, convinced of her wisdom. A temperate affection was all that was desirable, her cousin had claimed, adding the rider that men hate clinging wives. It seemed that the quickest way to send a young husband into another's arms was to be forever hanging on his sleeve.

"I am more usually called Libby," she replied gruffly. She was determined that her hated name, at least, would no longer fall from his lips.

"Libby? I like that! It's pretty and it suits you much better than Liberty," he added, once again recollecting his father's advice.

Francis Westwood had, after all, made several marriages, not to mention countless other, less regular unions. He was most surely an expert on the feminine mind. 'A few sweet words, Hal, gentle and pleasant manners at all times and attention to your duty as a husband, and you'll have her eating out of your hand in no time at all!' his father said, and Hal had been rigorous in following his advice to the letter, and yet something was lacking. What, he wasn't sure. In fact, that exactly summed up the whole situation since his return to England.

He listened intently for the slightest sound of the dog. "Well, he plainly isn't coming and I rather think we'd find that entrance too cramped for comfort, don't you? Shall we look for a door?" he suggested.

"Won't all the doors be locked? Your Aunt told me they were kept so," replied Libby doubtfully.

"I rather think my Aunt is being optimistic," he replied, turning to look along the building.

"Plainly everything has been allowed to go to rack and ruin. I doubt any door would hold out against a determined assault."

"Couldn't you call the dog again?" she suggested unhappily. She followed him reluctantly as he began to walk along to the door. "He might come to you." She had suddenly decided, having glimpsed again the darkness and general air of rank decay and neglect within, she'd sooner do almost anything than enter.

"Come to me? Why, he knows me rather less than he knows you." he laughed over his shoulder. "Come now, you could hardly expect a dog to know that I am family!" He halted before the door that was nearly grown over with ivy and tugged at the rusted handle. It refused stubbornly to turn and he looked most disappointed when it held out against his strength.

"The lock still holds then?" said Libby, joining him, relief in her voice.

"Not for much longer," he grunted, putting his broad shoulder to the door. To her dismay the door showed signs of movement, and suddenly he dropped to his knees, pulling back the ivy with impatient movements. "I thought so," he cried, in a satisfied manner, "Look, the wood is quite rotten here." He broke off pieces with his bare hands and then stood up to aim a few kicks at the remainder. "Yes, I'm sure I can make the hole big enough to get in. Yes. There now, we can crawl in through that quite easily."

"Crawl?" cried Libby, in accents of horror. "But I'd get covered in dirt!"

He glanced up at her from where he was busily clearing away the last of the decayed wood and ivy, his eyes alight with laughter again. "My, how prim that sounds. Surely that is Liberty talking—or is it that Libby is equally craven?"

She stared at him, amazed to see that his icy indifference could melt, and partly indignant at the suggestion. "I am no coward what ever I am called," she cried, "At least," she hesitated and then added, "will you go first please in case—in case there are any spiders?"

He chuckled at that, clearing away the last piece of wood, and ducked down to scramble through the opening. "Come on then," he called, "I am standing on spider duty!"

Libby wished she'd held her tongue and not given him so useful a weapon for teasing. With one last despairing look at her clean gown, she got down on her hands and knees and followed her husband through the broken door.

She emerged into a long, dim passage, which ran away to both the left and right, the floor covered in thick dust. Quickly she scrambled to her feet, a remaining sliver of wood neatly removed her starched cap from her head, revealing her dark hair caught back from her thin face with unwonted severity.

"Oh, my cap!" she cried in dismay.

Hal stopped brushing the dust from his breeches to pick it up and made a face at the soiled state of it. "I don't think you can possibly wear it in that state. Indeed, I don't know why you should want to wear such an ugly thing, anyway."

"All married women wear caps," she said, horrified to hear such heresy. She looked, with something akin to despair, from her dirty cap to her grubby hands and the ruined front of her gown.

"Not all married women," he corrected her. "It is no longer the fashion in France nor at Court. Smaller lace caps are worn by fashionable women now. My father's new wife, Jacqueline, wears beautiful lace caps no bigger than my hand which look most becoming." He glanced about him as he finished speaking, adding:

"Now, I wonder which way Worlsey went?"

Libby who had unconsciously bridled at this criticism, sniffed at the inferior ways of the French. She glanced doubtfully each way. "Perhaps we should try this way?" she suggested, indicating the right hand side that was faintly lighter because of the many holes in the roof.

Hal, however, was more interested in his surroundings as he peered through the gloom. The heavily shuttered windows let in nothing but chinks of light, but he could make out the badly stained panelling and where chunks of plaster had fallen from the ceiling.

"We should have thought to bring a lantern," he remarked.

"Yes," said Libby, shuddering and trying to stop her teeth from chattering from mingled nervousness and excitement. "Oh, look! Aren't those paw marks in the dust?"

"So they are, clever girl!" he agreed. He peered again and moving forward following them. "Going in this direction, too."

"It's even darker that way!" she protested. She glanced again hopefully toward the area lit by the clear blue sky, which now, as her eyes became more accustomed to the gloom, appeared quite light by comparison.

"Do you want to find your lost charge or not?" he asked, in a teasing tone.

"Why don't we just call?" she suggested again, nervously.

He cast her a glance of tolerant amusement and threw back his head to call lustily. The sound echoed eerily about the deserted gallery, but no little dog came panting to meet them.

Instead they heard a faint scrabbling of sharp claws against woodwork, and a distinct whine from the direction of the paw prints.

"There's no help for it," Hal said. "We must go this way! Come!"

Imperiously he held out his hand and Libby, after the barest hesitation, took it, drawing comfort from his firm, warm clasp. They walked forward with some difficulty over the floor, which was rotten in places, trying to place their feet carefully in the increasingly dim light. The floor was strewn with both decayed plaster and the leaves of countless summers.

"I think I can hear him whining again. He must be trapped," said Hal, who had been listening intently. "It's as well you saw him go in here or—"

He broke off as Libby gave a shriek of pure terror.

"What is it, what is it?"

Without thinking he caught her to him, holding her close, feeling her whole body shudder with revulsion as she frantically ran her hands over her face, crying: "Spiders! Webs! Ugh, how horrible! I walked into a web! Get it off me! Please, get it off me!"

Swiftly he brushed his hands over her face, inhaling the unfamiliar perfume of her body and feeling for the first time a sudden surge of desire for her as his thumb brushed her lips and he remembered their sweet surrender.

"Hush, hush!" he soothed, still feeling how she trembled and clung to him. He was strangely moved by the trusting way her hands fell from her face as she allowed him to remove any last traces of the sticky web. "There now, it is all gone," he said, and the words came unsteadily as he gave her a quick hug. "Better now?"

"Thank you." For a few seconds she leaned against him, her eyes closed, shutting out the horror, whilst he, his eyes growing more accustomed to the darkness, dimly made out her face and her tumbled hair. "Thank you," she repeated, straightening up. "I'm sorry, so silly of me!"

"Not at all," he replied politely. "Shall we go back? I can easily send one of the stable lads to fetch Worlsey now we've located him."

"No." Feeling she must now have lost all credit with him, Libby was determined to go on, if only to prove she was not a complete coward. "No, it's not much further now, for I'm sure I, too, can hear his whine. My eyes are more used to the dark now."

"Come then, I'll go first," he said. Seeing she was reluctant to let go of his hand, he held the edge of the short doublet he wore out to her. "Hang on to that if you will, only don't tug too hard on the ribbons, please, they cost me three francs the ell."

In single file, with Libby hanging onto the edge of his doublet as if it were a lifeline, they proceeded along the gallery; the dog's whine getting all the louder as they went.

"He is plainly shut in. Obviously that is why he hasn't returned the way he came," said Hal.

"Yes," agreed Libby in a subdued tone, disliking the way their voices echoed uncannily against the walls.

"Over there I think," said Hal, as a loud whine came again. "I only hope he isn't locked in somehow. Hold hard, Worsley, rescue is at hand!"

He advanced on a door from which a frantic scrabbling sounded, followed by one or two high-pitched barks. He lifted the latch and stepped into a roofless room, which was flooded with light. The dog bounded out, overjoyed to see them and be released from his captivity.

"Well, I don't know how he got stuck here, unless the wind closed the door on him," said Hal glancing up through another room to the sky. His gaze travelled to the collection of broken and discarded furniture, most of which was piled in the centre of the room, shrouded in dustsheets and a cover of fallen leaves. It was impossible not to feel discouraged by the desolation of it.

"What a terrible mess," he commented, as Libby bent to pat and sooth the excited little dog. "I can't help feeling it will take a lot of money to do anything with this. It would be better surely to pull it down and start again." He paused again sniffing the air, wrinkling his nose distastefully. "No, it's not damp and I guess I know what brought Worsley here. It must be a fox, I've heard that they smell badly."

Libby held her hand to her nose as she, too, caught a whiff of the smell. "A fox, in here?" she asked anxiously.

Hal looked about him once again and seemed to come to a decision. "Most probably, the place is plainly in ruins. Either way, this is most definitely a task for a stable lad. Dogs, I will find, yes, but not foxes! Come, now we've found our wanderer, we need prove our valour no more. Let's go back, before I disgrace myself by spewing!"

"The smell is bad." Libby moved thankfully to the door and paused to view the dark gallery with some misgiving. The dog however, remained by an old oaken chest, still whining.

"Come, Worsley, come! Don't be tiresome. Worsley, here boy! Come sir, at once, d'ye hear!" called Hal. Surprised at the dog's intransigence, Hal turned back into the room, and Libby followed.

"You bad dog, sir! Come when you are bid!" Hal cried crossly. Then he frowned as the little dog tugged at a cloth hanging from the chest. "Hello, what's this? Why, that looks like a tapestry!" he cried and threw open the heavy lid of the chest with a triumphant air.

Libby got a flashing view of a crumpled and ominously stained tapestry swathed about something solid. Then the smell, increased ten-fold, making her gasp. Hal pulled back a fold of fabric and a man's hand, a curious pearly-green colour with blackened nails, fell out limply.

A scream rose in Libby's throat and died on her lips. Her head began to spin and the blood to drum madly in her ears. She heard Hal retching a long way off as the spinning sky whirled to meet her and she fell.

Chapter Four

The next thing she knew, she was looking up into clear blue sky, watching tiny fluffy clouds scud across it with a feeling of unreality. Then Hal appeared and dabbed ineffectually at her forehead with a very wet cloth, sprinkling water all over her face.

Abruptly she sat up and saw with surprise they were sitting on the long grass outside. She covered her face with her hands as it all came back to her. "I saw a hand! It was horrible! Oh, Hal, was it a body?"

Hal wiped his mouth with the back of his hand and sank to the grass beside her. He was looking curiously shamefaced she noticed and tears glistened in his dark eyes. "Aye. It was a body! The body of my uncle!"

"Your uncle? Your uncle! But how?" Horror filled her voice again and she felt herself tremble as she stared at him, unable in her bemused state to take it all in.

Hal still looked green and she could see he was shaking too. "Stabbed!" he said hoarsely. "Murdered!"

"Oh, Hal, I'm sorry!" she whispered. Her hand slid down his sleeve to clasp his fingers in compassion and she was forced to resist the urge to stroke his dark head.

He dropped his head to his hands. "To find him like that, rolled up in the damned tapestry!" He shook his head and managed a grimace of a smile. "I still don't feel that I knew him that well. In truth I had grown up holding him in dislike, for you'll know he and my father had been at daggers drawn for years. But he has been most kind to me since our return. To find him like that! Dead!" He stopped and rested his curly head on his forearms. "Truth to tell, I don't know what to do for the best."

Libby quickly gave herself a mental shake and forced her numbed brain to think clearly "We should tell somebody," she said uncertainly.

Hal nodded. "Yes, the local Justice of the Peace, I suppose, or mayhap the Sheriff. Now I think of it, I am sure my uncle is a Justice, was a Justice, but there must be others."

He frowned suddenly. "That isn't the problem—I was thinking more of my Aunts!"

"Oh!" Libby couldn't stop a groan of dismay as she understood the full extent of the problem. His Aunts would, of course, be sent into a frenzy of grief by this news, and surely the clamour they'd send up would be dreadful even to contemplate. For a few seconds she knew a craven desire to suggest they walked away leaving the corpse to slowly rot in silence.

"We must plan this out," said Hal, in firmer accents, showing plainly that the first shock was now over. "Peterkin must be sent for a Justice. Will Longstaffe will know of the nearest. And I shall dispatch Tom, my groom, immediately to London to inform my father of this. He must come here now!"

"I'll go and tell Aunt Margery and ask her advice about how we break the news to Aunt Kate," said Libby, with more resolution than she felt.

"Will you do that, Libby?" he asked, thankfully.

She nodded firmly, her spirits lifting to see respect dawning for her in his eyes. "Shall I go at once?"

"No, give me a few moments longer." He paused, his long tapering fingers pressed to his forehead. "The body must be left where it is, I think, until seen by the Justice." He glanced to her. "Come with me now, I think I'd better first write two letters before we raise the alarm. Better surely to explain the circumstances by letter, than to entrust such news to a servant, who will have it all over the countryside in an hour. A short delay cannot affect my poor uncle now!"

He got to his feet, extending his hand to help her. Her legs were still a little shaky, but the desire to assist him, to be his helpmeet, was stronger. Holding hands for mutual support they made their way back to the house.

❧

Ned frowned at the sight of his brother and his new wife approaching the house with an air of secrecy about them. Naturally, they'd failed to notice him up here in all the greenery. He was an expert now in concealing himself; a talent he'd come to perfect these last weeks in preparation for the arrival of his tutor.

He watched them disappear, kicking one heel viciously against the bark of the tree, thinking fretfully of the recent changes which had come upon him and how much he disliked them. He wasn't disloyal. He'd been as much for the King as anyone, but the triumphant return of King Charles II from the Low Countries had had such a profound effect on him.

Since being sent to England as a small child, he'd made his home here at Westwood. He had divided his time between his grandfather and his Uncle Henry, until the death of his grandfather last year, and since then he'd been solely in his uncle's care. Both men had been indulgent of one who they saw as little better than an orphan. Ned had soon learnt how to bring each man and old Parson Bowyer, who'd given him his lessons, round his grubby fingers. One way and another, he'd coaxed and wheedled and so managed to learn very little at all. He had been quite pleased with himself until the arrival of his father. That critical gentleman had taken one look at him, listened to his stumbling attempts at his books, and announced him an ignorant clod who'd been allowed to run wild. He compared him very unfavourably with his elder brother.

Moodily, Ned picked off pieces of broken bark and allowed them to drift slowly earthwards on the light breeze. Hal had always been something of a trial to him. His father's infrequent letters home had always been full of Hal, and even then Ned had been jealous of the special regard his father had for the son he kept close to his side.

He had been prepared for his father to think Hal was perfect, but to see his uncle, who he'd come to feel was especially his own after his grandfather's death, fall under the sway of Hal's charm had been the final straw. It wasn't that he was jealous of the inheritance, for he'd never truly expected to inherit.

Hal was the elder, and it stood to reason he would inherit, but there had always had been the chance Ned might have. Hal could have fallen to one of the diseases which seemed to abound in foreign parts during those uncertain days of exile, or more likely that he be cut out of his uncle's will as his father had been by quarrelling bitterly with his brother, but now even that faint hope was extinguished forever.

Hal had returned in company with his father, tall, elegant and eager only to do his duty. Even when the inevitable quarrel had come between the brothers, Hal had stood aside from it, and remained behind when his father had returned to the capital. Why, he'd even been prepared to marry his uncle's choice, the daughter of a lawyer from the nearby town. Try as he did, Ned couldn't find that it was done with any ulterior motive, he just seemed to be a naturally good and obliging young man, as everybody said.

Ned's simmering resentment, brought to the boil by the foolish adulation lavished on his handsome brother, spilled over into hatred each time he thought of his father's scathing contempt of his younger son.

As neither Hal nor his bride reappeared, Ned's curiosity got the better of him. He swung down from the tree with cat-like ease and sped light-footed to the door, entering and slipping unseen into the shadows. Silently, he moved closer and could just make out the scratch of

a quill pen on paper. Hal's voice, well modulated and
so unpleasant to his ears, came from the room to the
left of the door, where Ned used to take the few lessons that had been taught him.

He straightened up from the keyhole and pushed
open the door sharply, the sudden movement arresting
Hal in mid-sentence, and startling him so that a blot
of ink dropped to the sheet before him.

"Bother you, Ned!" he said sharply, pouring sand over
it with a hand which still wasn't quite steady.

Ned, who'd secretly hoped to find them engaged in
courtship, felt disappointed at the loss of such a weapon
for teasing. As he glanced from one to the other and
took in their dusty, untidy appearance, this initial disappointment was followed by astonishment.

"Where have you been to get so dirty? You look as if
you have been rolling about in the hay!" he cried mali-
ciously, hoping to discomfort them, for to his chagrin,
after his first expletive Hal had paid him no further
attention at all, returning to his letter, whilst Libby
stood at his side, reading through one letter already
written before carefully folding it for him.

"Do go away, Ned, and don't pester," said Hal, with
something less than his usual courtesy,

Libby blushed at the inference, then rested a hand

on his arm and whispered, "Hal, do you not think perhaps Ned could help us?"

Only further irritated by this evidence of an intimacy which eluded him, Ned, not giving his brother time to reply, snapped, "Help him? Nay, I'll not help such a Frenchified beau! Though your reputation for elegance must suffer, dear brother, if you should be seen in that condition! What have you been doing, exploring the attics with your bride?"

His angry glance strayed again to Libby's crimson cheek, as Hal paying him no heed beyond a slight compression of his lips, continued steadily writing. "And you look as if you've been weeping," he added, in a disparaging tone to her.

"I—both your brother and I have had a shock!" said Libby quickly, before he could make another uncomfortable remark.

Hal looked up suddenly. "Libby, say nothing further! We do not know if we can trust him to keep a still tongue in his head."

Ned bristled indignantly. "I'll engage to hold my tongue for longer and under greater duress than you! I've learnt to hold my tongue well! I'm no over-dressed poppin-jay, all lovelocks and laces! I'd not give a care for what torment was threatened. I'd be the one—"

"Neither pain nor torment is threatened upon your small person, my dunghill cock!" said Hal sharply, roused to anger by the insults. "Less bravado and more silence would be required of you, if you were to help!"

"I don't know that I want to help you, anyway," retorted Ned, satisfaction in his voice, at seeing his brother lose some of his self-possession.

Hal shrugged, selecting a piece of wax and held it over the flame Libby had kindled. Intent on their task, they watched as a few drops of the wax fell on each stiffly folded sheet sealing it against prying eyes. Neither paid any further attention to Ned, whose curiosity got the better of him and he was forced to reluctantly ask, "Why, what is amiss, anyway?"

Hal looked up from the letters, his glance measuring, hesitation still in his face, then he said slowly, "I suppose you'll hear of it soon enough. We've just found a dead body concealed in the ruins of the west wing. The body of Uncle Henry."

Ned's jaw dropped in disbelief. "Uncle Henry?," he stammered. "Where?"

"In the ruined part of the old west wing," said Hal. "He'd been concealed in an oak chest, wrapped up in that curst tapestry the Aunts were so concerned about."

"I—I—don't believe you!" The words were ripped

from Ned, who was suddenly very red in the face. "This, this is just your idea of—of a foolish jest!"

"I can assure you I'd never think of jesting over such a tragic subject!" said Hal quickly.

Libby saw how close Ned was to tears from shock. She took a step toward him and put out a sympathetic hand. "Indeed it is true, Ned," she began uncertainly.

"I don't believe you!" He shouted it this time, his tears spilling over and angering him all the more. "It's just more of your lies! I'll—I'll go and look myself!"

Hal leapt to his feet at this and in one bound was at the door barring his brother's exit.

"No, Ned, you can't! You've not thought!" he cried, his voice jerky with emotion.

"Let me go! Let me go! I shall see for myself! It's not true! I know it's not true! Let me pass!" Tears streamed down his face as he struck out blindly at his brother and tried to push past him to the door.

Hal caught him in his strong arms, accepting the blows without flinching. He spoke quietly, hugging him close to his chest, as if to shield him from the pain of the discovery. "You don't understand. I cannot let you see him, Ned. We found him by accident! The body has been there at least a sen'night. I saw it and it was so terrible it made me spew!"

Ned paused in his struggle and glared up at his brother angrily. Then as he understood, he cried defiantly: "Aye, well, mayhap the likes of you couldn't stomach it! But I am made of sterner stuff! You'll not find me spewing like a wench at an ugly sight!"

Hal released him abruptly, real fury in his face. "In that case, go and see," he snapped curtly. "Only don't touch anything, the authorities must see the body as it is!"

Libby now caught Ned's arm, holding him fast. "No, Hal, you can't let him go! Oh, I know he deserves it and worse, the horrid brat that he is. But you can't let him see that!" She turned to the boy urgently as he tried to shake her off, caught him by both shoulders and was unable to restrain from giving him a sharp shake. "Your uncle has been dead a long while!" As she thought of it again, her face paled and she had to take a deep breath to still her spinning head. "The body is quite decayed, Ned," she ended quietly.

Ned stiffened and drew back from her, but made no further attempt to leave the room. "How long has he been dead?" he asked from a suddenly dry mouth.

Hal picked up the letters from the table and shrugged his shoulders, still angry.

"I am not certain, a week, perhaps, if not longer. I

cannot dawdle here discussing this with you. There is much to be done. The Justice of the Peace must be sent for and then our first care must be for Aunt Kate. If you want help, Ned, then come with me to find Will Longstaffe. He'll know the name of the nearest magistrate now my uncle is dead."

"I know that. It's Mr Fenton who lives over in the great house at Longburrow. He was on the bench with my uncle and a friend of his," said Ned quickly.

"You are sure?" Hal's eyes gleamed. He was pleased he'd not have to seek the assistance of Will Longstaffe.

"Yes, I know Mr Fenton well. He was a friend of my grandfather's too. Longburrow isn't more than three miles from Greencote, my grandfather's house."

Hal nodded and taking up his pen again dipped it in the ink and subscribed the name in clear characters above the seal, observing as he did so, "It could be useful that he is known to us and that we won't have to deal with nameless officials."

"There's no point in doing that, Peterkin cannot read," Ned, irked by the ease with which Hal accomplished this task, had to find fault.

Hal shrugged his shoulders and glanced at Libby anxiously. He was well aware she had the most unpleasant task before her but shrank from the awfulness of it.

"Will you seek out Aunt Margery now?" he asked.

"I'll go at once whilst you see the letters taken," she replied promptly. "Then Hal, you and Ned might like to try to recapture Worsley, if you please?"

Libby was so intent on accomplishing the task before her that she hurried away and gave no thought to her appearance. Impatiently, she tucked away a stray lock of hair that had worked loose and was annoying her. It was thus she burst in on Aunt Margery in the full glory of untidiness.

Margery glanced up from the careful count she was making of used candles, her eyes widening in disbelief as she looked her nephew's bride over. Hal had been married without her approval. Her brother Henry's conviction it was the only way to mend Hal's fortunes had not pleased her sense of what was due to the family. She knew that many had made fortunes during the war, but she'd prophesied they'd live to rue the day they allowed young Hal to enter into a marriage with trade.

She gave the girl no time to explain her mission, but launched headlong into her favourite lecture.

"I vow, Liberty, I cannot attend to a word you are saying for the horror which fills me at the sight of you!

I make no mention of the fact that you have obviously lost sweet Worsley. Perhaps in your family the entrustment of a duty doesn't carry the same significance as it does in this one! No! Say nothing!" she interrupted Libby's stumbling apology. "I am aware you have been with us a matter of days only. You can hardly be expected to know all our ways immediately. We probably do show undue concern for Worsley's welfare, or so Henry claims, but I do know I would be failing in my duty to Hal if I didn't make some comment upon your appearance! My dear child,—no don't interrupt! Why is it this modern generation must ever be listening to the sound of its own voice? My dear, you can hardly have failed to notice what an extremely personable young man your husband is! Neither can I deny he has been made much of in the past, living as he has amongst a set of people who are more inclined to attach importance to physical beauty than is necessary. Indeed one must confess to feelings of relief that Hal has grown neither vain nor conceited by all this attention and admiration. Now, as his wife, you must come to understand this one thing, if you are not to sow such seeds of trouble as will lead to much misery for yourself and loss of respect for Hal! The good Lord, in his infinite mercy, seems to have given you a sound head on your shoulders to compensate for your own lack of beauty. I have no doubt this gift will last the longer. You must understand I don't say this to be unkind, child, you are well enough, as I dare say you know, but a beauty you are not. Therefore, your task is to keep your husband's affections from straying to the many beauties he will meet in the course of his life. In my opinion, attention to personal appearance is of paramount importance. A woman neat and well-dressed may never be called a beauty, but at least she can neither be an object of scorn or derision! I do not say—"

"Ma'am—your brother is dead!" cried Libby at last, desperate to call a halt to the endless flow.

"What is that? What did you say, child?" Margery stopped in mid-sentence, looking utterly amazed.

"Ma'am, your brother Henry is dead," said Libby slowly. She wished she'd not broken it so brutally as the colour was wiped from the good lady's usually high-coloured countenance.

"Hal found his body in a chest in the ruined part of the house. He's been killed."

"Killed? Henry!" she repeated blankly, as if the words had no real meaning. She sank to a stool behind her, her face now grey. "Henry? Dead? So that's why he sent no word! Are you certain of this, child? I knew Kate was anxious; indeed, so was I, but Henry dead? Are you sure?" She turned her stern face to Libby, looking almost pathetic in her desperation to understand what had gone on.

Tears stung Libby's eyes. "Yes! Yes, I saw him! It was horrible—horrible!" To her own amazement she flung herself at Aunt Margery's feet and clung to her plump knees, sobbing wildly.

"Poor child, poor child! Yes, weep, weep," said Margery in soothing tones totally unlike her usual brisk ones. She patted the girl's untidy hair absently, her eyes fixed unseeing. Libby relieved her over-charged nerves with a storm of tears, which were of short duration, for she quickly recollected the errand Hal had given her. Wiping her cheeks hastily and leaving fresh smears on them, she gazed up at Aunt Margery imploringly.

"Hal has written sending for the Justice of the Peace, a Mr Robin Fenton, and also sent a letter to London summoning his father," she sniffed, sobs still shaking her thin frame.

"Robert Fenton!" cried Margery taken aback. "Dear God, why must the Justice be called in?"

"Your brother met death in a violent manner, Ma'am," stammered Libby. "Hal says he'd been stabbed!"

Aunt Margery clasped her hands and closed her eyes briefly. "Oh dear God! Poor Henry!" she murmured.

"Poor Aunt Kate, too, ma'am," said Libby.

The older woman met her anxious eyes, her own round with despair as she said dully, "Kate! I'd not even thought beyond my own simple grief for my dear brother. Yes, we must break the news to Kate."

"I—I thought you'd know best how to do that, ma'am."

"Mmn? Oh, yes, my dear, most certainly I will tell her. It was thoughtful of you not just to go running to her and blurt it out. Oh, my poor sister. It will be a grievous blow to her!" Margery said in an aching voice.

Once again she closed her eyes as if unable to face what confronted her. She sat so for a few seconds then announced with resolution, "I'd best go and see the body for myself."

"No!" Libby surprised them both by her firmness. "No, ma'am, forgive me, but you can do no good by doing so! It is not a pretty sight. It made me faint clean away and Hal was ill. Your brother is dead. There can be no doubt of that. Our concern must now be with the living. At all costs we must prevent Aunt Kate from trying to go to her husband!" Then as the older woman looked at her doubtfully, she added with some vehemence: "Let her memory of him be as a living breathing man, not like mine!" Again she shuddered uncontrollably.

Aunt Margery looked again at the young woman who knelt at her side clasping her hands. For the first time she began to acknowledge that perhaps Henry had not been so very far out in his desire to unite their blood with a more common stock. This girl may not have been all they had once hoped for as a bride to the heir of Westwood, but she could not deny she was beginning to look as if she might be promising material with which to work.

Margery straightened her shoulders and announced in much more like her usual manner, "The Lord sends burdens only for the shoulders fit to bear them! Poor Kate, her shoulders must be very broad indeed. Well done, you are right, I am the only person to break the news to her. Come with me, if you will. I may have further need of your admirable common sense."

Chapter Five

Libby stood watching the girl as she laid the table, for so belated a dinner it was almost supper. She needed something to divert her thoughts from the scenes of the afternoon. She knew Aunt Kate had been devoted to her husband, but never guessed that so calm and cheerful a lady could touch such depths of despair. She had thought that the widow would as weep but never so hysterically, nor rend her garments, and run half - demented, intent on going to her husband. Libby had caught and detained her with a fleetness occasioned by panic. If Aunt Kate had accomplished her objective, it would have completed her despair. To Libby's mind, no one, and most surely not a devoted wife, should see Henry Westwood now.

She shuddered once again as she remembered how Aunt Kate had not resisted her, but slid to the floor in the gallery, rocking herself back and forth in her misery. It wasn't until Hal came and lifted her tenderly, and bore her away to her chamber that any relief came. Aunt Margery coaxed her into drinking a herbal draught and blessed oblivion came to blot out her pain.

"Liberty!"

Hal came quickly across the hall to where she stood, his pale face still streaked with dirt. "Libby, Mr Fenton, the Justice is come, so has the sheriff, and he has brought the constable from the village with him, too."

He beckoned and she followed him into the privacy of a small chamber off the screens passage. "In my ignorance of custom, I fear I may have offended both," he confessed, looking harassed.

"I had no knowledge that they come from different arms of the county law, but Aunt Margery has just been explaining that the sheriff, Isaac Hughes, is the Lord Lieutenant's man and Mr Fenton, as we know, was on the bench with my uncle. I must confess I still don't understand the nuances of it, but it would seem to add to this; we were on opposing sides in the war! This fellow, Hughes, being a Parliament man, so we can expect trouble from him. As we know, Mr Fenton was for Parliament, too, but he accepted my uncle's parole, and was his friend. More lately still, he and Hughes have been in dispute over the matter of some land. Whether this will work for us or against us, I have no idea."

He paused to scan her pale, fatigued face. "I am sorry I cannot spare you this interview. I tried to keep you from it, but they insist on you telling your own story, in case you saw something I missed."

Libby nodded. Aunt Margery had said she would probably be called to give evidence and that she must face the ordeal with fortitude. She followed him back across the hall and into the small parlour, her heart beating uncomfortably fast.

Hal bowed formally. "Gentlemen, this is my wife."

Libby could tell by the tone of his voice he hated the whole procedure. She allowed Hal to lead her to a chair with arms, set before a table spread with a bright Turkey rug. She sat down, her fingers anxiously smoothing the silk of her dark gown. Mentally, she thanked heaven she at least had found time to change from her soiled clothes, wash the worst dirt from her face and brush her hair into some semblance of order. On impulse she had taken a lace confection from her chest. It had been the gift of her brother Justin and she put it on instead of her usual cap. It was so very light and dainty as to make her head feel naked, she felt immodest and so found it difficult to raise her eyes to the men who sat opposite her.

"Mistress Westwood, I'm afraid we must trouble you

with a few questions." The elder of the two gentlemen had a pleasant voice and the tanned, open face of a countryman, with a good head of thick grey hair.

"My companion here, Sheriff Hughes, and I are sorry we must condemn you to yet another ordeal this day, but you look to me to be a strong, sensible young woman, who will bear up and answer truly our questions as we are all bidden by the law and the Lord!"

His smile, as she darted a swift glance, flickered to Hal. "I assure you we are used to making allowances for the fears of a young bridegroom."

His companion, a thin, younger man, with a spurious air of meekness, allowed a dour smile to flicker across his narrow lips at that, but Hal, taking his stand protectively behind Libby's chair, clenched his fist tightly.

"However, we must not forget this is a serious affair," said the Justice in sombre tones. "Aye, we pause to smile, but is not tragedy peering at us also, through the mask? A sorry business and one that for me entails grief, Henry Westwood was a good man and fine friend. I shall not find his like again." He shook his head, and sighed over the death of his friend. Then, sensing his companion's impatience, he became brisk: "Mistress Westwood, what can you tell us of this sorry affair?"

"I hardly know, sir!" she stammered. "Only that which my husband will have told you."

"No, Mistress, we'd like your account, if you please." The sheriff's precise voice cut across the still chamber.

Libby, surprised into meeting his eyes, blushed under his cold, steady scrutiny,

There was no kindness or encouragement in his gaze. She dropped her eyes to her tightly clenched hands on her lap. Her voice quivered slightly, but she spoke quickly, wanting to get the ordeal over with.

"I was asked to take the pug dog for a walk earlier. When I was returning to the house, the dog ran away and got into the ruined part of the house. I did not care to go in there, and the dog would not obey me and come out, so I went toward the stables, thinking one of the lads or a groom would assist me in looking for the dog. On the way I met my husband, and he came to help me search for the dog, for he knew his Aunt would be angered should the dog become lost." She paused glancing up appealingly at Hal, who nodded in encouragement. "However, the dog still would not come to our calls, so we had to go inside the ruined part to look for him. It took us a long time to find him. He'd been trapped in a completely ruined chamber, and when he still wouldn't go with us, Hal went to see what was attracting his attention."

She paused, her breath coming fast as she remembered, tears filling her eyes. "The dog was barking at a coffer, a carved oaken chest, and when Hal opened it I saw—I saw—"

"She saw the corpse and fainted. Now that is enough!" cried Hal roughly, his hand coming to rest on her thin shoulder and gripping it tightly in reassurance.

Libby covered her eyes with trembling hands, trying to shut out the picture the words had conjured. She seemed to smell again the sickening stench of decay that rose up with the lid of the coffer.

"You neglected to mention the hanging, Mistress," said Sheriff Hughes softly. Libby dropped her hands. Tears glistened in her eyes as she stared blankly at the man.

"I did not recognise it, sir. I had never seen it so it made no impression on me! Its disappearance predated my arrival at Westwood Hall."

"Of course, of course," murmured Mr Fenton sympathetically. "Not a very auspicious beginning to your married life, Mistress!"

Libby shook her head uncertain of what to reply. She was conscious only of Hal's hand still resting on her shoulder and drew strength from it.

"Tell me, Mistress Westwood, who is Mr Henry Westwood's heir?" asked the sheriff quietly.

"Why, I don't know, sir," she faltered. She glanced up to Hal doubtfully and noticed how his eyes widened in dismay. "I believe there was some talk of him naming my husband after our marriage, but it must have come to naught, sir, as he never attended the ceremony."

The sheriff picked up a sheet of paper he'd been writing on and directed his gimlet gaze at Hal. "Who then inherits Westwood, if you don't?"

Hal frowned. He already disliked the man and could see all too clearly where his questions were leading. "I fail to see what bearing this has on the issue," he replied coldly.

"Don't you, sir?" The sheriff's tone was insolent. His cold eyes flickered over the young man's face. "But then I forget, you are but recently come to England! Your uncle, sir, was murdered. Stabbed in the back and left to moulder in a coffer in a ruined part of this house. I don't know if that sort of thing is permitted elsewhere, but in England it is an unlawful act. It is my task to seek out the murderer and bring him to justice using whatever means necessary. No one shall hinder me in this task. I repeat, sir, who inherits, if you don't?"

Hal found he disliked the man's manner more and more. "In that case, sir, my father, Francis Westwood, as my uncle's younger brother must, unless specifically excluded, inherit."

"Your father? And he is where?"

"In London," said Hal shortly as the sheriff raised an eyebrow.

He turned over the page and read something. "London? But surely sir, by your own admission, you are but lately married. He did attend the ceremony?"

"No." Hal spoke reluctantly. He glanced to Mr Fenton, whose expression was wooden. "The ceremony, in fact, took place at the house of my wife's cousin. My father was detained in London by affairs of some importance."

Mr Fenton puffed his cheeks out in a sigh. "Unfortunately that's not what is being said, young Hal. The talk is that Francis disliked poor Henry so much that he refused to attend your wedding if he would be there."

"It wasn't like that at all, sir!" interrupted Hal. "True, as you and many others well know, they never have been, on the best of terms. I think it was more that the match was so very much of my uncle's making that my father felt he was not needed. And I know my father did have very important affairs to attend to!"

"What could be more important than a son's wedding?" asked the sheriff.

Hal hesitated. "I hardly know," he said uncomfortably. "Possibly—the King's business?"

"The King's business," repeated the sheriff looking as if he didn't believe a word.

"I am given to understand it is so," replied Hal flatly. "And who am I to disagree?" Hal's glance swept over the man daring him to say a word. "You see, my uncle indicated quite plainly, when we first returned from Holland that if I would remain here with him at Westwood Hall and do his bidding, he would make me his heir. My father and I agreed it was in my best interests to do so. It is possible he thought everything would go smoother if he stayed away!" His glance included the Justice. "You know he and my uncle couldn't be in each other's company above an hour, sir, without coming to blows!"

He broke off, suddenly realising that this entirely innocent phrase would have been better unsaid and the more he talked, the worse he made everything.

In the sudden silence a clock ticked, then Mr Fenton said quickly. "So your father, Hal, has been in London ever since he returned from abroad in May?"

"To the best of my knowledge," replied Hal. "Apart

from the one visit we have already discussed."

The sheriff consulted his notes. "Returning to the matter of your wedding, sir. Did you not think it strange that your uncle missed the wedding ceremony after all the trouble he went to in arranging the match?"

"Not at all," insisted Hal stubbornly.

Mr Fenton, who was clearly weary of the formality of the proceedings that were getting nowhere, decided to change the tone.

"Aye, now, Hal, you must admit that was odd. I know it was not only his intention, but also his dearest wish, to see you wed. He told me himself everything was going forward exactly as he wished and that he was looking forward to seeing you settled when we were last together at the Petty Sessions."

"Yes, sir, I'll freely admit I did find it strange when my aunts arrived at my wife's cousin's house alone," he paused to explain. "Perhaps you'll know, sir," he continued, speaking pointedly to Mr Fenton, "that I left Westwood a full week previously, at my uncle's behest. He said it was advisable I make the acquaintance of my future wife before the wedding date."

Once again his hand tightened slightly on Libby's shoulder, and she darted him a doubtful glance. "I had fully expected my uncle to be one of the wedding party;

he'd promised me as much, but as I say, my aunts came, escorted by my uncle's groom, bringing my uncle's apologies. It would seem he had been called away on a matter of some importance only the day before; that we were to proceed with the wedding as planned and that he hoped to join us, if not in time for the ceremony, then for the celebrations. In the event, he came to neither and was not here on our return."

"Called away?" questioned the sheriff.

"To London, so I believe," added Hal.

"Ah, to London also—no doubt to meet with your father?" suggested the man softly.

"No, indeed no! Nothing would have induced my uncle to seek out my father!" cried Hal quickly, and as the sheriff with another lift of his eyebrows, noted that also, he had to restrain himself from crying out in anger. Each word he said was seemingly taken amiss. He folded his lips together firmly, determined he'd give no more away but keep a strong guard on his tongue.

"You have no idea what this matter of importance was?" asked the sheriff, than as Hal shook his head curtly, he added: "Where is your uncle's widow?"

"Abed, sir, in dire distress," said Libby sharply, as Hal glanced enquiringly at her.

The man met her determined eyes and acknowledged

defeat. "Then it seems I must return another day to question her," he said simply, making a note of it. He paused glancing through them and then turned to his companion. "Mr Fenton, are you satisfied as to the cause of death?"

"Aye, that's plain for all to see!" he retorted. "We hardly need an inquest for that! Stabbed clear through the heart he was, a nasty blow, of some force, I'd say. It wouldn't be advisable to hold up the burial long either. I dare say you'll agree with me, Hughes, now you've seen the corpse?"

"Yes," he replied grimly. "No doubt it will be best for all concerned if you summon your nine good men as soon as possible, say tomorrow morning? Then the funeral can follow in the afternoon." He glanced to Hal. "Does that meet with your approval, sir?" Then, as Hal nodded curtly again, he added: "In that case, I'll take my leave of you for the present. I have much to do. You have no plans to leave the country, Mr Westwood?"

"Leave?" said Hal blankly.

The sheriff nodded, his face cold. "As long as you have no thoughts on returning to France, sir, or Holland."

"Those of us who have tasted the bitterness of exile, Mr Hughes, do not long for its return. I shall remain here at Westwood," said Hal coldly.

♣

"What an unpleasant man," said Libby. They were standing together in front of the house some minutes later to watch their visitors depart in different directions.

"Hughes? Yes, very unpleasant, but I expected little of a fellow like that anyway," replied Hal.

"He appears to expect foul play," she observed.

Hal chuckled. "Who wouldn't when confronted with a corpse stabbed through the heart?"

"No, I meant that he appears to suspect us." She stopped short. She regretted the words and their implication that they were united. To her relief he didn't take them amiss.

"I suppose if he has to discover the murderer, his thoughts must naturally turn our way. If this is the case, I tell you this, I am very relieved my uncle didn't have time to name me his heir!"

"Why?" She was astonished for she felt certain he would be bitterly disappointed.

"It would mean I had a reason for wanting him dead. It is bad enough that they suspect my father, but at least we can be easy on that score. He was at least a hundred miles away in London."

"You, too, were miles away," she said quickly.

"Was I?"

"Not a hundred miles, but fifteen. Don't you see? If the body of your Uncle Henry was found wrapped in the tapestry, that proves he was killed after you left for the wedding. It was still hanging on the wall the day that your aunts left to join us."

"Yes, that's true," he said. "I had not thought that through. Therefore, logically, the murder must have occurred on or about the day of our wedding. That is good! Should Sheriff Hughes decide I might have a motive for killing my uncle, I have the perfect excuse. I can plead I was exactly where I should have been. Abed with my bride!"

Libby felt the colour flooding her cheeks. "We cannot be sure exactly when your uncle was killed. And as you are not your uncle's heir there can be no need for Sheriff Hughes to ask you such a thing."

Hal chuckled at the sight of her face. "He'll think of it sooner or later. He's exactly the sort of impertinent fellow who would ask such a thing."

She smiled a little, but still looked embarrassed. "I know you are teasing me, Hal, and I beg you will not."

The mischief died from his face and he became serious as he saw he had distressed her primness. "I beg pardon; that was ill done of me! You are quite right to scold me. I shouldn't tease you, not when it has been so terrible a day. Dreadful in all but that I have discovered something of my wife's goodness. I thank the Lord for that mercy."

Libby, though she was thrilled by his words at the time, found much to think of later as she lay sleepless in bed. So her cousin had been correct. Her beauty, or lack of it, hadn't mattered one whit. It was the size of her dowry they had been interested in. For repairs for the estate; and the promise of future wealth in the form of the inheritance of Westwood Hall. An inheritance he had now lost, it would seem. She had no clear idea whether he was disappointed at that loss, but then she had no clear idea of what went on in his head anyway. He was, in that, as in everything else, as elusive as ever. His protectiveness had surprised and thrilled her, but she was frightened of showing too much dependency on him. She didn't want to send him from her by being a nuisance and hanging on his sleeve, but it had been so good to feel the warmth of his hand on her shoulder as she'd faced the questions put to her by the Justice and the Sheriff. She fell asleep wondering how she could strengthen the bonds between them.

Chapter Six

The inquest took place the next morning as Sheriff Hughes had requested. Hal and Libby were bidden to attend by the Coroner's officer.

A similar summons had come for Aunt Kate too; but Aunt Margery over-ruled it in her high-handed fashion. She sent the poor messenger about his business sharply, with a message for his master to the effect that her brother's widow was still too stricken with grief to attend. She also added a rider to the effect that she would attend in her stead, to answer any questions they might see fit to put to her.

Hal and Libby were both glad that Aunt Margery was to go with them. Hal was taken aback by the Pandora's box he seemed to have opened, and unsure of his ground in a country whose laws were unknown to him. He knew she'd allow no impertinent questions to pass her by and would back him in all he said pertaining to the family honour.

Libby, for her part, was just thankful for the presence of another female and an older person who could show her how to comport herself in such difficult circumstances. In this, Aunt Margery was superb. Garbed in mourning clothes, her haughty bearing and grandiose air quickly over-awed the small crowd gathered to witness the inquest.

The murder of a local personage of note was an exciting event in a small market town. Idlers were out in force and the only impudent braggart who did venture on a cat call was so scorched by the power of her gaze that he promptly retired to a nearby tavern to steady his shaking nerves with a mug of home brewed.

The Crowner himself was only a little less afraid of so formidable a lady. He was upheld more by consciousness of his office than any personal esteem.

It was as Hal predicted, in a whisper, to Libby as they entered the largest inn, the Fighting Cocks, where such courts were by custom held. The Crowner was soon apologising to Aunt Margery for causing her so much trouble and distress.

The Sheriff was impressive in the giving of his evidence. Mr Fenton spoke well, Hal was merely pleased to get the ordeal over with and Aunt Margery voiced her dissatisfaction with the proceedings and the state of the country in general. The outcome was obvious, as Mr Fenton had predicted: Mr Henry Westwood was unlawfully killed by persons unknown. Sheriff Hughes was called upon to find such persons and bring them to justice.

Libby felt she was fortunate in not being called by the Crowner supposing she had nothing to add to her husband's testimony. The session was then ended and they were allowed to go.

In the yard of the busy inn, Libby stood with the others whilst Hal went to hasten his groom with the horses. Aunt Margery talked with sublime indifference about the weather to Mr Fenton while Libby, uncomfortably aware of the nudges and pointings of the crowd, watched with dismay the approach of Sheriff Hughes.

"Mistress Westwood," he paused at her side, bowing politely, but said with a slight sneer, "I trust you didn't find the inquest too insupportable. Is your husband at hand?"

"He has gone to hurry his man with the horses."

"Of course." He nodded his understanding, glancing about the busy yard, full of the bustle attendant on such occasions. "Perhaps when he arrives, you'll be good enough to remind him I am still wishful to speak with his uncle's widow?"

Margery, who had overheard, interrupted with an air of majestic patronage, "My dear sister is still inconsolable with grief. She is in no case to be answering impertinent questions. Rest assured my good fellow, when she is recovered I shall personally summon you to Westwood."

The sheriff reddened as some bystanders sniggered. "I beg you won't send a servant on such a sleeveless errand, ma'am," he replied ironically. "For I shall be at Westwood for some time to come. With your permission, I am instructed by law to ask questions of others involved in this sorry affair." With these words he bowed stiffly and walked away.

"How such a fellow got so high a position I shudder to think," observed Margery. "The war has a great deal to answer for! In my father's day such a rascal wouldn't have been tolerated. Impertinent jackanapes!"

"He is generally considered to be a sound fellow," replied Mr Fenton mildly.

Libby was only glad to see the man leave. She found his presence unnerving and knew Hal had taken him in equal, if not so vocal, a dislike. The events of yesterday had left her feeling bewildered and anxious. She felt a deplorable desire to hold fast to Hal's arm as he escorted her across the courtyard to the waiting horses.

Hal, in spite of her cousin's warning as to the dire consequences of such behaviour, did not seem irked by it. When he noticed her, he merely patted her arm in a kindly, absent manner as he helped to the saddle.

He even appeared to accept the sheriff's message without comment, appearing as exhausted by the proceedings as they were.

❧

When they returned to Westwood Hall, Hal went to prepare Will Longstaffe and the outdoor servants for the coming inquisition. He was pleased when he got to the stables to find that although it was its usual hive of activity; it was also free of the steward's presence.

He warned Peterkin, the head groom, of the sheriff's visit and as he watched him lead away the horses he saw Jack Turner, the carpenter, and called to him. "Jack, are you engaged on any task today?"

He loped across to him. "No, young master. Not now I've seen to Master Henry's coffin. Has thy aught for me?"

"Yes, the door leading to the ruined part of the house is rotted through. I made a forced entry yesterday, to find my Aunt's dog. It will need replacing. Either that, or boarding up."

The man opened his eyes wide, nodding his head slowly. "Aye, thy found more than the lost dog, it seems, young master!"

"As you say," replied Hal curtly, not wanting to discuss it again.

"Not a pleasant sight, so old Moll, as laid him out, said," he continued, shaking his head. "I don't know what ails folk these days, to be so wicked, I'll take my oath, I don't. Why, the Master, he were a good and true man. Now who would want to kill a good and true man like that and worse still, deny him a decent burial like a good Christian!"

Hal saw how grieved the man was and answered kindly, "I don't know, Jack, but that insult at least can be remedied this very day."

"Aye, but he'll not rest easy until justice is done. They never do. You mark my words, young master, unless his murderer is found, his ghost will walk!"

A shudder ran through Hal and he turned impatiently from the man. "There are no such things as ghosts. As for his murderer, he shall be found, of that I am sure, and he'll get what he so richly deserves."

"Aye, well I hope he does, young master, who so ever he be." He caught the sound of Will Longstaffe's whistle approaching and made haste to gather up his bag of tools. "I'm off then to find a nice bit o' wood for that there door. I fancy we've some oak planks in the yard, just matured right they be. They'll make a good sound door."

Will Longstaffe had ridden into the yard in time to hear the last of the carpenter's words. "What's all this then, Master Hal? Are you starting work on the west wing already? Ain't you a bit hasty with your uncle not yet laid to his rest?"

"I am merely ordering the replacement of a rotten door," replied Hal, "something I know my uncle would have wished."

Will looked him over with narrowed eyes. "Aye, well I'm not so sure. I reckon I've knew him the longer! Either way, your uncle is dead. Happen you should wait to see who's been named heir before you start giving out orders. Or do you think you know who inherits anyway?"

Hal frowned, seeing in the man's increasing lack of respect the first fruits of his uncle's demise. He was determined not to lose his temper with the man, whatever the provocation, but also equally determined the agent should not have the final word.

"No, I am aware my uncle didn't have time to change his will, although it was fully his intention. However I am still heir now to my father, who shall surely inherit."

"Oh, that's how you see it, is it? It seems you think to win either way, young master!"

Hal looked decidedly annoyed as the man almost turned his back on him. In spite of his resolve he would have rebuked him sharply, aware that if he didn't soon get the better of this man he would never do so, but the arrival of the vicar on his staid cob caused an interruption. Pushing down his annoyance he crossed the yard to greet the man.

The vicar clasped his hand warmly. "Young Master Hal, or rather Master Westwood, I should say! The very person I wished to see!"

"You wish to see me?" said Hal blankly. He'd imagined the cleric's errand with the grieving widow or his Aunt Margery.

"Indeed, sir, if you will be so good as to spare me a moment of your time."

Hal now remembered that the vicar's long tongue was legendary, but he also knew the office, if not the man, demanded respect so he replied politely, although with a marked lack of enthusiasm, "In what way can I serve you?"

"Ah, so good! So amiable!" murmured the vicar with a sigh. "Such gentle manners, if I may be permitted to say so, as we have long been lacking in our little community. You set an example to us all!"

Hal well knew his uncle had little use for the Rev. Mr Broxtowe, calling him a fool of a man, fit only for the company of females. If he did not stop his speeches, he would be there for an hour or more so he asked firmly, "You said you required a moment of my time?"

"So sorry, dear me, yes, but one moment, if you will be so good sir, to discuss the funeral arrangements for your dear uncle."

"Arrangements?" Again Hal looked blank. "I thought my Aunt Margery had already done so."

"Ah, yes, indeed, your Aunt has indeed kindly conveyed to me the wishes of both herself and the poor widow of your late uncle. But ladies, you know, in times of grief, find it difficult to make a decision, and it is usually the custom for the male next-of-kin to make the final arrangements."

Hal, who had never in his short experience of his Aunt Margery found her to have any difficulty in making a decision, blinked and answered the part of this he could agree with: "Yes, I had been hoping my father might arrive in time for the funeral, but I suppose one could hardly expect him so soon."

"No, indeed, sir, the journey from London is not

one to be undertaken lightly but it would be most un-
wise I fear, to delay the funeral any longer. However
we can always hold a memorial service for you uncle at
a later date."

Hal's brow cleared. "Of course, that exactly solves
the problem. Yes, we can have a service once my father
comes. That's well settled then. Now, to the matter of
the funeral. I'm afraid I am a complete novice in such
matters. What would you advise?"

❧

The next few days flew by so quickly that Libby was
surprised. There was so much to do, so many tasks to
be accomplished that there was little time for reflection. The funeral had passed off in much the manner
as such things do, and Aunt Kate, the first excess of
her grief burnt out, took up the threads of her life
bravely. She was supported by all of her relations except Francis Westwood, whose absence still continued
to puzzle them.

Gradually life began to resume more usual ordinary
routines, yet all had the feeling of being in limbo. The
first spate of talk faded to be replaced by more insidi-
ous gossip.

Hal began to grow more anxious, wondering why his father had not yet arrived or even written to acknowledge his letter.

Libby came down to the hall late one afternoon to watch for Hal's return. She occupied herself with a small task as she waited, not wanting any to guess her errand. She was surprised to see from his arrival he was both hot and angry.

"Is something amiss, Hal?" she asked. She could not see trouble on his face and not long to ease it.

"Naught of any significance," he replied curtly.

She blinked in surprise, for he seldom took that tone with any, but merely said quietly. "Kitty has laid out fresh linen and there is rose water in the ewer."

He nodded and strode on, whilst she made a parade of refolding the napkins for supper. Half way up the stairs he paused and turned back looking shamefaced.

"Libby, I beg pardon, that was ill-done of me. Why do you not chide me for my lack of manners?"

"You have much to fret you. Would my scolding help?"

"Fear of it might stop me becoming a tyrant, which I am like to do if you will be so forbearing. Are you busy?"

"No. I was merely finding occupation," she replied.

"Come then, be a better wife than I deserve and tidy away my clothes for me. I must wash and I'll tell you why I am such a bear."

Her heart leapt to think he wanted her company and she followed him happily. She was glad to think they had managed to achieve that easy intimacy which had first seemed so impossible. Some moments later, having found out his favourite doublet and put away his boots she asked, "Has something irked you?"

He paused in drying his hands, his expression reflective. "I was going to say it was something somebody said, but they didn't say anything. It's nothing as direct as that, more just a feeling. Yet I tell you Libby, it's tangible. I can almost taste it on the air!"

Libby frowned as she seated herself on a chest. "What is?"

"Suspicion!" he replied harshly.

"Of whom?" she asked blankly.

He shook his head. "I don't know, how could I? Nothing is said openly in my hearing or to my face. None speak out, yet I hear whispers, see men nudge each other as I pass by. I tell you I can sense it in the atmosphere!"

"But they cannot suspect you! Why, you weren't even here at Westwood when your uncle was killed!" she cried indignantly.

"Suspicion takes little account of facts. It feeds on half-truths and gossip! It dwells on the fact that I am not truly one of them. I was bred abroad, therefore I am the next best thing to a foreigner!"

"But you must speak out, Hal! Tell them openly that you weren't here, don't even let them think you could possibly be guilty of so wicked a crime!" she cried angrily.

"I would I had your conviction, Libby, perhaps then they'd believe me, if I did," he replied smiling wistfully as he buttoned on his shirt.

"Then I shall tell them, aye, and send them smarting about their business, too!" she cried wrathfully, leaping to her feet as if about to go and do so.

He laughed again, his ill-humour evaporating. "By heaven, I see I have taken a tigress to wife!" he cried, in mock dismay. Seeing his temper was mended she, too, laughed. But all too soon he was sobered and sighing again: "I would to God my father would come," he said, the anxious note back in his voice. "I hear whispers about that, too, everywhere. I expected him yesterday at the latest."

"Perhaps it was not possible for him to leave London immediately," suggested Libby.

"Surely if one's brother is foully murdered all other

concerns must be forgotten?" he countered. "Mr Broxtowe, who by the way, is the only one who is pleasant to me, was asking earlier when I expected my father. He is anxious to make plans for the memorial service. Will Longstaffe muttered something about his not coming this morning, which he would not dare do were my father by."

He broke off, shaking his head and began to pull his fine cambric shirt through the slashes in his doublet. "And as for Aunt Margery saying my father has always been unreliable and that she never expected any better of him!"

"I can see it grieves you to hear your father abused so," said Libby, with ready sympathy. "But you must remember Hal, what a terrible shock this has been to your Aunts, and how too they have had to bear the brunt of it all."

"The truth of it is she is right!" he interrupted. "My father is completely unreliable! Oh, he's a splendid fellow in a fight, or with a crowd of men, but he has no sense of responsibility at all! Living in exile, plotting for the King's return, that all suited him perfectly, but the mundane existence of daily living is not for him! Oh, I know I shouldn't be saying this. I know I owe a duty to my father, but by God, I wish he'd come now and do all that is expected of him before he falls into even worse repute! I am growing so anxious about this murder. The sheriff's man was in the yard yet again this morning, asking when my groom will be returned! What does he mean by it?"

"Don't fret, Hal," she soothed, handing him a comb. "Any hour now your father must come and he'll surely take all under his control."

He reddened at the inference he was incapable of handling the matter. "But will he? I fear not! I would take the responsibility myself, but I have no authority here, none pay me any heed. All look to Will Longstaffe and treat me as nothing but a boy!"

She glanced up at him and longed to take him in her arms and soothe his wounded pride. "I know it is difficult for you as things are situated. If only your uncle had named you as his heir you'd have none of this trouble."

He laughed bitterly. "Aye, if only. But it was not to be! I fear you have been badly taken in Libby, allying yourself to little better than a pauper!"

"I am content with the bargain if you are," she replied seriously.

He met her eyes, his own equally serious, as he held out his hand. "I believe I am more than content. Come;

let us go down to supper. If my feelings should get the better of me, and I look like to explode when Aunt Margery speaks out against my father again, give me a hint!"

Chapter Seven

Supper went forward in much the same way as it had anytime during the past few days. Aunt Kate was a little tearful, Aunt Margery absent minded and Hetta subdued. Libby was casting about in her mind for a topic of conversation, which would not bring about sharp words, when the sounds of an arrival were heard.

" 'Tis my father!" cried Hal with relief. "There you are, Aunt, I knew he'd come just as fast as he could!"

He hastened from the table into the screens passage, but fell back a pace in surprise.

"Jacqueline! Bess! Where is my father? Is he still with the horses?"

"Your Papa, he is not here," said his step-mother, with an accompanying gesture, which could only be Gallic. "Your letter, it comes, Hal, after he leaves with Jane to visit her new husband. So Bess, she reads your message and she writes also to your Papa and then she says we must come here. But this man of yours, Hal, he is so disagreeable! He goes so fast and will not let us rest. He is the imbecile, I tell him, but he shrugs only and calls me French. *Sacré Bleu!* Hal, what else can I be but French?"

Hal smiled at this ingenious history, and drew his step-mother further into the hall. "Come, ma'am, I beg pardon for the churlish fellow. He's a sad case, I fear. But come, let me make you known to your husband's sisters at last." He indicated his Aunts, both of whom had risen to their feet and were standing together, viewing the little French woman with varying degrees of doubt and hostility.

Jacqueline came forward as she espied them. "So, you are my husband's sisters, no? The ones he calls the old cats?" Her smiled died as she glanced from one face frozen in greeting to another. "What is this? I say something wrong?"

"Not you, dear sister," replied Margery majestically. "For you merely repeat the words of your degenerate husband!"

"Come, be welcome to Westwood Hall," said Aunt Kate. "You must be a hungered, and full weary, after your journey." She could not help smiling a little, in spite of her grief, to see the other's puzzlement.

"Weary? *Mais oui, merci!* I cannot say how weary I

am. Hal, I will take a glass of that wine, if you please."
Jacqueline nodded and walked forward into the candlelight so those at the table got their first clear view of
her.

Libby was already bristling at the familiar manner in
which she addressed Hal. She took one look at his step-
mother and confirmed her initial feeling of dislike.

Petite was the word for Jacqueline, petite and polished. She had all at once that finished air which pro-
claimed her a daughter of France. Libby had never to
her knowledge seen a French woman before and like
most of her countrymen was inclined to scoff at any
thing from that country. But even she couldn't deny
there was something about the visitor which made everyone else look dowdy and provincial. Dark-eyed,
raven-haired and imperious, she took Hal's chair at the
head of the table and command of the situation with
an ease which took their breath away.

Libby, frowning over the effect she had on them,
caught the eye of her travelling companion, standing
neglected in the shadows behind her. This then was
Bess, Hal's second sister. Libby was reminded again how
odd it was that none of the brothers or sister seemed to
show any resemblance to each other. Bess had none of
Hal's dark good looks or any of Ned's freckles and fiery

colouring, yet no more did she share the sleepy blue-eyed blondness of Hetta. No, Bess was an odd looking girl, with hair the colour of honey and hazel eyes. She was also extremely tall and very thin and showed to very little advantage beside her stepmother.

Jacqueline noticed Libby's interest. She turned in her chair. "Bess? Come here, girl, do not loom over me like the maypole! Make your curtsey to your Aunts. *Voilà!* That was not so very ill done, no? Sisters, you will not comprehend the trouble I am taking for this one. I tell you I am determined I shall find for her the husband!"

"Pray, won't you sit down to supper with us, we have barely begun," suggested Aunt Kate, casting Bess a sympathetic look as she blushed and looked more awkward than ever.

"Supper? *Non, non,* I could not swallow a morsel!" cried Jacqueline, casting the table an eloquent shudder. "Me, I am—how you say? Exhausted? My body, it is racked with the pain from the eternal jolt, jolt of the horse! You are too good, all of you, but non, nothing for me, less it be—the merest mouthful in *ma chambre.* You will forgive, I beg, but I must rest me. The smallest crumb, an omelette perhaps, should your man know how to make such a thing, and another glass of wine to refresh me. Or no, a little white fish in sauce would lie easy. I would not put anyone to any trouble for me! *Non, non,* I insist I shall do very well. None shall wait upon me, least of all my husband's sisters! *Non,* Hal shall bring me *le soupçon* to *ma chambre. Bon,* that will answer *parfait. Non, non,* just the suggestion of the headache, *non, merci, ma femme* can do everything for me. Hal, I depend upon your coming in a very few minutes!"

This last was almost a command over her shoulder, as she went with grace from the hall, followed by a dark maidservant.

Aunt Kate looked bewildered as she went to speak with the cook and said, "Had I better get cook to make an omelette—or some fish? Have we any fish in the house, I wonder?"

"Only salt herring, and depend upon it, that would not suit," said Aunt Margery, her voice only too clearly indicating her displeasure. "Come, Bess, sit down at the table. You, I am sure, won't be so foolish as to refuse food. Heavens, girl, how you have grown since I last saw you!"

Libby smiled encouragingly at the blushing girl and made room for her on the bench.

Aunt Kate was still undecided. "What should we do for the best, Hal? I think it would be beyond cook's power to make—what is an omelette?"

"Eggs beaten together, ma'am," he replied frowning. "In fact it isn't so very difficult to do so perhaps I should—"

"Sit down, Hal and eat your supper," commanded Aunt Margery sharply. "Presently Kitty shall take your step-mother a bowl of mutton broth. Mutton broth is what we eat after a long journey, and if it is good enough for us, I imagine it will do very well for your father's wife!"

Hal had a nasty feeling that he was about to become caught up in a maelstrom of domestic wrangles. It was something he was anxious to avoid at all costs. "I doubt very much that Jacqueline will appreciate mutton broth, ma'am. It's not something that I ever recollect the French eating."

"I expect they do, Hal, however, they'd just call it something different," said Aunt Margery, expressing by her words and tone, her opinion of everything French. "Anyway, your step-mother is in England now and must learn to do as we do. Liberty, pass the bread to Bess, if you please, and let us have done with this chatter!"

In view of the manner in which she spoke, there was silence in the hall for quite some while, but for the clatter of spoons against dishes and the cries of swallows as they whirled about the house. Then Hal said reflectively, plainly showing where his thoughts had been: "Did Jacqueline say you'd sent word to my father before you set out, Bess?"

Bess's voice was soft and low and she answered her brother without confidence. "Yes, Hal. He and Jane have gone to arrange Jane's marriage to Mr Eustace's son."

"Philip Eustace?" Hal was surprised.

"Yes," She lowered her eyes to her plate, biting at her soft under-lip.

"But surely my father wrote to me saying that he was destined to be your husband?" he said, in astonishment.

She swallowed, her eyes filled with tears and she made haste to explain. "He—he didn't care for me when we met in London. No more did I care for him! He isn't much more than five foot even now and so very childish that Father thought perhaps Jane might suit him better, being younger. So he took her down to their home near Malford to meet him."

"Jane is but fifteen, do you think she is done growing?" he asked, his mind diverted from his main preoccupation by this startling news.

"I hardly know," she said. "I only know she wept her heart out for three days before they left and that Father says he is determined to get the affair settled quickly."

"I can't think why," said Hal, his face inscrutable. "The Eustaces are as short of money as they are inches! Not a brilliant match by any standards. You'll surely do better, Bess."

Libby, seeing how Bess laughed with the rest of the table at this mild sally, was pleased with Hal for easing his sister's embarrassment. But Hal, in spite of his grin, still had his mind on other issues.

"The Eustaces live fifty miles from here, do they not, ma'am?" he said, appealing to his Aunt.

"Indeed they do, Hal, or so I believe for I have not personally had the pleasure of their acquaintance," said Margery. "However, I must say I am surprised at your father's determination to obtain the connection. A Parliamentary family I believe, who had their fingers in most of that rascal Cromwell's pies!"

Hal stiffened, his eyes flying to Libby face, certain she would be hurt by the round condemnation. "Then surely ma'am, his aim was to further the good work my uncle has begun, by allying his children with those who opposed us during the war. That by this measure the division in our country may more solidly be healed. My point is, if my father is but fifty miles away, mayhap I should ride and acquaint him of the tragedy here?"

"I am only amazed, Hal, if that is the case, he knows nothing of it already," said Aunt Margery. Two high spots of colour appeared on her cheeks as she realised the mistake she'd made. "For it is all over the country now. Will Longstaffe said he heard it discussed at the Gloucester horse fair yesterday."

Hal looked even more confounded. It was true the country was alive with gossip and rumour, but before he could answer, Aunt Kate came back to the table, a pucker between her sad eyes.

"Hal, your step-mother requests you go to her immediately with a glass of wine."

There was a silence as Hal, with an exclamation of dismay, jumped to his feet, caught up a glass and a jug of wine, and hurried from the hall.

"I set Kitty to coddle an egg for her," Aunt Kate continued, addressing the table at large. "I do hope that might serve. How very odd French manners are! Do you think it is quite the thing for young Hal to—"

Margery's warning cough drowned out her last words and she broke into speech as Kate resumed her seat. "They are very odd, my dear, but there, we have no choice but to bear it! You must find it as difficult as I do, to have such a woman arrive here and start issuing orders. Her audacity is beyond belief, but then what else could one expect from a wife of Francis! Liberty, my dear, I beg pardon for my words earlier. I had forgot you when I spoke."

As Libby, appeased by this handsome apology replied suitably, Kate, frowning, said: "Why do you say it will be difficult for me, Margery?"

"My dear, if Francis is Henry's heir, Jacqueline is now mistress of Westwood Hall," replied Margery looking at her sister-in-law as if she were simple.

"But he isn't," said Kate, cutting across Margery's heavy sigh. "Henry named Hal as his heir."

Margery, remembering Kate had suffered a great shock, spoke with patience, "Henry certainly intended to do so but recollect, he was killed before he had time to make a new will."

"No, Margery, Henry made a new will; I saw him do it. It was the evening of the very day Hal had left for the wedding. He was saying how pleased he was with Hal, with his obedience to his wishes and his general desire to please. And then, all at once he decided he'd not delay but make the will out at once. He sent for Mr Broxtowe and his wife to witness it. You must remember, Mr Broxtowe came that evening, for did we not discuss whether it would be advisable to allow the congregation to celebrate all the old feast days again, or keep strictly to those only recommended?"

"I remember that well enough, but knew nothing of this other matter. Are you sure Kate—and that you saw Broxtowe and his wife both witness it?"

"Oh, yes," said Aunt Kate, "It was to be Hal's wedding present, so he wanted it kept secret. Then he thought he might make Rushley Manor over to him as well, and so in the end Henry decided to take the will to London and consult his man of business."

"Well, I knew he intended to settle Rushley Manor on Hal at his marriage, but I didn't think he had time to do it. This is splendid news!" cried Aunt Margery, her face lightening. "So, young Hal is master of Westwood? This will not please Francis, if he should ever come!"

"You know Henry never did have any opinion of Francis's ability to manage land. Whereas Hal, even in the few short weeks he has been with us has shown himself so biddable, so willing to learn. Now of course, I don't know how Hal will manage alone." She sighed as her face crumpled and tears filled her eyes.

"Will Longstaffe can teach him much," said Aunt Margery. "I have a good opinion of that young man."

"He is no fool. It is, of course, a pity his birth should be so unfortunate, for it appears to have given him what can only be described as a chip on his shoulder. I understand he can be most unpleasant to deal with, if one doesn't know how to handle him, which, of course, Henry always did, and Hal must quickly learn," agreed Aunt Kate.

Libby noticed reservation in her voice, and mentally agreed with it, thinking she must remember to tell Hal of it. She knew he found the man very difficult indeed to handle.

Whilst the sisters talked on, Libby tried to settle her confused thoughts. Hal master of Westwood, and she its mistress! It was amazing! She knew he would be pleased and excited by the inheritance, but the more she thought of it, the more glad she became that he had not been here when his uncle had died. If the talk had been bad before, surely it would get worse once this news was out.

Hal, in ignorance of his good fortune, made his way to Jacqueline's chamber.

"Hal, is that you? Come in! Marie is just going. See, I am already in my bed, being full weary!" She made a face. "French manners, my dear!" she mimicked, in a passable imitation of Margery's tone. "Ah, how they do hate me already, the cats, your Papa's sisters, Hal."

"I rather think it was calling them cats which set up their backs, ma'am. In England one doesn't call a lady a cat," Hal explained with a grin.

"Why not? Are they not beautiful creatures, with more grace than any of Francis's sisters will ever know? Oh, this England, Hal, it is not the place for me!" She sighed heavily and patted the bed. "But do not stand there in the door, come pour me a glass of that wine and sit by me. Tell me all the gossip. How went your wedding? Which was your bride? I do not recollect her. Did the wedding night live up to your expectations?"

Hal poured her a glass of wine and reluctantly sat as far as was possible from her on the bed. "Everything went very well, ma'am," he replied. "Libby was sitting near the foot of the table."

"*Non*, she made no impression, but then I am weary. Now, tell me all the gossip. What happened at your wedding? The aunts, they attended, no? She yawned and stretched her arms above her head, showing her pearly white forearms in the candle light, whilst Hal shifted uncomfortably, thinking that few women could be so totally unaware of their beauty than his father's wife, or unaware of the effect she could have. Once again his thoughts backed away from the suggestion that he found her desirable.

"Everything went well, ma'am," he replied.

"So, Hal, you don't say, how do you like your bride?" she repeated, casting him a sly look from beneath her eyelashes.

"I like her very well," he replied steadily. "She's a good sort of girl."

"A good sort of girl? Oh, Hal, this no love match, then," she laughed. "Ah, but that I had noticed her. Describe her to me."

"You'll see her for yourself tomorrow ma'am. She's tallish, slender, with darkish hair and blue-eyes, I think." Suddenly he felt embarrassed that he couldn't remember.

Her lips twitched. "She is no beauty then?" she remarked.

"She has a pleasing sort of face, and a nice smile," he replied stiffly, not want to be disloyal.

"*Mon Dieu!* I have much to do, then, for what you describe to me is plain," said Jacqueline complacently.

"It would be unfair to call Libby plain," he said, stung by her words.

"If a woman she is not pretty, she is plain," said Jacqueline, in a manner to end all argument.

"But do not fear, most women, unless they be truly ugly, can be made to look a beauty!"

"When did you last have the pleasure of my father's company, ma'am?"

She made a face and shrugged her elegant shoulders. "Marriage has sobered you, Hal. Already you take on the role of the husband. As for mine—it is some ten days since I last saw him."

"He is long overdue, ma'am, I think I must seek him out."

"He will not like that, Hal. Francis, he like to play the lone hand!" she warned.

He glanced to her in some astonishment. "His brother has been killed, Jacqueline, under highly suspicious circumstances. It is imperative he comes here not only to take command, but to put a stop to all this talk!"

Again she shrugged the candlelight making her shoulders gleam. "You know your Papa, Hal, he comes in his own good time and not before."

"Never the less, I must seek him out. Rumours are growing apace which, if not soon scotched, will mean the devil to pay!" Hal insisted firmly.

She sighed and stretched languidly. "The devil is a master who must always be paid, Hal. Tell me more of your wedding, be not in such a great hurry to be gone."

Chapter Eight

In the hall the supper finally drew to a close. Bess, who watched her aunts bustle off with their heads close together, made haste to follow Libby into the parlour.

"Excuse me, it's Liberty, isn't it? Nobody thought to introduce us. I'm Hal's sister, Bess."

Libby smiled, taking the hand she extended. "How do you do? Yes, my name is Liberty, but I prefer to be called Libby; it's less formal!"

"Rather like Bess, as opposed to Elizabeth. When I am called Elizabeth I feel I must be solemn," replied Bess with a shy smile.

Libby laughed. "Exactly! I see we think alike! Are you to make a long stay here, Bess?"

"I hardly know. I am at my step-mother's command. She, as you may have gathered from her conversation, came prepared to take possession of her house."

Libby looked dismayed. "Oh dear! Do you think she will be angry?"

"Oh, furiously so!" Bess giggled at the thought, then seeing Libby's shocked face, she added quickly, "I beg pardon; that must make me sound quite horrid! But if you only knew the furore she will create! No, I'll say no more, you'll find out the rest all too soon!"

Libby digested this in silence as she crossed the room to the window, then she turned to confront her new sister-in-law. "You do not like her?" she asked bluntly.

A closed-look flitted across Bess's young face. "No, I do not like her," she admitted. "That is why I must say no more. I do not like her, but most people do. She can be very charming! May I sit with you?"

"Oh, please do," Libby made haste to remove the scattered silks of her embroidery and waited whilst Bess arranged skirts of her gown. "Your step-mother appears to be on great terms with Hal," she remarked airily.

"Oh, yes, she is mightily fond of Hal. Hal is so very decorative, you see, and his attentions add to her consequence. But there, I'll say no more! See, here comes Hetta! It is so long since we were last together! What is this, have you so soon forgotten your sister, sweetheart?"

Hetta came forward to embrace her sister. At first she was shy, it was some months since they had been together, but presently her tongue grew looser and soon she was happily chattering to them both.

A pleasant hour passed and then, when Bess went to see her sister into bed, Libby sat on alone in the twilight. As she sat waiting for Hal to return she thought on all she had heard. She was angry with herself for the jealousy that flared in her heart the very moment she had set eyes on Jacqueline. She realised she had no right to expect Hal to be in constant attendance on her. She was also aware he had a duty to his step-mother, but what could be keeping him so long if Jacqueline was, as she declared, so exhausted.

A welcome diversion came in the form of Aunt Kate and Aunt Margery. Their conference over, they came, workboxes in hand, to spend the evening much as they always did. They sat down at the well-polished, gate-legged table and began to sew steadily. Whereas Kate worked with a concentration which had its roots in misery, Margery darted several looks in Libby's direction as she, her work forgotten, gazed silently from the window into the darkening landscape.

Then as Tobias came to light the candles, Libby rose to her feet, saying quietly, "If you'll excuse me, I think I'll retire now."

"Are you quite well, child?" Aunt Kate asked as she looked onto to the young face illuminated by the light of her candle.

"Thank you, ma'am, yes," she replied softly.

"Come, give me a kiss then," said Aunt Kate, and held out her arms.

Libby looked surprised, but complied, bending submissively to the older woman's embrace. Then with a curtsey in Margery's direction she hurried from the chamber.

"Why did you do that, Kate?" asked Margery.

"I don't know, except that I felt a sudden kinship with her. She looks so lost and forlorn!"

"Aye, and we don't have to look far to seek the author of her misery! Really, the behaviour of that French woman is more than enough!" snapped Margery, then she broke off as Hal came into the chamber.

"How is your step-mother, Hal? Is she quite comfortable?"

Hal came to sit with them at the table. He felt a little uneasy that he had been gone so long, but he tried to carry off the situation with aplomb. "She is well enough, thank you, ma'am, but she was never happy to leave France. I don't think she ever realised we would actually one day go home. The restoration of the King has been a nasty shock to her, and everything English has become distasteful to her."

"Hardly a satisfactory state of affairs!" remarked

Margery, with the awful restraint of one whom could say so much. "However, to more important things! Hal, your Aunt has something to say you should hear!"

Hal glanced to Aunt Kate, surprised and a little on guard. "Ma'am?"

"It's about your uncle's will, Hal," Aunt Kate began slowly.

He interrupted her swiftly. "You need have no fear, ma'am. I do not care, I assure you. Before I was to be my uncle's heir, now I am my father's. But that I've lost an uncle I was growing to love and respect, there is no difference."

Margery glanced shrewdly to his handsome face as he spoke, wondering if he was ever at a loss for a smooth phrase or a courtly gesture. Had he ever in his entire life been taken at a disadvantage.

"No, Hal, I wasn't about to explain how your uncle didn't have time to make you his heir, but to tell you that he did."

Hal stared at her, the colour suddenly flooding his cheeks. "He did?" he repeated, excitement leaping into his voice.

"Yes, Hal, he did. Indeed that was the reason he set out for London to take the will to his man of law," Aunt Kate frowned anxiously. "However, if he never left Westwood, as the Sheriff suggests, I begin to wonder what has happened to the will."

"Of course Henry left Westwood, Kate," said Margery impatiently. "Did we all not stand before the door in all that dreadful heat to see him on his way?"

"Yes, but I was wondering if perhaps he wasn't attacked and killed and then brought back here," replied Kate slowly.

"In that case the will would have been found on him surely, and given into Hal's hands with all his other possessions," said Margery logically.

"Not if—if the person who killed Henry wished to prevent us from knowing about the new will. Surely, if some one was trying to keep Hal from inheriting, the will must have been destroyed?" said Aunt Kate.

Hal glanced to her swiftly. "Have you someone in mind, ma'am?" he asked sharply, thinking he saw the direction of her thoughts.

She met his eyes frankly. "No, Hal, I don't know for sure whom your uncle had named as his heir in an earlier will."

"Why, it must be Francis," said Margery blankly. "He is his brother!"

Aunt Kate shook her head. "I only know Henry swore he'd not let Francis have Westwood to bring it to ruin."

"So you think Henry was killed by someone who knew him," said Margery frowning over her thoughts. "Why else would the murderer return him to Westwood?"

Hal couldn't resist a faint smile. "I think we'd near all ruled out footpads, Aunt," he said. His eyes travelled from one to the other, as they exchanged glances and his smile died. "You suspect my father, don't you?"

"No, but it looks so bad, Hal, his not coming," said Aunt Kate simply.

"It is of course, exactly the behaviour I would expect from Francis," said Margery, her voice hard. "We'd do better to face it Hal. Your father is the sort of man to kill his brother rather than let his own son inherit!"

"It cannot be so! I know my father. I'll even agree with you, Aunt, that his character is far from perfect. But he would never stoop to such a thing!" Hal was passionate in his defence.

"In that case Hal, where is he?" demanded Margery, with devastating logic.

"He can only be ill or even dead himself!" cried Hal desperately.

"I trust he is Hal, even if it must be by his own hand," she replied grimly. "For if he should be found and brought to trial, every man's hand must be against him."

"Every man's save mine," he replied stiffly.

Margery sighed wearily. "You are very young Hal. And that brings me to another matter. You are, as I've said, both young and inexperienced, so you'll not see what she is about, but have a care of your step-mother!"

"As my father bade me, ma'am," he replied curtly, his face suddenly rather white with anger.

"I don't think he meant that sort of care Hal, I mean look to her, for she is bent on making mischief!"

"She is not the only one, Aunt!" he snapped.

Margery glared at him. "You may be the new master of Westwood Hal, but you are still young enough to be an insolent puppy!"

Hal inclined his head in a stately manner.

"Your Aunt and I are concerned for both your and Libby's welfare, Hal," said Aunt Kate, hastening to pour oil on the troubled waters. "Jacqueline, she is, well, the sort of woman who would thrive on intrigue and secrets! Pay her no heed, Hal!"

Hal rose to his feet and said, "I beg you will both forgive me, but I am weary and would away to my bed."

"A place you should have been an hour ago with your bride rather than dancing attendance on your step-mother. You'd do well to remember, Hal, you've a duty to produce an heir now!" snapped Margery.

He looked thunderous, but made no further remark; merely bowing with meticulous grace and walking from the room.

"One can't deny he has excellent manners, Margery," said Kate into the silence, which followed his departure. "His looks said things unspeakable!"

"I think I might almost prefer it if he wasn't so very well-mannered," remarked Margery with a short laugh. "His iron control strikes me as just a little bloodless!"

Kate shook her head decidedly. " Oh no, he has the temper of the Westwoods, but it is as you say, kept under iron control. You know, I don't think I'd much care to be around him if he ever lost it!"

Hal, meanwhile, crossed the hall and mounted the stairs prey to a black fury which was, as his aunt suggested, all the fiercer for being kept rigidly under control. The implications of their remarks were not lost on him. The element of truth lashed his sensitive conscience on the raw. There was no denying Jacqueline was a beautiful woman, and living as they had done in France, it was surely natural theirs should be an amicable relationship. As he loved his father, it was no more than that. He couldn't allow it to be more than that.

Still angry, he thrust open the door to the bedchamber and so disturbed Libby. She immediately sat up, rubbing her eyes "Oh, Hal! Have your aunts told you the news?" She yawned sleepily.

"My aunts have told me many things!" he growled in response.

Libby looked dismayed. "Are you cross?" she asked.

"Cross! Cross? Dear God!" In irritation at the silliness of the question, he crashed his clenched fist into the side of the press. The pain flared up his arm, yet there was a certain satisfaction from the violence.

Tears filled her eyes, part of fear to see his anger, yet more of pain to see him hurt.

"Are you hurt?" she asked timidly.

"No!" he growled. "Let me be!"

She sat back in the bed in silence and watched warily as he walked to the window to nurse his throbbing knuckles and stare at the black void which was night.

"Where are you?" The cry burst forth from him as if he could contain it no more. "Where in God's name are you?"

His voice echoed tensely in the silence and Libby closed her eyes, letting tears seep silently into her pillow, then as more minutes ticked by, she slid from the bed and came to him.

"Come to bed Hal," she whispered, still half-afraid.

He turned from her. "Let me be!" he warned.

"But you are weary," she persisted. "You need rest!"

"Rest!" He spun round on her, catching her by her thin shoulders, his fingers pressing into her flesh, bruising her to the bone. "What rest can there be for me? Do you know what they say? Do you? They say my father has killed my uncle rather than let me inherit!"

"You know it's not true, Hal!" she cried, her teeth chattering.

"Do I?" he cried. "Do I? Then where in damnation is he?"

Tears spilled from her eyes and down her face as he shook her hard in his fury. "I don't know!" she sobbed.

"Do you know what else they say, those cats, my aunts?" he cried furiously, his face close to hers, "That Jacqueline wants me in her bed and that I should be in yours getting an heir!"

She began to tremble now, very afraid as sobs shook her frame. She'd never seen any man truly angry before. She could not believe that one so usually gentle and courteous could behave in so frightening a manner. "Let me go, Hal!" she begged in a terrified whisper. "Let me go. You are hurting me!"

He released her at once. He was horrified and ashamed as he realised her terror, yet in a way that made him still angrier.

In her fear her legs began to tremble and she staggered and nearly fell. She caught the back of a chair to steady herself. "I'm sorry, so sorry! I thought you would be so glad to inherit!"

"What have I inherited but suspicion and calumny? There is as yet no proof of a will. I can inherit naught until this slur on my father's name is cleansed!" He threw himself into a chair by the window. "Go to bed! I must think!" he commanded.

Chapter Nine

When Libby awoke at dawn the next morning Hal was sleeping soundly in the bed beside her.

She lay quietly for some moments looking at him. She had sobbed herself into oblivion last night. Now as her eyes dwelt tenderly on his beloved face relaxed in sleep, she began to consider what lay before her. His anger had surprised and bewildered her. He had always appeared to be a kind and gentle man, yet as she looked at him, noticing how the anxiety of the past few days was wiped away, she wondered just how much she knew him.

Unconsciously she reached out a hand to stroke his lean cheek; her fingers very nearly brushing against him as he suddenly opened his eyes.

He stared at her blankly for a few seconds and then yawned saying thickly: "Oh, good morrow!"

"Good morrow," she replied quietly.

He stretched, yawned again and was then still as his

brain began to work. Libby pushed back the covers and moved to get from the bed, but his hand came out to detain her.

"Stay!" he commanded.

She glanced doubtfully at him, but he had turned over on his back so as to not meet her eyes. He stared up at the elaborately carved tester. "I think I owe you an apology. I'm afraid I was rather ill-tempered last night and that you unfortunately bore the brunt of it. I beg your pardon. I'll never treat you so again."

Tears filled her eyes. It was a coldly formal apology, spoken in so wretchedly distant a manner. It was difficult to believe they had shared the same bed. All at once she felt she was back to the first few days of their marriage, with all their later intimacy forgotten.

"It is no great matter," she replied in a suffocated voice.

He was still formal. "I am relieved by your forbearance. I trust in my anger I did you no injury?"

She felt like screaming, but she bit it back and replied much in the same vein as he. "I am somewhat bruised."

A flicker of emotion disturbed his face. "Then I must beg pardon for that also."

"I have said, it is of no great matter. No doubt I bruise

too easily. May I go now please?"

His grip on her wrist seemed to tighten, but then he released her abruptly. "As you will."

She got from the bed, going first, as was her custom, to the window to mark the day.

Hal remained in bed silently and when he did speak it was politely, as if he were conversing with a chance met stranger. "Have you any plans for the day?"

"No, none," replied Libby, beginning to brush her hair.

He watched her covertly from under his eyelids, aware that her unconsciously graceful movements made a poem in the early morning light. "I am resolved to ride over to Dunhill, on the far side of Chipping Barbury," he said grittily.

She swung round to face him, surprised. " Dunhill? Is that not a full fifty miles from here?"

"Yes, I know it will take me the better part of the day to get there, but I must have more information of my father. He may have told Mr Eustace of his plans, or someone may have seen the direction he took on leaving. He must have ridden, so I'll try to trace his route, find his horse. A man can't just disappear from the face of the earth!"

"True enough," she agreed. Feeling utterly miserable

she watched him becoming more passionate as he spoke. Plainly his coldness was just with her. Perhaps she had offended him in some way? Or more likely, that with Jacqueline here, she could share anxieties and confidences and he would have no further use for her.

"I would ask you to ride with me, but the distance is considerable and you do not ride well." He felt rather uncertainly of her. He had an uneasy feeling the violence of his temper last night had shocked her profoundly and was the cause of her coldness.

"No, I do not," she agreed and there was a hint of tears in her voice.

"So I shall be obliged to leave you for all of the day. Have you any commissions for me before I go?" he concluded lamely. His life appeared to be falling in ruins about him, but he could think of nothing, do nothing, until he felt certain in his own mind his father was innocent.

"None, thank you," she replied with quelling formality. She lifted her chin, determined he'd not see her weep. Of course he must be glad to leave her, she realised that. She could never have hoped to retain his affection for long. "Does your step-mother accompany you?" she asked, unable for her life to resist the question.

"Jacqueline? No, she rides no better than you do.

Why?" he asked bluntly. He was aware that in some-way the question was important, but found it just be-yond the grasp of his understanding.

"There was no particular reason. I merely thought she might."

"She will still be weary from her journey and I do not think it would be suitable," he replied, too con-fused and weary to do anything but take this at face value. He got from the bed; he was anxious now that he had come to the resolve to get on and try to find his father. An inner voice warned him that he should stop and take time to unravel this tangle, but his anxieties drove him on. As he made his preparations, he seemed to put all thought of it entirely from him and presently rode away without waiting for breakfast.

Libby ate hers in company with the aunts and Hal's sisters. She hoped to have the opportunity in the course of the day to get to know Bess better. They were of an age and Libby felt they might have much in common. Aunt Kate, who sent them all to gather raspberries from the kitchen garden helped in this object, and whilst thus pleasantly engaged, all last remnants of constraint fled. Bess confided the horrors of her meeting with Philip Eustace, and Libby talked with longing of her old home and her father and brother.

Margery, having commented unfavourably on Jacqueline's habit of spending the best part of the day in bed, began her usual daily round. Tobias was summoned to her and she was in the midst of her instructions when Jacqueline came slowly down the main staircase and into the hall. To her intense irritation the young woman was dressed in the very height of fashion in a very becoming shade of green. She had plainly shown no regard for the fact it was a house in mourning.

It was part and parcel of her unsatisfactory younger brother, that he should have married yet again and this time to a French woman. None of the family had ever complained when Francis had shifted the responsibility of his wife and children on to them. No, they had borne the load, be it light as in the case of dear Catherine and her daughters; or heavy, as with Ned, who could be troublesome. This last, this final, imposition was too much.

Jacqueline glanced from the patient Tobias to Margery curiously. "What goes on here?"

"Nothing which need concern you, Sister," replied Margery in her usual haughty manner. "I am merely discussing with Tobias the meals for today."

She came to sit down beside Margery at the long

table. "Meals? How you say? Food? Then be assured it does concern me! Pay attention, *Monsieur!* The food here—it is horrible!" She shuddered eloquently as Tobias stared open-mouthed and Margery bristled angrily. "I do not know what was offered to me last evening but it was impossible to eat! Broth? And some eggs 'alf cooked! Ugh! And again this morning, something, I know not what. It had the taste and texture of pig's swill!"

"That was oatmeal," said Margery in arctic tones. "It is eaten by many at breakfast and knowing of your delicate constitution we thought it best to send you some. Of course, had you left your bed and come down to the table like the rest of the household you would have found a better selection of food."

Jacqueline cast her a thoughtful look. "*Mais oiu*, that is another thing which must be changed. The times of these meals—they are ridiculous! Breakfast at dawn? Dinner at noon, supper at sunset! *Mon Dieu*, it is intolerable! No wonder the English have the bad temper. They always have the indigestion!"

"Meals have always been served at these times at Westwood and will continue to be so served! We want none of your French ways here! This is England Jacqueline. You are married to an Englishman. You had better conform to *our* ways!" cried Margery.

"Conform?" She frowned over the word. "This word I do not know, but this I do know. Henry is dead. Francis my husband is the master here now and I shall say what time is supper!"

Margery couldn't prevent a small smile of triumph curving her thin lips. She'd not asked to be the one to break the news of Hal's inheritance to Jacqueline. She'd fully expected Hal to do that but by heavens, if he hadn't and Jacqueline still thought Francis would inherit, she was going to enjoy disillusioning her. "I fear you are labouring under a misapprehension, Sister," said Margery. "Yes, thank you Tobias, that will do, we'll discuss the other matters another day." She waited until Tobias had reluctantly taken his leave; fully aware he'd gone only as far as the screens passage.

"Jacqueline, you speak of Henry's tragic death, for which we all mourn, and of Francis's inheritance, which I fear doesn't follow! Henry recently made a new will. Francis isn't the new master of Westwood Hall; young Hal is, and his wife sweet Liberty is the new mistress. She, if anybody, will be the one to decide upon innovations!"

Jacqueline blanched and the complacent smile was wiped from her face. "It cannot be so! You lie!"

Margery turned a dull red. "I have never told an un-truth in my life! It *is* true! If you do not believe me, then seek out Kate, who will verify all I say; or the vicar, who witnessed the new will!"

Jacqueline said not another word, although her dark eyes glittered angrily and she sat clenching and unclenching the arms of her chair.

Margery sat for some moments recovering her tem-per and enjoying the other's discomfiture under the cover of writing down the menus in her accounts book.

"So— it makes nothing!" Jacqueline said at last, with a shrug. "Hal has Westwood Hall, not Francis. It makes nothing! Hal will look to Francis for guidance, I think. And this Liberty, her I must meet! Together we can do much!"

"I do not think you'll find Liberty easier to persuade about changes than any of us. Liberty is too unsure of her position to make changes or oppose tradition," re-plied Margery shrewdly.

"Tradition? Bah! Where will I find me this Liberty?" Jacqueline got decisively to her feet.

"In the kitchen garden, picking raspberries with her husband's sisters," replied Margery in a satisfied tone.

Jacqueline frowned, and after some thought wan-dered away from the hall and summoned a maidservant to conduct her to the kitchen garden.

She greeted her small step-daughter Hetta, with pro-testations of delight, making much of her, patting and kissing and standing back to inspect her and finally allowing the girl to lead her to a sunny seat and feed her plump raspberries.

Hugging the child to her, Jacqueline exerted herself. She began to weave a spell about her, dazzling her with her exotic, foreign beauty. She predicted she'd have no trouble at all in finding such a *petite jolie* a husband.

Occasionally she glanced up to consider the young women who had continued steadily picking through all this. Bess and Libby were aware of how many rasp-berries must go to make just one bottle of cordial and could not afford to dally. Jacqueline watched Libby, frowning over her, her agile brain wondering what could be made of her. When she turned her eyes on Bess, however, they became cold and she sighed heavily.

"*Le Bon Dieu,* Bess! I fear me I shall never have a like success with you! Only observe the condition of your gown, all stained with berry juice and caught by thorns!"

"It is naught but an old one!" protested Bess indig-nantly. "Aunt said to put on old clothes! I have worn this gown many times these last three years!"

"I marked indeed that it is much too small for you!"

replied Jacqueline with a tinkling laugh, which had little humour and no kindness behind it. "I don't know what I shall do with such a—what is it your dear Papa calls you, a hoyden? Only look at your brother's wife, she is as neat and precise as the nun!"

"But ma'am, the only reason I borrowed an apron from one of the serving wenches is because I have no old clothes, only these rather plain gowns which—" She stopped, rather dismayed by the unkind comparison and not caring to admit she had no inclination to wear the costly, but plain, gowns her father had so approved, because they were obviously not fine enough for her new family. "Because they are too plain for my present company," she ended reluctantly.

"Non, you look perfectly attired for your present occupation!" said Jacqueline. "Bess would do well to follow your good sense. There is nothing wrong with that gown that *ma femme*, Marie, couldn't alter with a ribbon and a lace. A snip here, a touch there and you'll see. A little more frivolity in your dress and perhaps your hair dressed in a different style and you'll be *à la mode*."

Libby was effectively silenced by this damning faint praise and turned back with a sullen Bess to continue picking. For both girls, who had barely stopped talking ever since they'd entered the garden, all the lightness and the good humour had gone from the day. They picked in brooding silence whilst Jacqueline continued to lavish her attention on the younger girl. Hetta, unused to such attention, was only too happy to suddenly have the position of favourite. In no time at all she was Jacqueline's willing slave. Jacqueline however, was not used to children and certainly not fond of them. Very soon the child's high spirits began to irritate her and she became bored.

"Have you not enough of the berries yet, Bess? My how slow you pick!" she cried. "Come, I want you to take your sister to the house, too much sunshine in the heat of the day is not good for her and I want to make better the acquaintance of Hal's wife."

Reluctantly Libby and Bess left their occupation. Bess carried the basket of raspberries and escorted the little girl back to the house, whilst Libby, upon invitation, gave Jacqueline her arm as they strolled around the formal garden.

"So, you are the daughter of what my husband used to call a 'scurvy Roundhead' are you, chérie?" she asked with a twinkling smile, which robbed the words of offence.

"No!" Libby was unable to prevent an answering

smile even though she bristled instinctively at the inference. "No, my father didn't fight in the war. In the
beginning we were still in Virginia, which is where my
brother and I were born. It was only after the death of
my mother and baby sister that we returned to England and by that time the war was nearly over. My
father is a lawyer. When we returned home and he took
up law in Adamsholme, which is his birthplace. He
never was a Roundhead, but he was, before my mother's
death, a Puritan. He now says he is a man of good
sense!" She smiled at the thought of her astute, wily
father.

Jacqueline agreed with a nod of her dark head. "As
must be all men of the law! So, your Mamma, she died
many years ago, *oui*? This I understand! Yet you have
the brother, I think?"

"Yes, Justin, he is very clever studying law, but in
the vacation he helps my father," she replied, a proud
glow lighting her eyes.

"Justin?" said Jacqueline, wrinkling her nose. "Here
is something odd. Did my husband not say you both
had strange names?"

Libby blushed as she agreed. "We were both named
by my maternal grandfather. He was very much a Puritan. He named us Liberty, Justice and the baby who

died shortly after my mother, Democracy. Justice is my brother, but he prefers to be called Justin, as I prefer to be called Libby."

"Libby! *Ah bon!* That is much better! *Oui*, Libby that suits Hal's wife! Ah, now I can do something for Libby that I could not for Liberty, I think!"

Then as Libby looked at her puzzled, she made a comical face and continued, "*Chérie*, you have grown up the motherless child. Your father, an excellent man in his way, can have no idea of such things, especially if he was one of those cheerless Puritans. Your clothes, *chérie!*"

"They are of the very best quality, ma'am," said Libby quickly.

"*Mais oui*, I do not doubt it! A country lawyer allying his daughter to a gentleman's son, they will be of the best, but so dull, *chérie!*"

As Libby's face closed, she quickly added, "No, do not look like that. Me, I do not say this to wound you! My uncle, he is such a one as your papa, he tends the legal business of his fellows. My papa, he is dead now and with the Holy Virgin, but he was no more than, how you say, Master of the Horse?" She smiled as Libby nodded, frowning. "Like you, I am not *la grande dame*! Therefore we cannot afford the dowdy clothes! For us, *chérie*, we must have that touch of—" She waved her hands as her English failed her. "Not like the aunts, so fusty and dull, but smart and to attract the eye!"

Libby looked doubtful. "I don't think a lady of quality wishes to attract the eye," she said rebelliously.

"A lady of quality? *Le Bon Dieu! Chérie*, the Duchess of Cleveland is a lady of quality, no? Does not she attract the eye?"

"But ma'am, that is the point! The Duchess is not a lady of quality. She is the King's mistress!" said Libby sharply.

Jacqueline glanced to her nodding. "*Oui*! The King's mistress! So, only the trollops must look pretty and inviting, yes?" Then as Libby looked confounded by this reasoning, she quickly followed up her advantage. "No true lady of quality would wish to be mistaken for such a one as Barbara Castlemaine, you say? *Oui*, this is so, but between Barbara Castlemaine and the Aunt Margery, there is perhaps, the middle way?"

Libby, mentally comparing the two, gave a choke of laughter.

"Ah, you laugh, this is good! I tell you this Libby, not to hurt you, but for your own good! Hal, he is the handsome man, no?"

Libby sobered abruptly, "Yes."

"*Bon!* You had noticed!" she remarked ironically. "And it is good you make me no speech about handsome is as handsome will, or some such silly thing, like the Aunt Margery!"

"Does," supplied Libby with a giggle. "Handsome is as handsome does!"

Jacqueline frowned over the words, shrugging her elegant shoulders. "So, it means nothing to me! Hal is handsome and he does handsome?"

Libby couldn't stop a small laugh. "It means that those who are good are the prettier!" she explained.

"Pooh!" said Jacqueline. "Never will I understand this English! What I say is that Hal is handsome, so you, his wife, must keep his attention."

"I hope I know my duty, ma'am," said Libby stiffly, having endured this lecture now on several occasions.

"Duty? Poof!" she cried rudely. "This I will show you how to do."

"I am very sensible of your kindness, ma'am," began Libby.

"*Oui*, you will be when you see the changes I make!" interrupted Jacqueline "But come, why do we walk in this gloomy place? There is no sunshine and these trees give me the horrors!"

"The yew walk is generally thought of as one of the

finer features of the garden. It enhances the prospect."

Jacqueline cast a cursory glance at the distant view. "It is no more than trees and fields," she replied, her eyes turning back to the yews which lined the walk with more interest. "For me, I do not like so tall trees. I will tell Hal to have them chopped down!"

Libby opened her eyes wide at the thought of the uproar this decision would make. "But they make a nice protected walk in winter. And the birds depend heavily upon the berries. It looks as if there is a heavy crop of them this year."

Jacqueline eyed the berries, shrugging her shoulders once again. "The walk could be planted with limes, or perhaps the beech."

"Neither give winter protection," said Libby.

"Walking out in winter is injurious to the complexion," returned Jacqueline, as they quitted the walk and entered the flower garden. "You have the good complexion now *chérie,* but if you walk in the cold winds in ten years time you will look like the Aunt Margery! Take me to the herb garden. There we will find the marigold and the camomile. For you I will make the lotion for the face." She turned once again to look at Libby. "*Oui,* I can see I have much to do!"

Chapter Ten

Jacqueline seemed determined to keep Libby at her side all day long; first instructing her as they strolled about the herb garden on the uses of the many herbs there, then later, talking of her childhood in France. As Bess had said, Jacqueline was an amusing companion and could be entertaining. Yet as Libby listened spellbound, she remembered Bess's words and realised that for all Jacqueline could spin a good tale and make her laugh, she did not really like her. There was vindictiveness in the older woman's tongue and a single mindedness which Libby found frightening. She was relieved when supper preparations finally brought her release.

She hurried to the stable yard hoping to see if Hal had arrived, but his horse was still missing. She was turning back wistfully as she was called:

"Excuse me, Mistress Westwood."

She was so deep in thought, she'd not noticed the figure of Will Longstaffe until he was directly before her. She stared at him a little dismayed. He was so very antagonistic towards Hal that she fully expected his hostility to extend to her, yet his manner was bordering on pleasant.

"Master Longstaffe," she said blankly.

"I'm sorry to trouble you, Mistress," he said politely removing his hat, "But I was wondering, hoping like, that I might be able to have a few words with you."

"With me?" Libby's tone echoed her incredulity.

He grimaced and flashed her a rueful half-smile. "I could hardly expect Master Hal—Mr Westwood, to listen to me, could I? Not when I've been such a damn —oh, I beg pardon, Mistress—silly fool in my dealings with him!"

Libby nodded, accepting the truth of his words, but still bewildered and curious, "What do you want to say Master Longstaffe?"

"Well, ma'am, even though I've made an idiot of myself with regard to the young master," he said with a fine air of manly frankness. "That don't make me not care for Master Henry. I want to find out who did this dreadful thing to so fine a gentleman! We all feel the same in the yard and I wanted to say to the young master that we was all behind him, so to speak. He could call on any of us at anytime to assist him. The only trouble is I've made such a dog's breakfast of things that I doubt Master Hal would even give an ear to me."

Libby privately thought that in Hal's present mood this was most likely correct. She was rather swayed by the agent's humility in one who had previously been so very superior and arrogant. She said slowly, "Well, I could always pass on your message to Hal or you could, of course, speak directly to him if you wished," she added, recollecting that Hal was hardly likely to listen to her either.

"Why, thank you, Mistress, I'll try again to talk to him. Thank you, too, for listening to me so patient like. You see, I can't always get the right word or tone Mistress. My book learning were good enough for the usual run of things, but the Parson, he didn't bother with fine manners and etti—etiquette," he stumbled over the word. "I guess he knew he couldn't make a silk purse from a sow's ear," he ended with a guileless smile.

"Not at all, Master Longstaffe," she replied politely, "I'll be sure to try to speak to my husband for you."

"You are too kind, Mistress," he replied. "I'm anxious because—" He broke off and looked about him carefully, "Master Hal has not been at Westwood long, nor more have you, Mistress. There are things in the past that happen you should know about."

"Know about?" asked Libby taking up the bait.

"Aye, all is not as it seems, Mistress. No, nor will they be spoken of now. Not now Master Henry's dead."

"What sort of things should I know about?" said Libby.

Again the agent glanced about to Jonas dozing at his post, to the yard quiet in the warm afternoon sun. "Things I can hardly say here, ma'am," he hissed. "None now speak of the quarrel between my Master Henry and Justice Fenton, do they?"

"Mr Fenton? I understood him to be Mr Henry Westwood's great friend," she said in surprise.

"Aye, that's what is said, Mistress. All is forgot now. I wager Mistress Kingscott won't have spoken of it either, no, nor the magistrate himself!"

Then, as Libby stared at him in amazement, he added quickly, "It were long ago before the master married again, so likely Mistress Kate wouldn't know either. Few remember how Master Henry and Justice Fenton fought a duel when he tried to elope with Mistress Kingscott!"

"Aunt Margery?" cried Libby. She could not believe Aunt Margery had ever loved anyone with enough passion to elope, let alone a sombre man like Mr Fenton.

"This were years back, so I were told. Master Henry fought and wounded the Justice, aye and for many years they were at daggers drawn."

"When was all this?" asked Libby in disbelief, "How do you know?"

"I had it from my foster mother," he replied, "She used to be maid to Mistress Kingscott when she were a girl. It all happened before she wed Master Kingscott, of course. That's why they married her off so quickly to the master's brother-in-law."

"I—I cannot believe this to be true!" said Libby, her impression of Aunt Margery suffering a complete revision, "They actually eloped together?"

"So the story goes, but that's gossip! My concern is Master Hal should not overlook anything," said the agent eagerly, "What with Master Henry and the Justice being of different sides in the War, too, there were scores to be settled, I'm thinking. Indeed 'tis only since Master Henry took his parole that he and the Justice have been on terms." He broke off as voices were heard in the yard. "Someone has come, Mistress, I'll best back to my work. You'll tell Master Hal then? Warn him to trust nobody."

"I'll certainly relate all you've told me, but can you not tell me more?" she asked anxiously.

"I am waited upon, ma'am," he replied, "I'll speak with Master Hal somemore if I may, at another time."

"Yes, please do. I'll tell him to seek you out."

She hurried away, her head spinning in amazement. She could not grasp all that she had heard. The whole idea was too amazing and fantastic for words. In spite of her desire to immediately share the revelations with Bess, she realised she must first consult with Hal. All at once her anxiety to see him was intensified.

She took her place at the supper table; her head still in a complete whirl. She was so silent and preoccupied throughout the meal, that her plea of the headache was easily accepted and she was able to make her escape to the solace of her chamber.

Once there she still found she couldn't rest, and as the summer evening drew to a close and night came down, she began to pace back and forth between the door and the window. Dusk was long gone and the moon risen to glow like a great lantern in the sky, yet still Hal had not come home.

What really troubled her she decided, was that none seemed to treat the matter as being one for concern. When she had mentioned at supper his lateness, the aunts had passed it off lightly. They all seemed to think it was likely he would elect to remain at Dunhill to see his father and sister, to rest his horse and take supper with them and possibly even remain over night.

Libby had thought this was highly unlikely, but had been too unsure of her company to say so. Now, after pondering over it for some hours, she thought that Hal, in the fretting mood he'd been in that morning, was not like to be so easily soothed by the mere sight of his father. Surely Francis Westwood, hastened by his son's arrival to a belated sense of urgency with regard to his brother's death, would decide he must return to Westwood immediately. And in that case wouldn't Hal ride on ahead to give warning of the fact?

Her steps took her to the window once more and she leaned her heated brow against the panes, fighting off a sense of undefined foreboding. She was weary of trying to reason out Hal's actions. Their acquaintance was still too short for Libby to feel as if she knew or understood the actions of her husband or any of his family. Reluctantly she conceded Aunt Margery was probably right; everything would look better in the morning.

As she gazed before her, wondering if she got into bed she might feel sleepy, her attention was caught by the sight of a light dancing in the still reflection of the pond, which formed the centre of the formal garden. Unlike the few other lights of the house, which were steady in the calm of the night, this light moved hither and thither with a frenzied haste and appeared to come entirely from the wrong direction. Libby frowned and opened the casement wide in defiance of Aunt Margery's ban. She leaned out as far over the window-sill as she dared, trying to seek out the source of the light. As realisation dawned slowly on her, the blood in her veins began to run chill and she was aware of the hair on the back of her neck prickling, for the light was coming from the ruined west wing.

All at once every ghostly story, which Justin had ever relayed to her with ghoulish relish, darted into her mind and lodged there regardless of her efforts to oust them. She turned resolutely away, banishing from her mind's eye the chief favourite of his, which had told of a dead man's hand with lighted fingers chasing it's unfortunate victim until it sought relief in death, and glanced longingly to her bed. It would have been better by far to put all anxiety from her mind and seek repose, but now that option was denied her.

She stood hesitating for a few moments, then she put back her shoulders and with great daring slipped a cloak on over her nightgown. She was no longer a foolish maid, she told herself severely, to be frightened by childish tales, but most likely the mistress of this great house. As such it behoved her to seek out the author of the light and take them to task for trespass.

Having made this resolution, she could not forbear one more glance from the window, nor stop the shudder, but she forced herself to pick up her candle and hastened from the room.

It wasn't that she was afraid to go alone she reasoned, more that she felt she would like a companion, so she hurried along to Bess's chamber. The room Bess shared with her little sister was bare and furnished with oddments left over from other chambers. Libby had no time to make more than a surprised note of this, before shaking the sleepy Bess and putting a finger to her lips when she would have cried out in wonder.

"Shush!" she murmured, indicating Hetta who was sleeping the deep, dreamless sleep of childhood in the great curtained bed. "Bess, there is a light in the west wing! A flickering light!"

"My uncle!" Bess opened her eyes wide in horror.

"Your uncle is dead!" said Libby firmly.

"He is not yet revenged! They say the spirits of those murdered walk, unable to find rest until their murderer is brought to justice!"

Libby felt her own faint courage ebbing. "Shush! I am sure it is no more than thieves or perhaps a vagabond. I think we should go and see!"

"Go and see!" squeaked Bess in disbelief. "You and I? Why not call a servant or wake the aunts?"

"Only think of the fuss they would make! As for servants, whom do you suggest? Will Longstaffe must be fetched, and Tobias, once he knew what we feared, would not set foot outside the house! I know Hal wouldn't hesitate and I don't think we should either."

"But for us to go?" asked Bess, unable to deny the truth of this.

"Well, if you are too afraid," began Libby.

"Yes, I am afraid," admitted Bess frankly. "I think it is foolhardy for us to think of going alone. I know, we'll send Ned! You can't doubt his courage, of that I am sure!"

"Ned?" Libby asked, with some reluctance; not sure now she'd screwed her courage up, that she wished to relinquish the idea of going. "I suppose we could ask him to go with us."

Bess seeing she was determined, clutched at this concession. Getting swiftly from the bed she hurried to fetch her cloak. Thus suitably attired, they tiptoed along to the far end of the corridor, knocking lowly on Ned's door.

The rousing of Ned took some minutes, but once his indignation at the disturbance to his sleep was over and he grasped what was afoot, he entered into their plans with great enthusiasm. As he scrambled inelegantly into some clothes, he began issuing orders, taking the expedition entirely out of Libby's hands.

"It's almost certain to be ruffians!" he said confidently, tucking the folds of his nightshirt into his waistband. "Give me down my sword, Bess. I'll deal with the matter!"

"It may only be a beggar seeking shelter," Libby suddenly had the feeling the matter was getting out of hand.

"I'm convinced it is the shade of my uncle!" hissed Bess ghoulishly.

"Stuff and nonsense! There are no such things as ghosts!" cried Ned scornfully.

Libby warmed to the boy in an instant. "But you will take care, Ned!"

He ignored this warning, snatching his sword belt from his sister and drawing the sword from the sheath in a practised manner.

"Yes, I'll take care," he returned impatiently as Libby repeated it in growing anxiety. "What a work you females make about everything! Right, now you two wait here, this shouldn't take—"

"We are coming with you." Libby was firm.

He glanced to her, his look measuring. "You'll have

to hold your tongues," he said flatly. "I want no screech-
ing and such like!"

Giving no heed to their indignant protests, he ush-
ered them out of the house into the brightly moonlit
night. Soft-footed and hugging the shadows, they left
the safety of the house making their way across the
damp grass to the older building.

All was silent and dark. Ned had just begun to mutter under his breath about the over-worked imagination of females, when a light suddenly showed at the
window before them. It seemed to perform a stately
dance before being whisked away to suddenly appear
at another window.

"There!" breathed Bess. "No human hand ever held
that candle. See how it moves so fast it seems to glide!"

"Hush!" commanded Ned. To Libby's ears he sounded
less sure, and glancing to his ruddy face she thought he
looked very pale. "Come, we'll soon find out!" In single
file, with Ned leading they made their way to the door,
which stood thrown open wide.

"There!" Ned muttered in some satisfaction and relief. "No ghost I know ever bothered to open a door!
It's ruffians for sure! Now, take care. Bess, be ready to
run for help if there should be more than half a dozen
of them!"

In trepidation they crept again in single file down the dim gallery. Libby's candle cast ominous shadows on the walls and the flickering light made patches even darker in the gloom.

"Hist! He's in here," whispered Ned, his voice suddenly high in mingled fear and delight. He leapt forward, his sword at the ready. "Stand fast, villain! I have you covered!"

Hal swung round, startled, "Ned? Libby? Bess?" The lantern he held on high swinging drunkenly casting soft, mellow light over all.

"Hal! You are returned!" cried Libby, and the patent relief was there in her voice for all to hear.

"Yes, this hour past. What are you all doing here?" he replied, in a distracted manner.

"What are *you* doing here?" Bess was indignant. "We thought you a ghost!"

"I never did! I was certain you were a vagabond!" Ned was determined he would not be caught up in what he thought of as feminine nonsense.

"Or thieves," put in Libby, who felt quite faint with relief.

"I am neither," he said, a little irritably. "I'm looking for—" he hesitated and then explained. "When I got to Dunhill earlier today I found my father had indeed been there, and long gone."

"Gone?" cried Ned. "Where is he then? Back in London?"

Hal, his face pale with weariness, sighed. "Hopefully, but he told Mr Eustace he intended coming here to Westwood first."

"When did he leave then?" asked Bess, seeing his unease.

"He left two days after his arrival. On the eve of the feast of Corpus Christi, to be exact." Hal's expression was wooden.

"The eve of Corpus Christi? The day before our wedding? That was weeks ago!" cried Libby.

"Exactly," Hal said, looking grim.

"Where is he then? Where has he been all this while?" demanded Ned.

"I know not. I left Dunhill within the hour and traced his movements as far as I could. I got almost to Maucester, but after that there is no sight of him. As I rode on from there I had such a fear rise in me that I'd find—"

"Find, find what?" Ned interrupted fiercely.

"I thought I'd find him here. Dead." He glanced about him at the crumbling walls. "Dead and hidden, like my uncle. That is why I've been searching and searching, but I have found nothing." Exhausted he slumped back on a broken table.

"Have you searched every chamber?" Ned asked quickly.

"All but these last few."

Ned held out a grubby hand for the lantern. "I'll finish looking for you," he said.

Hal met his eyes frowning and then silently surrendered the lantern. As Ned pushed past, Libby and Bess entered the dusty chamber more fully.

Libby went to him, longing to take his weary head in her arms and kiss him, but she contented herself with resting her hand lightly on his bowed shoulder and asking, "Have you eaten today, Hal?"

"I ate some bread on the road."

"Then I shall find you some food the instant we get back to the house," she said quietly. "Shall we not go back now?"

"Yes, once Ned is done. For there is plainly nothing here—" He stopped as Ned gave a shout.

"Hal! Come quickly and see what I have found!"

In one bound Hal was through the door, tripping in the darkness and almost falling into the last chamber where the light of the lantern showed. Ned held up a blood-stained weapon in triumph. "Look! The dagger that slew our uncle!"

Hal clutched at the doorpost to support himself. "Dear God, I thought you'd found another body! Thank God! Oh, I thank God!"

"Where was it, Ned?" Libby eyed the dagger with distaste.

"Over in the corner there amongst that pile of old armour," said Ned. "I came in and thought I'd look through it to see if there were any pieces with bullet holes. This is the stuff which was worn during the siege of the house, you know. Then suddenly I came upon it!"

"How can you say it's the dagger which killed Uncle Henry if it is amongst the armour from the war?" asked Bess practically.

"The blood on it isn't that old, see, it's hardly rusted." Ned held the gory knife toward her. "Anyway all the weapons are kept under lock and key and well-oiled, I can tell you, for Will Longstaffe showed me once. Besides, this was concealed inside that cuirass."

As Bess made a wry face Hal held out his hand. "Let me look at that dagger more closely, Ned," he said.

Ned handed it to him. "Is that not a pretty toy with which to take a man's life?" He was unable to keep a note of satisfaction from his voice that he had made so useful a contribution. "Although by my guess it is not English workmanship."

"No," agreed Hal, turning it over and examining the blade carefully. "It's definitely not English."

"Why, it is very like the one Father carries, Hal," said Bess, leaning over his shoulder to look at the dagger. "You must remember. We bought it for him for his birthday some five years ago now. Don't you remember Mary insisting on having one just like it because the design of birds caught her eye?"

"Yes, I do," he said grimly. "I remember very clearly. Only it isn't *like* Father's dagger, it *is* Father's dagger! See, here is the broken blade where I borrowed it to take the stone out of my horse's shoe on the road to Calais!"

There was a dead silence at this as they all stared at the dagger with its tell-tale blood and broken blade.

"There must be an explanation," said Ned blankly. He took the dagger back and examined it again as if he could extract the secret from it.

"Of course," said Hal curtly.

"Father must have lost it!" said Bess, in a puzzled tone, her anxious eyes going from one to the other as Hal turned away hiding his face. "Yes, that will be it," said Hal, but Libby could see that he, like she, had remembered that Francis Westwood had been at his old home but once since his return to England.

"Come," she said briskly. "There is no point in remaining here any longer. We must go back to the house. Hal can have some food and we should all go back to bed."

"I couldn't sleep a wink!" declared Ned. "Hal, do you think—"

"Bring that dagger, Ned," said Hal. His face was grey with anxiety and fatigue as he turned out of the room. "I must first go and stable my poor mare. I left her standing in the yard and she is sore weary, poor beast!"

"If you wish, I could do that Hal," Ned offered awkwardly. "I can see you are equally weary."

"Would you be so good? I thank you, yes, suddenly I feel I have strength for nothing."

"Go you up to bed Hal, I shall bring food and drink to you," said Libby, seeing how leaden his steps were.

"I'll come with you to help," said Bess. Her troubled eyes went to Ned as he stood frowning, still considering the dagger.

Silently they all followed Hal back out of the ruins and into the moonlight, pausing only whilst Hal remembered to lock the door.

As they walked back across the grass to the house, all their sense of adventure and excitement seemed to fall from them, leaving everyone tired and worried.

"Come up to my chamber, Ned," said Hal as the boy turned aside to the stables. "We must talk about this."

Chapter Eleven

Libby was concerned for her husband as they entered the darkened house. She said, "Do go up to bed, Hal. Bess and I will see what can be found in the kitchens."

"Bread and cheese will suffice," he said with a yawn and without another word went across the hall and disappeared in the darkness.

"Poor Hal, he must indeed be weary, I have never seen him look so dismayed," said Bess thoughtfully as she struggled with the tap of a barrel of ale.

"Yes," said Libby. She added a few slices of beef to the half a loaf and heel of cheese she had already on a plate.

Bess half-turned to her, a question in her eyes, then she sighed and made haste to change the subject. "Libby, how glad I am that you came to wake me. I quite thought once you'd been with Jacqueline you'd not want me for a friend again."

"How so? You think I am a fool to be dazzled? No,

she is, as you said, fascinating but so cold, too. I would not want to think of her as a friend."

Bess smiled back at her. "I am glad Hal has wed you," she replied.

"Come, enough of this chatter. We must take food to Hal; he is half-starved," said Libby with a laugh.

When they entered the chamber, Hal was slumped in a chair in an attitude of complete exhaustion. For all that they laughed and tried to keep light-hearted, it was obvious the findings of the night weighed heavily upon them all. Libby quickly set the food before him and encouraged him to eat, whilst Bess poured him a mug of ale. By the time he'd drunk that and eaten a little, Ned was amongst them again.

"I did no more than unsaddle her and give her some water and hay, Hal," he said, as he came to join them. "I thought time enough tomorrow to see her groomed, but she'll need resting a good few days, too."

"Aye, I know right well I rode her hard," he replied. "Come, take a mug of ale and sit with us."

As Hal returned to his food, seeming suddenly to realise how truly hungry he was, Libby pressed Ned also to eat, knowing by now he could easily eat at almost any time.

When Ned had swallowed his last mouthful of bread

and washed it down with another mug of ale, he said bluntly: "Things look bad for Father, Hal."

"I know it," he replied quickly. "But that is all they do; look bad. I know there will be a reasonable explanation."

Ned nodded in agreement, but his eyes never left Hal's handsome face as he asked: "Where is he, Hal?"

"I would to God I knew!" Hal replied bitterly. "He cannot still be in London, for I wrote to him there days ago. But now he is not at Dunhill, and hasn't been for two weeks. I know not, only that, thank God, he is not here at least—and not dead!"

"But what of the dagger, Hal?" Bess blurted out the words as if she could contain them no longer. "Do you think Father lost it when he came here? Or was it perhaps stolen?"

"Again, I know not," he replied quietly. "I cannot remember the last occasion I saw him with it, try as I might."

"It must have been back in the Spring when he came here with you," maintained Bess stoutly.

"I do not know, I have not been in his company since that time," said Hal wearily. "I only know my father is innocent of this crime, however bad it looks." He glanced from face to face, as if daring them to disagree.

Ned sat frowning fiercely over a private thought. "I would to heaven we had not gone to that fair! I never wanted to go anyway, but Hetta kept talking about it. And Kitty desperately wanted to go, so she encouraged her. Kitty is supposed to look after Hetta, you know, but is like most females, useless at any given task. She went off after Will Longstaffe almost as soon as we reached Maucester."

"Will Longstaffe?" Hal asked in surprise. "I would never have thought him the sort of man to run after wenches!"

"No, he doesn't as a rule. Usually it's the wenches running after him. They think he is a fine fellow. Indeed, he didn't run after Kitty then, for she came back in a rare old taking and was weeping and spitting fury all the way home, too," said Ned.

"Why?" asked Bess curiously.

"Oh, Tobias said about seeing Will with another wench which put her in a flame. I don't believe he did, but she swore Will had promised to meet with her and take her to the dancing. And that he never came, but left her there to wait for him for hours."

Libby was amazed at the amount of gossip the lad had picked up and at the readiness with which he was prepared to relay it. She glanced to Hal to see if he had noticed, but he was too busy brooding over his father to notice Ned's tale.

"Father cannot have killed Uncle Henry," interrupted Hal, proving he'd not heard one word of this ingenious history.

"Why not?" asked Ned.

"Because it is not the sort of thing Father would do," said Hal, speaking with conviction. "He would *never* stab his own brother in the back and hide the body. If Father had killed Uncle Henry it would have been in a *fair* fight, with others watching!"

Ned nodded slowly, turning his thoughts over; thinking of his flamboyant parent. "Aye, there is much in what you say," he agreed. "But I don't think your friend the Sheriff will accept that as an excuse. He'll demand proof!"

"Then proof he shall have! Father must be found!"

"I *do* wish you'd stop stating the obvious," snapped Bess. "He *can't* be found, not just like that, or you would have done so already!"

"I don't think it would do any of us any good to quarrel. It is very late and we're all extremely tired. Why do we not talk again in the morning? Things might seem clearer then," said Libby peaceably as Hal glared at his sister.

"You are not as foolish as you look," Ned said simply, without any rancour as he got to his feet. "I'm for my bed. Goodnight!"

Bess chuckled as she made haste to follow him. "I don't think he truly means to be rude, Libby, it seems to come naturally to him. No wonder Father despairs of him! Goodnight, Libby. God Bless, Hal!"

There was an awkward silence once they'd gone. Libby made haste to put the chamber to rights. "I am sorry, Hal that you are so tired, but I do feel I should tell you something. I don't know if it is important or not, but I gave my word to Master Longstaffe."

"Will Longstaffe?" said Hal with foreboding, smothering a yawn.

Libby nodded and as swiftly as she could, told him the facts of her meeting with the agent that day. Hal listened at first with a face of scepticism that slowly turned to amazement and was replaced with a frown as she finished her account.

"What did you think? Did you believe him?" he asked.

She was surprised he asked for her opinion, "Yes, I did. I mean I was astonished, but, yes, on the whole, it was too shocking for disbelief."

He nodded, still thinking, then with another yawn

cast aside his doublet. "No—it's no good," he sighed. "My head is too stupid to think anymore tonight. I'll consider it in the morning."

Libby made no reply, still feeling there was a measure of constraint between them. She snuffed all but the last candle and made ready for bed herself.

"Goodnight, Hal," she said as she got into bed, but there was no reply as he was already asleep.

Chapter Twelve

The knocking on the door jolted Libby awake. She sat up abruptly, still confused by the nightmare that had wracked her dreams. In it ghostly hands illuminated Hal's blood-stained body, stuck through with the slender dagger they had found the previous evening.

"Oh! Who is there?" she cried in panic.

"It's me, Mistress Libby! That there Frenchwoman, Mistress Jacqueline's maid, says Master Hal is to go to her mistress at once!" Alice the maid's voice expressed her indignation at being commanded by another servant.

"What is it?" Hal sat up, his hair all on end, showing he, too, had spent a troubled night. "Who is there?" he demanded thickly.

"It's Alice," replied Libby, her tone carefully neutral. "Marie, your step-mother's woman, bids you attend her."

He fell back against his pillows, in an attitude of

weariness. "Damnation! What o'clock is it?"

"I don't know. It's late," said Libby. She went to open the door. "What time is it, Alice?"

"Gone nine of the clock on a fair morning, Mistress, if you please," she replied, with a saucy look. "Not that any of us would have dreamed of disturbing you and Master Hal, but that Frenchwoman says—"

"My compliments to my step-mother," Hal interrupted from the bed where he still lay with his eyes closed. "Tell her I shall be with her in five minutes."

Alice bobbed a curtsey. "Yes, sir. Will I bring you fresh water, Mistress?"

"If you please." Libby went to the window, still a little confused by the rude awakening, whilst Hal got reluctantly from the bed groaning.

"I see I am well paid out for my recent laziness. At one time, a day spent in the saddle would not have left me so stiff. It would seem I am growing soft and must take up my riding again." He glanced to Libby uncertainly as she made no reply to this and added: "Perhaps you and I could ride together each day. That way you would soon become proficient."

Libby hid a sigh as she turned from the window. "Yes, I suppose we could," she said, but without any enthusiasm. "As long as you don't think it would bore you."

He grunted as he tucked his shirt into his breeches, offended by her so patent lack of interest. "I don't see why it should. Tell Alice to leave fresh water for me, too. I'll make myself more presentable once I've seen what Jacqueline wants of me."

"Shall I wait breakfast upon you?" she asked, a note of jealousy in her voice.

He frowned, detecting something amiss in her tone. Then as she turned away from him, he shrugged and smoothed down his unruly hair. "Breakfast? No, don't do that. I don't know how long I am likely to be." With these words he hurried away, leaving Libby to shed a few hot tears.

He found Jacqueline also still abed and looking both wide-awake and extremely beautiful.

"Good Morrow, Hal. There, is that not right?" she asked, holding out both hands to him. "Is that not what these English say? Good Morrow!" She made a face and then glanced up at him in mock concern. "But what is this? My Hal to look like the rustic? Hal to be all unbrushed and unshaven!"

He bowed politely over her hand. "I beg pardon ma'am, for coming to you in so untidy a state. I have only just awoken and I gathered you wished to see me immediately."

Something flickered in her dark eyes and she laughed slyly. "Oh, Hal, a wearying night, eh? I think perhaps I have the envy of your bride!"

"I did not return from Dunhill until a late hour, ma'am," he replied stiffly.

She chuckled to see his discomfort and patted the bed beside her. "Sit, Hal. It is about your visit to Dunhill I wish to hear."

He sat down reluctantly, only too aware of her beauty and wishing there was some way he could keep her more at a distance without offending her.

She patted his knee and allowed her hand to rest there. "So Hal, you found no sign at all of your Papa?"

"He had been with Mr Eustace, ma'am. Indeed, I spoke with both he and my sister, Jane, who, as you know, has been left in Mistress Eustace's care to better become acquainted with the son, Philip. Both agreed my father was in excellent health and spirits when he left." Hal resisted the desire to wriggle away from her. He felt acutely uncomfortable, yet he could not deny how his pulses quickened at her touch.

"But *where* then is he gone, Hal, if he is not there?" she cried quickly, consternation spreading to her face for the first time.

"Alas, I cannot say," he replied. He felt himself getting rather hot under the collar as she leaned forward imperiously, her nightgown slipping from her pearly shoulders and revealing the soft roundness of her breasts. "I managed to follow his route as far as Maucester with ease. Then on the far side of the city I lost it. I cannot think if he were intent on returning to London he would have come so far out of his way as Chipping Barbury. Besides which—"

"Yes?" she prompted gently, looking up into his anxious face.

"Mr Eustace appears to have formed the decided opinion this house was his destination. My Father said something to him about not breaking in on the wedding where he wasn't wanted, but coming to Westwood Hall to see me settled and happy," he admitted reluctantly.

"He said nothing of this to me Hal." She leaned back against the pillows and wound the end of one long lock of jet-black hair about the tip of her forefinger. Her eyes met his in a knowing smile. "He promised me he would come straight back home, just as soon as he could."

"I do not doubt that such was his intention, ma'am, and it is that, in part, which worries me most. It makes me fear he has perhaps met with an accident."

Her eyes widened at this clearly original thought, and she took her plump under-lip between her little white teeth as she considered it. "An accident you say Hal?" she murmured lowly.

"Some mischance, either to his horse or to himself, which must have delayed him," he said quickly, not wanting to frighten her.

She stared at him horror-struck. "*Non!* The horse, he could get another. It is to him the mischance must have occurred!" She met his eyes again, her own now sombre. "You fear he is dead, Hal?"

"No, no," he replied too quickly. He glanced at her, all the anxiety of his heart plain on his face. "Not that; but injured perhaps; or taken ill. Ma'am, there must be something to account for his not coming!"

She nodded, not as he'd half-feared going into hysterics at the suggestion, but staring ahead, her eyes suddenly distant as she reviewed her situation. Hal was right; if Francis hadn't come, either to claim what he looked upon as his own, or to his son's aid or most important of all, to her side, then something dire must have happened. He must be either insensible, or dead, and if it were indeed the latter, where did that leave her?

She allowed her gaze to linger on her step-son as he

sat with his head in his hands, trying desperately to convince not only her, but himself that all was well with his father.

Hal was a very handsome man. She had long felt more than a mere admiration for his looks and his easy, unaffected charm. True, he was unsure of himself and untried, but with the right guidance such faults could soon be rectified. She was a stranger in a foreign land and must look to herself. If Francis were indeed dead, she must find another protector and quickly. Hal was not only convenient, but also very desirable. Unless she read the signs wrongly, which she had never yet done, he was strongly attracted to her.

She considered her best approach. Hal, for all that he looked the part of a Royalist, had almost a Puritan sense of right and wrong. Francis had often commented upon it, saying he'd little fear of the lad going astray with his principles. Yes, she could see that it might well be tricky, but Hal did have his weaknesses.

Slowly two tears formed in her eyes and trickled down her cheeks, followed by another two and then another. Hal, catching the sound of a sob, looked up in horror. He reached out impulsively to take her hand. "Oh Jacqueline, don't weep, I am sure in my own mind he is safe somewhere! I beg you will not weep!"

"Oh Hal, how can I but weep?" she cried. She took his hand clasping it in both of hers and holding it to her breast. "I fear me my beloved husband is no more! Oh Hal, what shall I do? Where shall I go? All alone as I must be, a stranger in this cold, unfriendly land." She cast herself expertly against his chest.

He held her to him, his arms coming about her reluctantly, his head suddenly light as he inhaled the heady scent of her perfume. "No, no, he is not dead, Jacqueline, I promise you. I swear to you I will find him! He is hurt perhaps, yes, injured somewhere, but I'll not fail you! I'll scour the countryside to find him and bring him back to you!"

She raised tear-filled eyes to him, her head resting on his shoulder, her lips moist and quivering. "Oh Hal, you are so good to me. You bring me such comfort. When you hold me close, I am no longer afraid! I know you will not desert me!"

He stared back down at her, trapped by her eyes, his blood pulsing at her nearness. He gave no thought to what he did, but answered the mute appeal of her lips, losing himself in their yielding softness. The kiss seemed to last an eternity, until she made a small movement to pull away, her tears coming into play again.

"Oh, Hal, Hal, do not! It is wickedness! See what

you make me do, Hal! I am lost—lost entirely!"

A look of incredulous horror came over his face as he, too, realised the enormity of their actions. He swallowed, his arms falling to his side in dismay. "Jacqueline, I beg your pardon! I never meant, oh, dear God, I never meant it! I cannot think what possessed me! Ah, Jacqueline, can you ever forgive me?"

She cast him a rueful, beguiling look over her sleek shoulder, before turning to him more fully. Her smile was coy; her eyes limpid. "Forgive, Hal? It is *I* who must go down on bended knee! It is *I* who am the wicked sinner! What? Have you never guessed at the longings of my wicked heart, Hal?" She gave a small, bitter laugh, as he looked utterly dumb-founded. "No, you who are so good, so free from all sin, how could you ever begin to think of such a thing? But me? Ah Hal, I think for me, once I saw you, I loved you!"

He stared at her in undisguised horror, his face pale. "But—but you love my—my father!" he said as if to deny her words.

"*Non! Non,* once I have seen you Hal, it was all finished for me." She managed to make it sound tragic.

"But I'd swear you love my father! You behave as if you do!" he cried desperately.

"*Bon!* Then my little deceit, it is successful and if it is so, all is as it should be and we need say no more of the matter," she replied with a brave smile.

"You mean—you mean—" he stammered.

"That I live the lie? Yes, Hal," she interrupted him. "Oh, you men! How little you know of a woman's feelings! Do you think me the first young woman tied to an old man, who has loved where she must not? The world is full of such as I. Full of women hiding despair under a brave smile. It matters not!"

He got to his feet, his brow contracted, whilst Jacqueline watched covertly. She rather thought she'd cast her line exactly right and that the bait had been well and truly taken. She was a consummate fisher of men. She knew when to give enough line before hauling in.

"Come, Hal, do not look so distraught. The world does not end. I should never have let you see into my heart. And but for my confession, you would never have guessed, now would you?"

"No," he replied with stark honesty.

"So! We will cast them from our mind and be as we were before. *Bon*, then we can be comfortable again!"

"I—I do not know that I can put them from my mind." He got up and walked away to the window.

She rose from the bed and followed him, her hand

coming to rest on his arm, soothing him. "Of course you will, Hal. You are still weary, exhausted by worry, by your endeavours to find your *Papa*. Tomorrow, when you are more rested, everything will look better."

He averted his face from her; aware his pulses were still racing from her kiss. Her fingers dug into the flesh of his arm burning like the touch of a hot poker. "No doubt you are correct, ma'am," he stammered. "Forgive me. I —I must go!"

Her other hand reached to detain him, grasping at the linen of his shirt. "No, wait Hal, do not leave me like this, so cold! Oh, Hal, I see you think me the trollop, the fallen woman; You have no more the respect for me you used to have!"

He looked down into her face. She saw enough in his eyes to be convinced of her success. "No! Madam, I assure you I do hold you in the greatest respect! It is not you at fault, but me. *I beg you!* Let me go before I disgrace us both!"

She released him and watched his hasty retreat with a smug smile of satisfaction.

⚜

As Hal returned to his chamber to make ready for the day he took time to compose his thoughts. His inclination was to escape, to get away entirely from the house and the problems which, far from easing, seemed hourly to become complicated, but first came his duty. The tale Libby had related to him the previous night was still on his mind. He needed to find out the truth behind it and there was but one way to be sure. He sought out his Aunt Margery and interrupted her with less than his usual tact.

"In fact, ma'am, I do need to have some words with you," he said as she paused expectantly. She was on her way to oversee Hetta's lesson, but if Hal expressed a need for her company he, as head of the household, had a right to her time.

"Words with me, Hal?" she repeated. She was aware from his abrupt tone something was amiss.

"Yes," he hesitated at first, hardly knowing how to broach the subject and then realising he had no choice, began firmly, "It's not that I want to distress you, Aunt, nor come to that, rake over old sores, but a tale has come to my ears. Rather than going behind your back to seek gossip from others, I thought you would prefer me to come directly to you for the truth."

"I am always a friend to veracity, Hal, as you well know," she agreed looking astonished.

"The tale is from a few years ago, Ma'am, before you were married," he said.

"Always the polished manner, Hal," she remarked in wry amusement. "Why not say many years and have done with it? You refer, I gather to my spring of May madness when I allowed myself to be persuaded into a clandestine match with Robin Fenton."

"Persuaded, ma'am?" he said, a question in his voice.

She sighed. "I fancied myself in love with him," she said baldly, "and in consequence embarked with him upon a course of folly."

"Course of folly?" he repeated, "You strip the tale of all romance, Aunt."

"I was a vain young woman and, but for my family, might well have lived out my life in regret. By the good grace of my father, I came to see the error of my ways and I had the strength of mind to recognise it and to act upon it," she said bluntly.

"What happened?" said Hal. He was taken aback at her detached manner.

"Robin Fenton was but a year my senior," she replied, her voice harsh, "We were both full of youthful high spirits. It was all for love and the world well lost!" Her voice trembled over the words, but she coughed and continued sublimely, "My father and your Uncle Henry were appalled at the damage to my good name. They pursued us and came up with us at Oxford."

"But what happened?" repeated Hal as she fell silent, her face suddenly hard in the sunlight.

"My father pointed out the evils of my situation and I returned home with him," she replied calmly.

"And Mr Fenton?" he asked, "It is a lie then? Did Uncle Henry not fight a duel with Mr Fenton? Did he not leave him wounded, thus ensuring they were at daggers drawn most of their lives?"

"You did mean gossip, didn't you," she replied tartly, with a sigh. "A duel? No! Fisticuffs? Yes. There was, I believe, an unseemly tussle, in which Robin was worsted. A slight he nursed, I gather, until wisdom came with the years. Certainly by the time I was widowed and returned home to assist Henry in the nursing of his first wife, they were firm friends again."

"Their differences over the war did not affect their friendship?" asked Hal frowning.

"Not to my knowledge. There was a coolness, but then so there was throughout all England," she replied, "My husband, Thomas, was for Parliament, too, Hal. Henry, like many, fought for the King initially, but became increasingly disenchanted by the political games the King played. Henry was glad to take his parole and pay fines. It was as well some men did, or all would have been ruined as your father was."

"Indeed, ma'am, I do not think to criticise my uncle," he said hastily, "Recollect I was not in England since I was a child. I do not understand the nuances of the war, but I do know my father's course has not always been—" he hesitated, "I was going to say the wisest— but I am no judge—so I'll say it was not the one I would have chosen."

"It was your likeness to my brother Henry in outlook, which most pleased him and convinced him you were a worthy heir to his estate, Hal," she agreed.

Hal paused, running over in his mind the little she had told him. "This was in the year 1626, Aunt; the year you were married?"

"Yes," she replied picking up her embroidery. "I was married in the November of 1626."

"Your husband was a widower, ma'am?" he asked as she said no more.

"A widower with a ten-year-old son," she agreed.

"Not a young man," he said pointedly.

"No, Thomas must have been one and forty the autumn we married," she replied calmly. "However Hal, I would not want you to imagine that I was in anyway opposed to the match, for I knew my duty to my parents. They were entirely correct. Thomas was a kind, steady husband; a man to depend upon. I was indeed gratified that he honoured me by taking me as his wife and trusting me as a mother to his child. My one grief was that I was not able to repay his goodness by further increasing his heirs."

Hal frowned again. He still felt he wasn't getting to the heart of the truth. "Did Mr Fenton marry, ma'am?" he asked idly.

"Yes, I do believe he made a good marriage with a young lady of fortune and impeccable breeding," she replied. "I never met her, I'm afraid, but reports made theirs a most successful match. Certainly Mr Fenton has shown no indication to replace her in his affections, or so common gossip suggests."

"No," he agreed, recollecting how comfortable a widower the Justice appeared to be. Yet Hal had an increasing feeling that he was just missing something obvious. He sat in heavy silence for some moments, trying to think of further questions. His aunt continued to sew until he felt obliged to say, "You've nothing further to add to the tale, ma'am?"

"I keep my embellishments for my hand work, Hal," she replied serenely, rethreading her needle and snipping off the length of wool.

"Then I'll detain you from it no longer, Aunt," he said getting to his feet and bowing, "I beg pardon."

Margery nodded as he went from the chamber and bent to her task; her face composed, concentrating as she couched a length of wool across the canvas.

Aunt Kate, coming in a few moments later, glanced to her in concern. "Is the light good enough for your work, my dear?" she asked, "I thought you said it was too overcast today and that you'd set Hetta to writing out a psalm as a gift for Jacqueline."

Aunt Margery hastily wiped away a few tears with a scrap of wool. "Yes, Kate, you are quite right," she said quickly. "But young Hal wanted a word and I took up my sewing to occupy my hands whilst he talked. See what an old fool I am! I've strained my eyes, making them water in this half-light. Better I leave it until to-morrow."

"Indeed, you should not attempt such fine work on a dull day, Margery. However, Jonas says the clouds are going over and the sun will be out within the hour. And you know how reliable he is with regard to the weather."

She crossed the chamber coming to look at her progress, "My, I don't know how you achieve such regular tiny stitches; you put mine to shame."

"My eyesight for close work has always been good, but I do notice the strain more now," Margery said in agreement. "I'll put it away and take up some hemming to do in the evening. Did you not say you had some of Ned's linen that requires repair?"

Aunt Kate laughed, "When do we *not* have torn shirts of Ned's? I vow I don't know what that lad gets up to with his clothes."

"Torn clothes are easily mended. It's torn hearts that cause trouble," said Margery. "I had better go and find Hetta. That child wouldn't even take up a pen if I were not there."

Chapter Thirteen

Libby had sat long dawdling over her breakfast, hoping against hope that Hal would join her. She'd ignored Aunt Margery's displeasure at Hal's apparent slothfulness, and refused Bess's tentative suggestion of a walk. She was finally forced from the table by Aunt Kate's determination to make her a tisane for the headache she plainly had.

Disconsolately she wandered from the parlour to the hall door and back again, her thoughts warring with her inclinations. She knew it was pure stupidity to object so violently to Hal visiting his step-mother, that she was a fool to let her jealousy ride her as she did. She knew, too, she had no ineffable right to Hal's affections, but even so, her scolding served no more purpose than to make her even more miserable. On the third journey to the door, which coincided with a burst of sunshine, she decided Bess was right. A walk in the fresh air would be the best remedy for her headache.

She set out in the direction of the park. She passed the dovecote and called out dutifully to old Jonas, then stood watching the pigeons whirl up in a cloud, as they always did. Very soon she met up with Bess, who had the good sense to remain an undemanding companion whilst they strolled the lawns.

They ambled for more than an hour in the parkland. As Libby's headache disappeared, she became more talkative and, as time went on, an amicable companionship was well-established between them. They had just decided, as they reached the furthest extent of the mown grass, to make the large oak in the outer park their destination on the morrow, when they saw a lone rider drawing near it.

"Is it your father, think you?" asked Libby, as both put up hands to shield their eyes from the sun. Her mind was on Hal's overriding anxiety.

"I think not. It has not the look of him somehow," Bess replied. She squinted short-sighted eyes in an effort to make out the distant figure. "Surely that rider is too slender a man?"

"He's slender; Taller than Hal, too, although not so broad," Libby paused as the rider came closer, waving his hat. Gradually recognition dawned on her and she exclaimed, "Why, it's Justin! It's my brother, Justin!"

Bess turned again to look in surprise. "Your brother? What does *he* here?"

"I can have no idea, but, oh it's so good to see him!" replied Libby, waving now and jumping up and down in delight at the prospect of seeing her brother.

Bess glanced to her radiant face, seeing the shy mouse suddenly come alive and look pretty with her flushed cheeks and sunny smile. "I'll go and leave you alone to greet him."

Libby caught her hand detaining her, knowing well how shy she was. "Please, do stay! I want to introduce you to my brother. Oh, Justin!" she called, as the rider came within earshot. "Justin, how glad I am you are come!"

Justin reined in his mount, his rather pale face flushed with the unaccustomed exercise. "Hello there, Libby! Are you well?"

"Indeed I am, and ever more so now I've seen you!" she replied as he pulled his horse to a halt and slid from the saddle into her arms. "Although I cannot think what brings you here! But first, let me introduce Hal's sister. Bess, this is my brother, Justin!"

Bess, her cheeks much flushed, sank into a curtsey and rose to find her hand in the clasp of a tall young man with serious eyes, who was, if possible, even red-

der-faced than she. In wonderment she raised her eyes
and looked up into his face, enjoying so novel an experience. He gazed down at her in delight and stammered
that he was happy to make her acquaintance.

Libby embraced him again and tucked her hand in
his arm. "What brings you to Westwood, Justin? You
are most welcome, of course, but I never expected father would let you come so soon."

Justin hesitated and glanced uncertainly to Bess. "Father, as you know, is most anxious not to encroach on
your new relations, but he is rather concerned and—
well, not to put too fine a point on it, he is worried
about your welfare."

"Welfare?" echoed Libby blankly, as Bess, too, turned
a questioning eye upon him.

"He is concerned about the events here," he said
looking embarrassed and as they merely stared at him
mutely, he added uneasily, "The scandal is pretty bad,
you know. I mean about Mr Henry Westwood's murder. All manner of rumours are being bruited abroad!"

"We know of them!" interrupted Libby.

"Aye? Well then, you must in some measure understand father's concern," he replied quickly. "After all,
as he said this morning, we don't know him. True, we
met at the wedding, but then only briefly. One can't

truly hope to form an opinion of a man's character in a few hours! Then, well, your letters have hardly been full of nuptial bliss. So when Widow Brewster came to see us all full of the latest gossip father grew very anxious—"

"Father grew anxious? One moment!" Libby stopped him in mid-sentence. "What do you mean? What rumour? What gossip has reached your ears?"

"Why, that Henry Westwood has murdered his uncle! Your husband, Henry—I mean, Hal do you call him?'

"Hal?" she repeated in astonishment, then in growing anger., "Hal? My Hal? As if Hal would kill his uncle! Are you mad? As if Hal would do any such thing! Why, you fool! Hal is a dear, sweet, gentle—oh, I have no patience with you! I will not listen to you!" Angrily she thrust aside his detaining hand as he tried to stem her mounting anger.

Justin ducked away swiftly from her fists. "Wait Libby! No, listen, I beg you! Hold, Libby, hold!" he cried desperately.

As Bess stood gaping in amazement, he caught first one hand and then the other, holding both fast. His horse, taking fright at the commotion, began to shy, so that Bess had to come to their rescue. She went to the animal's head and spoke lowly, soothing it whilst

Justin tried a like thing with his enraged sister.

"Pax, Libby, pax! I beg pardon, my dear sister, I swear I never thought your Hal could have done such a thing! I guessed how it was with you from the first, but Father thought your letters sounded as if you were unhappy. From that it was but one step to your husband neglecting you, and from there, to him being a monster!"

"My father is a well-meaning fool!" snapped Libby, who was still too angry to give regard to filial deference.

He released her hands, still keeping a wary eye on her face as he agreed diplomatically. "Possibly, but you must see that he has your best interests at heart. What if your Hal was a monster, rather than the darling you plainly think him?"

Libby blushed, realising too late she'd betrayed that which she would have rather kept secret. She put up her chin defiantly. "Why then I'd still be married to him and would by now have learned better than to bewail my fate!" she replied loftily.

He hid a smile. "Spoken like the true daughter of a lawyer and the wife of a gentleman," he responded, taking the bridle from Bess's hand with a murmured word of thanks.

Libby laughed abruptly, and then shook her head. "Now see how you have disgraced me Justin!" she cried reproachfully. "I had Bess here convinced I was a well-mannered lady. Now she knows me for a termagant."

"Aye," he agreed, "and worse still, can warn your husband of the harridan he has married, if you've not yet lost your temper with him!"

"It is not necessary to lose one's temper with Hal," Libby replied wistfully.

"He sounds a pattern card of all virtue!" remarked Justin with a grimace, glancing again to Bess.

"Hal is a good brother," she admitted with a chuckle. "If not quite the paragon Libby would have you believe. He is certainly a man to trust, and not most definitely not a murderer!"

"I am most relieved to hear it. However, if it was not he, then who *did* murder Mr Henry Westwood?" asked Justin astutely.

"That's a question Hal has been trying to answer. Come, we'll walk with you to the stables and explain things."

Justin hesitated, glancing toward the house in the distance doubtfully. "I am not sure in my mind that I should come to the house. Neither father nor I wish to intrude upon you and your new family."

Libby stared at him as they turned toward the house. "Don't be foolish. It seems quite likely this will be Hal's home now, and, as his wife, I know my family will always be welcome. Why, did he not invite both you and father to spend Christmastide with us when we parted at the wedding?"

"Yes, but that was mere courtesy," Justin hesitated and then fell reluctantly into step with them as they left the park. "So, father *was* right, Hal has inherited?"

"We are still not entirely sure until we hear from the lawyers in London, but it seems likely," she agreed.

"That's what the rumour hinges on, you know. In order to inherit, Hal killed his uncle," he said softly.

"Unfortunately all too many are ready to give credence to rumour and circumstance!" snapped Libby, her eyes flashing again. "However, as it happens, Hal knows where he was when his uncle was most probably killed. What is more, you can swear to it, too, for he was at our wedding."

"What? He knows when his uncle was killed? Come, this is excellent!" cried Justin, who sounded more cheerful. "But how can you be so sure exactly when Mr Henry Westwood was killed?"

Bess smiled as Libby hesitated, "I see no help for it Libby; we must tell your brother about the tapestry."

Between them, as they walked slowly through the park, past the dovecote with its pigeons and round to the stable yard they explained. There were many pauses for further explanations, but at the end Justin sighed, saying, "Father will be so relieved to hear all this. It is excellent the time of death can be fixed so clearly and that Hal is so plainly out of it."

As they walked under the arch of the stables their gaze turned to the figure of a horseman there.

Hal, for his part, looked at the group in astonishment, his eyes going to the arm the young man had about Libby's waist with a black look. Then as he suddenly recognised her brother, he jumped down from the saddle, and walked forward to meet them; forcing his voice to sound cordial, as he held out his hand, "It's Justice, isn't it?"

"Justin Danvers, Mr Westwood. Libby and I agreed some years ago that, although we may have been burdened with odd names, we did not have to keep them." He met Hal's eyes with an air of apology, and shook his hand firmly. "I beg you will forgive this intrusion on you sir, but rumours of what has occurred here have reached my father's ears and filled him with concern for his daughter's welfare. Thus you find me here, his envoy."

"You are very welcome, too, Justin," said Hal with an affability which did not reach his eyes. "I bid you make free of this home, which will most probably be mine. I know that my family and my wife will give every care to your comfort."

He turned his gaze to Libby, but once again his eyes were veiled and his manner distant. "I beg you will hold me excused, my dear. I have certain duties I must attend to and doubtless you'd like some time alone with your brother. We'll meet again at supper time, Justin, if not before!" Touching his hat in salute, he swung himself back into the saddle of his waiting horse and rode off, leaving Bess frowning and Libby looking miserable.

Justin watched him recede into the distance. "Poor Libby, now I understand. I'm sure he is a darling indeed, if ever the ice meltes!"

"Pray leave your horse to Peterkin to tend, Justin," said Libby. She made no reply to his remark, but she couldn't help recollecting just how shrewd her brother was. "And then we'll go to the house and tell the aunts you are come."

❦

Hal could not deny he was glad to get away from Westwood; his feeling of guilt when he looked at Libby threatened to overcome him. He rode his borrowed horse hard as he pounded across the sheep-filled meadows and on to the open heath above them. He galloped for some miles, then slowed his sweating horse to a walk, finding as he did so he had no choice but to consider his problems.

They seemed to be growing daily, and this last problem was most certainly one he could do without. Half of him couldn't believe he'd sunk so low as to kiss his father's wife. The other half of him was thrilled to the marrow by the heady rush of passion Jacqueline had unleashed. He could lie to himself no longer. He desired her with all his senses and had, if truth be told, done so ever since his father had first bought her home. Until this morning he had always managed to keep his feelings tightly under control, but now he could keep up the illusion no more. He desired Jacqueline with an intensity that still had every fibre of his being quivering, even though he knew such a longing was a deadly sin.

Yet he knew such thoughts, such longing, must be kept under control. He must find something, someone in whom to put his trust. Anything, which could save him from the maelstrom of destruction, which threatened to engulf him. There was no doubt in his mind; a betrayal of his father, whether in thought or deed, would lead to dishonour or worse.

Could Libby be that saviour? Could her sensible ways and practical ideas fill the void in his heart? True, she didn't fill him with a wild longing that half-frightened him by its intensity. She was good and gentle, and grateful for the slightest smile, but that spark which made every encounter with Jacqueline one of vibrant passion was missing.

Libby, however, was his wife and he owed her a duty. The logical side of his brain acknowledged that, even as his emotions swept over him once again. For a few minutes he wondered if he were verging on mania, as his desire threatened to consume all his good intentions and noble longings. He lifted a hand to his head, which was aching fit to burst, and made a mental effort to break free. He was a man full-grown. He knew right from wrong. He must remain true to his aspirations and not give way to baser instincts. He was not a woman's plaything or a mindless fool to be dragged into the pit of Hell by lust.

Jacqueline was but a woman, and furthermore, his father's wife. To desire his father's wife was wrong, therefore he must not do so. He sat for some further minutes concentrating on future actions, then he straightened in the saddle and faced up to his responsibilities with resolution. With all the strength of his character, he put thoughts of Jacqueline to one side. His infatuation with her was over. He would heed his aunt's advice and make sure he was never alone with Jacquline again. He didn't need to test his hard-won control past endurance.

Hal returned to the house calmer, but very weary. He had lost best part of the day in his deliberations, but at least he was finally at peace with himself.

"Hal? Is that you?" Aunt Kate called, coming from the parlour. "Oh good, I am so glad you are come at last. Libby was growing quite worried. Never mind that now, for Mr Newcombe has arrived from London."

"Mr Newcombe?" Hal took off his hat and gloves in a manner which showed how exhausted he was.

She came to clasp his arm and smile bleakly up into his face. "Your Uncle's man of law, Hal. He brings the will with him and says Henry left London two whole days before Corpus Christi. Other than his murderer he must have been the last person to see Henry alive!"

Hal covered her hand gently. "Courage ma'am," he said kindly as her voice cracked.

She cast him a fleeting, grateful smile; took the fine

linen handkerchief he offered and mopped her brimming eyes. "Dear Hal, what a considerate boy you are. I assure you, it is comforting to me just to have news of him, even if it does make me cry! It is such a relief for us to have someone as dependable as you!"

Hal looked bleak, thinking how far he might fall in everyone's expectations. Then, as she blew her nose she added, "Mr Newcombe tells me Henry left him in the very best of spirits, full of energy and vigour!" Once again her ready tears spilled over, but she wiped them quickly saying, "And that is most certainly because of you Hal, for he told Mr Newcombe that at last he'd got himself an heir to be proud of, one he would gladly call son if he could!"

Much embarrassed and feeling even more that he was despicable, Hal smiled uneasily and pressed her trembling hand, saying, "Pray, ma'am, come with me and introduce Mr Newcombe, if you please."

"Oh, yes, of course I will Hal. Give me but one moment to dry my eyes, or Margery will scold me again."

After such a hint as this, Hal wasn't really surprised to see his Aunt Margery sitting in state in the large parlour, giving the family lawyer the benefit of her advice on sundry matters. The lawyer stood up as soon as Hal entered. He was a large, shambling man with pudgy features and the myopic vision of one who spends his days shut off from the sun with books. He appeared relieved the *tête-à-tête* was over.

"Mr Westwood, I'm delighted, delighted, to make your acquaintance," he said, taking the hand Hal held out in a cold, damp grasp. "Your uncle was full of your praises on the last occasion we met. The last, now in retrospect, melancholy occasion!" he added dolefully.

Hal nodded, and unable to think of any thing to say in reply, courteously invited the man to resume his seat.

"Oh, yes, yes, indeed. I'm vastly obliged—vastly obliged! And, as I've just been explaining to this dear lady, your aunt here, I've come post-haste. Yes, post-haste, to tell you that your uncle's will, the new one, naming you heir, is indeed valid. And that you inherit this worthy house, its contents and lands." He paused to bow, and turn a face of acute melancholy in Aunt Kate's direction. "As for your uncle's widow, dear Mistress Westwood, was already previously provided for by various settlements of her own marriage contract. Yes, yes, already provided for."

Hal nodded solemnly, biting his lip in an effort to quell a reprehensible desire to giggle at the man's absurd trick of repeating himself.

"As the will is a lengthy document and concerns

mostly your good self, Mr Westwood, I will refrain from reading the whole thing at this date. There is nothing of note, merely a few smaller legacies to faithful servants. And the slightly larger one in the form of Rushley Manor to your younger brother Edward, whom I understand is more commonly known as Ned, which I might add, you will be required to manage until he attains his majority."

"Rushley Manor?" Hal was surprised, for this had been his father's property. His uncle had promised to make over to him and he and Libby had expected to make it their home.

"Yes, Rushley Manor, the property your father lost and later your uncle was able to repurchase. Now you are thinking no doubt, young sir, that your uncle had intended to leave it to you for a wedding gift?" The lawyer continued as Hal nodded, "Yes, indeed it was his initial intention. Indeed he actually carried the deeds of it on his person when he left me, but he had decided in the course of our time together that it was to be loaned to you only. It was his intention that Rushley Manor would be a place for you and your young bride to learn the business of running an estate. Then, in turn, on his death it was to come to your brother if he had attained his majority."

"Yes, thank you, I understand," said Hall, nodding. "Pray continue."

"As I was saying, since so few people are involved, and in view of the tragic circumstances in which we find ourselves, it is my proposal to read the document to you and your guardian only."

"My guardian?" asked Hal blankly.

"Indeed sir, you are a little short of your majority, I do believe?" The lawyer raised his brows in an inquiry.

"I am not one and twenty until October," agreed Hal.

"Your uncle was a man well-used to listening, and may I say, profiting from advice. He saw no need to insert a clause pertaining to his early death, but I— with perhaps what can be termed melancholy foresight, insisted that he did."

"Who is my guardian? My father?" asked Hal quickly. A frown creased his brow, as he realised, yet anew, that until his father came he was powerless to act.

The man cleared his throat delicately. "I fear not, sir. Your father, excellent man though he undoubtedly is, did not find favour with his elder brother, but this is no news to you! You of all people must be aware of the discord between your uncle and father. So it will not be a surprise when I name your uncle's friend and fellow magistrate, Mr Robert Fenton, as your guardian."

"Robin Fenton? A man of straw! I would have thought Henry had more sense! " cried Margery.

"Henry had the highest opinion of Mr Fenton, Hal. He is a good man. You may put your trust in him!" said Kate gently.

"I have indeed met Mr Fenton, ma'am. I was most impressed by his kindness and good sense. It was he that came here initially with Sheriff Hughes. I think he is the man to stand my friend over the next few months."

"So, Mr Westwood, if you will be so good as to agree, then Mr Fenton can be summoned here, we'll meet again and I'll do myself the honour of reading your uncle's will—yes, reading the will!"

Hal nodded again. "Thank you," he said gravely. "I will write to Mr Fenton at once and communicate this to him."

"All done, young sir, already in hand! I took the liberty of doing so," the lawyer said. "It being my duty, so to speak. I am given to understand Mr Fenton will be pleased to join us tomorrow at noon to settle the business."

"In that case you leave me nothing to do, sir, but invite you to take supper with us," said Hal politely.

"Thank you, Mr Westwood, but I must crave your

indulgence," he replied quickly. "I partook of a heavy dinner, as is my custom, at an inn on the road and now ask nothing but that I be allowed to retire to a chamber at the inn in the village. I must look over some more papers before seeking the solace of my bed." He heaved a sigh and patted his solid buttocks. "A London lawyer gets precious little exercise. I shall pay heavily for my hours in the saddle this night I think!"

Chapter Fourteen

Justin came down into the hall shortly before the appointed hour for supper and had the good fortune to find Bess and Hetta there.

"Oh, Mr Danvers," Bess smiled faintly. "My aunts send their apologies. Aunt Margery is making a tisane and will join us later, whilst Aunt Kate has gone to see her cook about something being burnt."

Justin looked inordinately relieved. "I met your Aunt Margery earlier, but have not seen Mistress Westwood yet. I imagine she must be greatly grieved by her husband's untimely death."

"Oh yes, she is," agreed Bess simply.

As he stood talking to Bess, Justin became aware of the steady scrutiny of the younger girl.

Then as the silence lengthened and became uncomfortable, she observed, "You are very tall, sir; even taller than Hal. Ned will not like you."

"Ned?" said Justin. He was taken rather off balance

and unable to think whom Ned might be.

Bess made haste to explain. "Ned is my and Hetta's full-brother, sir. He is somewhat short in stature and of a consequence, has a dislike of tall people. He always calls me a Long Meg."

Justin smiled, having been the butt of many such names himself. "Plainly it is all a matter of degree, Mistress Bess, for I must confess I think your height quite perfect. You are the first young lady I have not had to crick my neck to talk to. No more do I feel like a maypole when I stand beside you."

She laughed, blushing a little at his look of admiration. "It is a relief to be able to look up when I speak to a young man. Other than Hal, everyone I know is shorter than I!"

Justin was delighted to see how her eyes lit up as she laughed. "A strange disfigurement, Mistress Bess. How odd that we two correctly proportioned humans should be lucky enough to meet. It must be fate!"

Libby entered in the wake of Aunt Kate and noticed how at ease they were in each other's company. She realised she'd never seen Bess look so handsome, and a sudden idea took wing over the supper which followed.

Upon Aunt Margery's appearance at the appointed hour they sat down, even though neither Hal nor

Jacqueline was yet of their number. Margery grimly took note of the fact and that Libby was aware of it, too. They had not begun long however, before Jacqueline made her entrance, staged as Libby became convinced, for her brother's benefit.

"Good evening, Sisters, I am glad you have not waited on me," she said, pausing on the stairs so that the full glory of a gown of yellow taffeta, which would not have disgraced a court ball and set off her dark colouring to great advantage, could be admired.

"Supper, as I explained to you this morning, is always at the same time, Jacqueline," replied Margery. Her lips tightening at the sight of her sister-in-law, for all about the table, save Justin, who wore a russet doublet, were dressed in sober hues in deference to the recent death of Henry Westwood.

"*Oui*, come rain or shine, comment or catastrophe, the supper it must be at the same time!" she replied with a sigh, coming to the table.

"Do people in France not observe mourning as a sign of respect, Jacqueline?" asked Margery coldly as the servant helped to her some mutton.

"*Mon Dieu*, always the dead sheeps!" sighed Jacqueline. "What is this you say? Mourning? *Naturellement*, we French observe the mourning, but me, I have not the mourning clothes. I have ordered them and they will come—but not yet!"

Margery hardly knew how to express her outraged feelings. "In the meantime have you not something more sober to wear?"

"Sober? What is this sober? You say I am the drunkard?" cried Jacqueline, wilfully misunderstanding her.

Bess interrupted quickly, observing that her Aunt Margery looked deeply offended at even the suggestion. "No, ma'am, my aunt wasn't saying that you were drunk. She is asking if you did not have a gown in a darker, more sober colour."

"Francis, he likes to see me *à la mode*. At Court we do not wear the black and the grey. That is for the Roundheads. No, at Court everyone must be gay!" she replied with airy indifference.

"I fully appreciate what you say Jacqueline, but this is not the Court. I am only pointing out the discourtesy you do to your husband's family. Ah, Hal," Margery stopped her patient explanation as he entered the chamber. "I am glad you are come at last. Perhaps *you* can make your step-mother understand that she insults Henry's memory and poor dear Kate, too, by wearing the colours she does!"

Hal looked pale and exhausted. He glanced from his

Aunt's angry face to the satisfied one of his step-mother. "Jacqueline doesn't yet have mourning, ma'am. Once it arrives I am sure she'll be as ready as any of us to show respect for Uncle Henry."

Jacqueline applauded her stepson; her eyes triumphant. "*Bon,* Hal that is what I say! But your aunt, she cannot understand my words!"

"I understand you very well, Jacqueline," snapped Margery. "I don't need to understand the French language to know what you are about! Your tricks are as old as time itself."

She turned again to her nephew, who was contemplating with distaste the food before him. "Hal, please explain to your stepmother, as she claims she cannot understand English as I speak it, that to wear a yellow gown to supper in the house where a relative has recently died is a grave insult."

"Yellow is a colour of mourning in some countries, I believe, ma'am," he replied wearily.

"But not in France, Hal, and most certainly not in England," retorted Margery.

Hal turned reluctantly to Jacqueline, speaking lowly and fluently in French. She retorted swiftly, her eyes dancing, to which he replied with a curt answer and returned his attention to his supper.

"So, it is the prettiness of my gown you object to, Sister," said Jacqueline. "A compliment, I think, if not reluctant! Would you say it is a compliment, Hal?"

Hal gritted his teeth. "I cannot say, ma'am, for I do not know what is in my aunt's heart."

"I shall take it as a compliment, for it is a pretty gown. The King Charles, himself said so, and there is no greater authority!" she announced, as Margery cast up her eyes in exasperation. "Do you think it is pretty, Libby?" Jacqueline turned to her suddenly.

Libby blinked at the tone of interrogation and replied politely, "Yes, ma'am."

"And this young man, he is your brother, I think? He thinks I look pretty?"

"Oh, I beg pardon, ma'am. This is my brother, Justin Danvers. Justin, this is Hal's step-mother, Mistress Francis Westwood."

"I am Jacqueline," she said. She pulled a face at Libby. "So, you are Libby's brother? *Bon!* Now, Libby's brother, is not my gown pretty?"

Justin looked dismayed by the question. He felt he was in no position to make a comment on anything. Before he could get lost in an embarrassed morass of sentences, Margery interrupted. "I think far too much discussion has gone into a very trivial matter. If you would just present yourself in future more suitably gowned, we would be grateful, Jacqueline."

"*Mais non*," she replied. "I canvass opinion, me. I ask Libby's brother what he thinks. I have already asked Libby, who is mistress here, and now I ask Hal, who is master. Am I not beautiful, Hal?"

There was an abrupt silence at this, all turning to Hal to see how he would deal with this challenge to Margery's authority, which had been implicit these last twenty years. He looked at the smiling, beguiling face of his step-mother. He recollected that he had been reared to think of the truth as sacred. "Jacqueline, you know very well you are beautiful, but you are causing my aunts grave distress. Please dress in darker clothes in future."

Jacqueline flashed him a knowing smile and bowed her head in feigned obedience, whilst Margery tried hard to believe her authority was undiminished.

Libby, who had seen the look on Hal's face as he spoke, grew quiet over the remainder of supper. She was disconcerted by the jealousy that flared in her heart. Hal had never once looked at her in that manner. Most of the time he hardly appeared to notice her at all. She longed for the uncomfortable meal come to an end and was glad when it finally did.

❧

Libby led Justin away to the parlour. She needed a few moments with him to regain her sense of balance, but before she could say one half of it, Bess joined them in the window seat. Libby very quickly understood why Bess had followed them and couldn't feel cross that she'd interrupted.

Soon they fell to discussing the events of the last few days. It was the arrival of the Aunts and Hal and Ned that brought this to a close, then the conversation grew more general.

It was only after the aunts retired that Libby and her brother drew closer to the table, and the talk began to be more openly of what was on their minds. At first Hal resisted the conversation, snubbing Justin's opening remarks with a haughty arrogance. Libby instinctively knew his bad manners were caused by the despair he felt and tried her very best to pour oil on the troubled waters.

Justin bore this pretty well although his eyes began to sparkle a little and he was privately coming to the conclusion Libby's husband was an unpleasant fellow. Ned, who'd been seated at a distance lovingly shining an old flintlock pistol, came to join them.

"It looks bad for your father," observed Justin, with a grimace.

Hal had been sitting pretending to read a book and interrupted sharply, "Only on the face of it."

Justin disregarded Hal's words as he had his behaviour. "It is a thousand pities your father cannot be found. Wild rumour already abounds. It is something which should be discredited as soon as possible."

Hal turned about to face them. "Do you imagine I don't already know that? I have been doing every thing I can to disprove them."

"You'll forgive me for saying so Hal, but all you've done so far is to run mad over finding your father," said Justin, with disastrous frankness.

Hal drew himself up, deeply offended. "It struck me as important that he be found," he replied curtly.

"No doubt it is," agreed Justin pleasantly, "but surely not as important as finding out exactly what happened here on the feast of Corpus Christi?"

Hal felt aggrieved. It had been a difficult and trying day. The last thing he needed was a bumptious brother-in-law to find fault with his actions. He put aside his book and came to the table. "Contrary to what you seem to believe, I have made such enquiries and established a few facts. When I questioned Tobias, some days ago, he told me of all that was known at the time, including the odd occurrence of sand between the flag-stones, and further questioning prompted him to produce this," Hal struggled briefly with the purse at his belt and finally produced the metal tag attached to a scrap of ribbon, which he held out with an air of mild triumph. "I have yet to talk to Jonas who—"

Bess snatched the ribbon from him in horror. "That's a ribbon from father's new doublet! I know it is, for it is the exact shade of green and tipped with silver. It is the latest fashion from France. He wore it when he took Jane to visit Mr Eustace's house at Dunhill!"

There was a deathly silence as the implications of her words sank in. Hal turned very pale indeed, but Ned's eyes glittered as he pursed his lips, saying: "Add that to my father's blood-stained dagger being found and I think you—"

"Hold your tongue!" cried Hal. He rounded on the boy in a voice none had ever heard him use before. His eyes flashed and dared Ned to utter the words, which hovered on his lips.

All looked startled, none more so than Ned, who flushed scarlet and looked sulky. Justin however, remained unawed. He took the ribbon from Bess's nerveless hand and examined it carefully, before saying: "So, one can't deny, Hal, evidence is mounting up against your father. Surely this makes it more imperative we discover all we can! Don't you see? Until we discover the truth—the whole truth—things look very black for him?"

"I utterly refuse to believe anything against my father," snapped Hal, looking thunderous.

"Yes, that sounds very noble," remarked Justin, with biting sarcasm, "but to my mind your very bearing refutes your belief. If you truly thought him innocent, you'd not be forbidding speech, but encouraging it. The truth of the matter is, you are terrified. You fear that we've hit upon the truth: Your father *did* murder his brother for the inheritance!"

Justin, very much the more slender of the two, felt a moment's qualm as Hal's eyes blazed with fury, "I very much regret that you are not only a guest in my house, but my wife's brother. Otherwise I'd thrash you soundly for those words!"

"Oh, don't be such a fool!" cried Justin impatiently. "By all means hit me, if it will make you feel better! In truth, I don't relish violence, but I'd sooner that, than have you continue to hide behind this icy facade of good manners! Don't you see? This is all far too important for such play-acting foolery!"

"Justin—please! Hal—don't! Justin, can't you see they are not used to plain-speaking?" Libby caught his arm, and Hal stared at his outspoken brother-in-law in disbelief.

"Aye, more's the pity!" sighed Justin. "Well, I'm sorry to have offended you Hal, but I tell you this, if it were *my* father in such a fix, I'd not give a damn for fancy words and honour. I'd just set to and find out the truth. To quote the Greatest Authority of all: 'The truth shall set you free'!"

Hal, who was speechless with fury at the accuracy of Justin's words, merely glared at him and would have walked from the room in dudgeon, but that Libby begged him not to leave. As he stood trying to regain control, the justice of some of his brother-in-law's words sank into his consciousness. He hesitated and finally said through gritted teeth, "I must beg pardon for my conduct, Justin. Plainly it is inexcusable."

If there was an edge to this, Justin wisely ignored it, forcing himself to speak pleasantly for Libby's sake, although he would have liked nothing more than to tell his arrogant brother-in-law exactly what he thought of him. "Don't fret, old fellow, I can see you are worried to death about your father, and with good reason. Now, let us all be friends again, and sit down and see what exactly we have in the way of ideas about what did happen that day!"

Hal took a seat with a faintly injured air. Justin exchanged a speaking-glance with his sister. "Now, you'd already left for your wedding Hal, and your aunts and their retinue followed, right?" He nodded as both Hal and Ned assented.

"So basically Ned, you and your sister, your Uncle Henry and the servants were left here. Is that correct?"

He took a tablet of paper from his pouch and a pen whilst Libby fetched an inkwell from the cupboard. Ned answered after some consideration, "No, my uncle left for London after Hal, but before my aunts. So it was just me, my sister and the servants left."

"Mr Henry Westwood most certainly went to London. We have your lawyers testimony for that, Hal, and he certainly intended to return," said Justin. "At least it would seem he did. Did he ride home? I believe Bess told me he rode to London, so is his horse here?"

"His horse?" Ned looked blank. "No, his horse is not here."

"He did ride to London? You *did* say, did you not, that he rode off to London?" Justin looked at their faces.

"Yes, he always did!" said Ned.

"Uncle Henry hated to travel by coach," said Hal. "He'd ride as far as Oxford the first day and stable his horse there at the Golden Lion, leaving it well cared for, and then proceed to London the following day on a hired horse, picking up the beast again on his return journey."

"Did he ever take a groom with him?" asked Justin.

"No, he never did," said Ned. "He said they fidgeted him unbearably. They were always wanting to stop to eat or sleep. He said no modern youth, except me, would have made a good soldier."

"So your uncle's horse is still at the inn in Oxford?" asked Justin.

"It would appear not," said Hal. "My aunt sent Sam, the groom, to Oxford yesterday to collect a parcel. He stopped at the Golden Lion to inquire, but the landlord told him my uncle had collected the beast, just as he said he would. Sam said they were all shocked by news of my uncle's death.

"So where is the animal?" asked Justin. "We know your uncle returned, for his body is here, but where is his horse?"

Hal frowned. "Perhaps the murderer hid the horse."

"How can one hide a horse, Hal? A horse is too large to go in a cupboard," Ned replied with a grin.

"But if we remember the dagger, Ned, we know a horse could easily be hid, in a field with other horses for a few days. A saddle and a bridle, too, if need be, and both later sold off!" Hal's frown deepened. "Wasn't there a horse fair last week?"

"Aye, there was one at Gloucester. Will Longstaffe went; he always does." Ned's grin faded and he suddenly looked serious.

"Then he must be the man to ask about it," said Justin making a note of it. "I imagine he would recognise your uncle's horse, would he, this Will Longstaffe?"

"He is my uncle's man, his agent," said Hal. "He would surely have recognised the beast at once. I will talk to him about it."

"Good, we begin to make some progress," Justin made another note. "Now to get back to the day in question. It seems that your uncle *did* return, but none of you were here. I am right in thinking none of you knew of it, for you'd all gone to the fair. Whose suggestion was it, by the by, you all went to the fair?"

Ned frowned, as if the thought had never occurred to him. "I don't know. The serving wenches had talked of nothing else since the King's return. My uncle wouldn't allow them to celebrate May Day, you see."

He shrugged, frowning all the more in an effort of concentration. "From what Kitty said, Will Longstaffe announced that my uncle had given permission for us all to go."

"Your uncle? Yet he'd left the day after Hal," said Justin. "So that means he either wrote to Will Longstaffe giving permission, as I suppose he might well do, needing to keep in touch with his agent. Or he saw him sometime after he left."

"Or Will Longstaffe made it up because he wanted to go to the fair," suggested Bess.

"Why should Will Longstaffe do such a thing? He's hardly the sort of man to want to go fairing!" protested Hal.

"Aye, but he is a man. Don't you recall me telling you of the fuss Kitty made because Tobias said he saw Will with another wench?" said Ned bluntly

"But this Will Longstaffe is your uncle's agent, isn't he?" asked Justin, as they all exclaimed over this. "He, of all people, would not need to go to a fair. He, surely, could see his ladylove whenever he chose. Do any keep a check on his movements?"

"No, neither they do," Hal sounded depressed at the loss of what had seemed a promising idea.

Justin turned to a fresh page and made a note of

Will's name. "I think we should both talk to this Will Longstaffe."

"That won't be an easy task," remarked Hal. "He already views me with dislike and suspicion."

"I'll do it," Ned offered. "I talk to him a lot anyway. He wouldn't hold me in suspicion because he thinks I don't like Hal either."

Hal held his brother's eyes for a few seconds, seeming to question him. He then transferred his gaze to Justin, saying quietly: "Write Jonas's name down too, if you please."

"Jonas, the blind dove keeper, I think you said," replied Justin. "What use can he be?"

"I don't know," said Hal. "He was the one person who remained at Westwood on the feast of Corpus Christi. He may be able to tell us something."

Justin was glad to see Hal was beginning to think rationally. He wrote the name down as bidden. "Right, now we have the dagger." He nodded to the dagger Ned held in a grubby handkerchief. "And this piece of ribbon to add to it." He continued, "This next piece must be speculation, of course, but the murderer, having found or contrived a deserted house, proceeds with his plan. Was your uncle being lured here? Or more likely, he just returned unexpectedly, to find—"

"The tapestry being stolen?" interrupted Bess.

"I suppose it could be that simple," said Justin frowning.

"But that wouldn't explain my father's dagger, nor the ribbon. Unless you wish to suggest my father is a thief now, come to steal a tapestry from his brother before killing him?" asked Hal sharply.

Justin looked uncomfortable.

"A thief wouldn't steal a tapestry," said Ned, "He'd take silver, or money."

"Unless he intended to wrap the silver in the tapestry to carry it away," said Libby,

"Ours is rather a methodical thief, is he not?" remarked Justin, with a smile. "No, to my mind a thief coming by chance on a deserted house, doesn't first pull down a tapestry and then proceed to collect the silver. He'd grab what he could before he was disturbed and then think of some method of carrying it away. You said, Hal, nothing else was taken?" Hal nodded and Justin continued, "So, what do we know?"

"We've discovered that my uncle was found murdered, wrapped in a tapestry last seen on or about the feast of Corpus Christi. He was probably stabbed to death by a dagger we later found hidden. This dagger is exactly like the one my father carries, down to the nick in the blade. On the floor of the hall a tag from my father's new doublet was also discovered, which is odd as he hasn't visited Westwood since May," snapped Hal. He got to his feet again and walked to the darkened window.

Justin looked dismayed at the manner in which all the pieces slotted so neatly into place. He realised that Hal, far from not thinking about it, had thought it out only too well. "So, we'll say that your uncle and his murderer met in the hall. And from some cause or other started a fight?"

"As my uncle and father invariably do," said Hal over his shoulder.

Justin continued less surely. "And in the course of that dispute, your uncle was stabbed, perhaps by accident?"

"Daggers don't accidentally find their way into hands," said Hal, a shade contemptuously.

"The murderer panics," continued Justin, disregarding this and warming to his theme. "Looks about him in dismay. He might be discovered at any minute. He sees and grabs the tapestry. He rolls the dead body into it, and hurries away to hide it, where it won't easily be found, in the deserted wing of the house."

"You've forgotten to mention how he first lost the

ribbon from his doublet, either in the fight, or perhaps as my dying uncle clutched at it, whilst falling at his feet." Hal spoke in the same bitter tones.

"And the murderer returned later, to rub away the blood stains from the flags with sand!" said Libby suddenly, as another piece of the jigsaw slotted into place. Once again the silence was absolute, as they each seemed to see in their mind's eye these desperate actions.

"That last piece is the only one which doesn't fit my father! All else, I can believe of him acting in a passion, but not the returning to remove the blood. My father wouldn't even *think* of it. In fact I don't think he would have hidden the body either. He would have just ridden off, never to return," Hal added under his breath.

Justin began to look more cheerful. "Then if that is out of character, the whole thing must be. Depend upon it; we shall soon discover other inconsistencies. Tell me Hal, who would have inherited if your uncle hadn't changed his will?"

Hal frowned over the thought. "I don't know. It might, indeed, have been my father, yet my uncle was so much against the idea that I doubt it." He hesitated and then without looking at the boy, said softly, "Ned, perhaps?"

Ned started rather violently as they all stared at him.

"Hey! I didn't do it! I know when I was younger my uncle sometimes talked of me being his heir, but that was years since he and my father first quarrelled! And I am sure I only would have inherited if Hal had died or been killed abroad! *I* had no reason to kill my uncle, who had been so good to me!"

"Nor the opportunity, I guess," said Justin. "Didn't you say you spent all your time at the fair with your sister, Hetta?"

"Yes. Kitty went off looking for Will Longstaffe without so much as a by-your-leave! A pretty fool I must have looked, playing nursemaid to a wench!" he replied tartly.

Hal came to rest his hand on his brother's shoulder and said gravely, "I had not realised you had such just cause to complain of neglect. Nor such burdens to shoulder. I can understand why you dislike me, Ned, and I am sorry for it. It shall be different in future, I promise you."

Ned stammered: "I don't know that I exactly dislike you! Not now that I know you better. It's just that my father thinks you so perfect. And then my uncle did, too, but now I'm more used to your fancy words and ways, I suppose I like you well enough!" He broke off, looking miserable and ashamed.

Hal gripped his shoulder hard. "I am glad to find in you an ally whom I hope will be as formidable against the enemy as he formerly was against me!"

"So, if neither Ned nor your father were due to inherit in the first will Hal, then who was?" asked Justin.

Hal shrugged. "I can have no idea, can you, Bess?"

She shook her head, her fine hair falling silkily across her shoulders and disturbing Justin's logical pattern of thought. "I cannot think of anyone, unless it be Aunt Margery's step-son, Tom Kingscott. He must inherit if all other male heirs fail, I suppose."

"Yes, but there is Ned and I before him. Tom Kingscott has a substantial property of his own, of far higher status than Westwood. And not to mention he is the kindest of men and nothing like a murderer." Hal smiled at the thought of his mild-mannered cousin cast in such a role.

"Might not Mr Fenton know, Hal?" asked Libby. "He was your uncle's close friend and he certainly seemed to know all the circumstances of his affairs relating to our marriage."

Hal considered the idea. "Yes, possibly. I suppose he may be the one person, other than Aunt Kate, who'd know my uncle's secrets."

"Your uncle's wife? She must surely know! Why have

you not asked her before?" asked Justin.

"I will not have poor Aunt Kate distressed further," Hal said. "She has been knocked asunder by all this. I could not see what possible excuse there could be for asking what can only be impertinent questions of her."

"Then you are not thinking logically," said Justin, "Look, your uncle made a will in favour of—we know not who. Then, you come along after an absence of years and he announces that if you'll only marry at his bidding, he'll name you his heir. Then, the moment you ride off to be married, so the promise becomes a certainty and your uncle is suddenly killed. Surely it indicates that the previous beneficiary of the will is the murderer!"

"I suppose so. And all we must do is identify this person and prove he did it?" Hal asked, but he didn't sound convinced.

"That's all," said Justin. He glanced to the other faces, which registered differing degrees of doubt, but there was a general murmur of assent as if they were glad to have something tangible to do.

"I will talk to Aunt Kate," said Libby. She knew Hal could never bring himself to intrude upon her widow's grief.

"And you, Hal, must seek advice of this Mr Fenton,"

said Justin. "Ned has promised to tackle Will Longstaffe, and I, with the help of Mistress Bess, if she will be so good, will talk with Jonas to see if we can discover if he knows anything. I think these must be our next tasks. When we meet again tomorrow, we will see what we've discovered and discuss further tactics. Until we next meet again, then, good hunting and good luck."

Chapter Fifteen

Hal glanced about the comfortable parlour curiously. It was filled to overflowing with books, documents and dogs. He couldn't help wondering how it would have looked if Aunt Margery had ever been the mistress of this establishment. His eyes travelled uneasily to the older man; wondering just what went on in his head, for his face gave no clue to his thoughts.

"So, young Hal," said Mr Fenton jovially. "You don't like that sack, hey?"

Hal looked down into the tawny depths of his wine, which was largely untested. "No sir, indeed sir, it's the finest I've tasted since leaving Paris, although I must confess I am no great drinker."

"No, taken all in all, you favour your mother Hal, or even your Uncle Henry," Mr Fenton shook his head sadly. "A bad business this, Hal, a bad business! I'll not try to conceal my concern from you, my boy. You'll know of the rumours as well as I do. It is absolutely essential your father come forward to clear his name. Either that or he must flee the country." He was aware of the boy's clear eyes fixed on his face and squirmed a little under the reproachful gaze. "Yes, I know you don't like to hear that, but the fact remains, Hal, it looks very bad for your father!"

"I'll not bother to deny that, sir. Instead, I'll ask for your help in clearing his name," said Hal.

"I'll help you all I can, lad, within reason."

Hal hesitated. "It's a delicate matter sir, I hardly know how to begin."

"Ah," Robin Fenton smiled interrupting, "You refer to the scandal of many years ago, I imagine? To how I carried off your Aunt Margery to Oxford. You'll have heard all the gossip of how I was there overtaken by your grandfather and uncle and how Henry and I came to blows in the midst of the yard, before a gaggle of stable lads."

"Well, yes, sir," said Hal in relief. "I mean I spoke to my Aunt Margery about it."

"Did you, by God?" cried Mr Fenton, "I'm impressed by your courage, lad! Your uncle needed to have no fear for you then, if you bearded that den!"

Hal chuckled and relaxed, confessing, "I did so with great trepidation. But you, sir, I am amazed at your temerity in running off with so august a person!"

"Oh, Maggie wasn't half so grand in those days." he replied cheerily, "She was a fine hunter, with her own kestrel in her youth, and she could sit a horse with the best of us in the chase. No, it was marriage to Thomas Kingscott, which turned her into the great lady of to-day. The Kingscott's have ever thought of themselves as the next best thing to minor nobility."

Again Hal chuckled, "So this tale, sir, of my uncle saving your life?"

"Oh, that was true enough," he agreed. "It was at Ledbury in 1645. I was with Edward Massey and your uncle was with Prince Rupert. Neither of us gave it a thought. Well, one could not consider such things in those days." He fell silent for a space and then shook his head, "So many killed, Hal, or ruined and all for nothing! We must do better this time."

"Yes, sir," he replied and glanced to him expectantly.

"It was a skirmish and Prince Rupert already had the day. Massey gave an order to charge the guns; a last ditch attempt. I suddenly saw Henry charging toward me,and stopped dead in surprise. I never expected to see him there and so I completely missed seeing the damned pikeman, who was about to have me from my horse. Henry shouted a warning to me and I deflected the blow and took out the fellow. That made Henry feel bad; it was one of his own men. He damned my eyes and rode off and I didn't see him again until after the battle. He was one of the wounded prisoners. I'd been wounded, too. I took a bullet to this shoulder, Hal, and it still gives me grief each winter. I knew that if Henry were hauled off to prison with the sort of wound he had, he'd die. I got him to sign a parole and brought him home myself."

"You were friends again from then, sir?" asked Hal.

He smiled. "Yes, we'd both faced death; that puts quarrels into perspective. So you see, young Hal, there's no bad blood between us. If I'd wanted revenge for what occurred at an Oxford inn, I could have ridden away and left Henry to his fate, the same as he could have let the pikeman run me through. But enough talk of the old times. We must get back to today and your father's problems. Is there anything more I can tell you?"

"I am obliged to you sir, for you frankness. But I do have a few other questions, I'm afraid. Perhaps you can tell me if you were privy to my uncle's former will? Not this latest one, which leaves Westwood to me, but the one before that?"

Mr Fenton got up and kindled a light, holding it to the long, clay pipe, which had lain propped up in the hearth. "Why do you ask that, my boy?" he asked slowly.

"We've all been thinking hard, sir, Libby, my wife, Ned and Bess and Libby's brother, Justin Danvers and myself, trying to understand how this all happened. It seems to us that if we could find out who was to have inherited Westwood, why, that person would have a very good reason for murdering my uncle. Especially as it was not thought that my uncle would change his will until after my marriage."

Mr Fenton pulled thoughtfully on his pipe. "You may have a point there, my boy, but what if that person should also be your father? What if it had all been left to him?"

Hal shook his head. "If it were all left to him? Is that what you are saying? Why then, I suppose I would have to be suspicious, but no, no, I *know* my father. He'd never kill his own brother! Or, at least, not in that manner!"

"Now there I agree with you," said Mr Fenton. "I knew both your uncle and your father. God, we grew up together as boys. And Francis, for all his faults— and he had many—Francis was never the man to hold a grudge. He has a temper, that none could deny, and in that temper he could kill a man—but never his own brother. That's not Francis's way!"

Hal nodded impatiently. "But you have not answered my question, sir!"

Mr Fenton agreed. "No, I've not and I don't know that I can. I only know that in the years following the quarrel—which was in 1646 remember—in those years, right up until, what, three or four years ago, he swore he'd never leave Westwood to Francis! Now I know for a few years he'd toyed with the idea of making young Ned heir, but then he seemed to think better of it. He said to me that he knew he was no longer a young man, and that he could not think but that it would be folly to leave the place to one so untried as Ned. As to whom he might have decided upon, I don't know. I only remember what he said to me one night when we'd drunk a few bottles together at Westwood after we had both been on the Bench that day."

"Which was what, sir?" asked Hal, with a faint glimmer of interest.

He chuckled. "Why, he said that the way he'd left things would cause quite a stir! 'That'll stir up the old tabby, my sister Margery. Aye, and my sweet Kate, too, I'll swear.' At the time I gave it no thought. He was as hale a man as I am. I expected him to live many years!"

"He said no more than that, sir?" asked Hal.

"I'm afraid not, Hal," he replied, shaking his head.

Hal sat silent for a space, turning it over in his mind, then he asked: "Have you no idea who he was referring to?"

"No, I've not, my boy," he said firmly. "As I've said, at the time we'd sunk a fair few bottles of claret, and I gave no heed to his words, beyond thinking that it would do Margery good to be stirred up a mite!" He cocked an audacious eyebrow at Hal. "I was quite heart broken, you know, when she was married off like that after our elopement, but your grandfather worked on her and convinced her she was too good to countenance my suit for long. A few kisses stolen one summer—" He sighed as Hal stared at him open mouthed. "All water under the bridge, my boy! So, as I say, at the time I gave it no thought, and when I spoke of it again on another occasion, he passed it off."

Hal looked despondent. "So, for all that you have told me, we are no further forward."

"Well, I wouldn't say that," said Mr Fenton, in bracing tones. "At least we know he was thinking of someone unlikely. So all we must do is think of a candidate who would offend your Aunt Margery most! Ah, I see your point! Of course, your father and Margery have been at odds for years and Margery always insisted it was Francis's imprudence, which ruined her chances of a brilliant match! Still, that's all in the past!"

He clapped Hal's shoulder affectionately, as he got to his feet to take his leave. "Now don't you worry, my boy. The truth will out! Remember, if you've any problem you can't handle, as your guardian I am here to help."

Hal said all that was necessary and presently took his leave much depressed. He hoped that the others had fared better in their quest for information.

❧

Justin did remember the reason he was to spend time with Bess, but as the matter wasn't so vital to him he was quite happy to spend an hour pleasantly wandering about the garden with her. When Hetta, released from her lessons, came to join them, they made their way to the dovecote to visit the old man who sat there.

As they entered the tiny garden, situated between the stables and the fine front of the house, the pigeons rose up in a cloud as usual. They circled overhead in a flutter of wings and Bess made haste to call out, "It's me, Jonas, Bess Westwood."

"Ah, Mistress Bess?" said the old man, turning his head toward them. "I thought it weren't Mistress Libby. You are not alone, hey?"

"No, Jonas, this is Mistress Libby's brother, Justin

Danvers and my little sister Hetta, of course."

"Ah, I heard he were come. Welcome, Mr Danvers, welcome!"

Justin gripped the old man's gnarled hand in his and sat down beside Bess on the neatly trimmed turf, as the pigeons began to settle back down.

"Well then, little Mistress, have 'ee come to feed my birds?" he asked of Hetta, fumbling in the bag at his side for some corn.

"Yes, if you please," she replied, as with a flurry of soft wings half a dozen doves settled about her.

"Really we came to talk to you about my uncle's death, Jonas," Bess said.

"Ah, well, that were a bad business," he agreed, shaking his old head sorrowfully as he gave Hetta another handful of grain. "A good man, thy uncle, Mistress Bess, thy'll not see his like again in a hurry, I'm thinking!"

"No indeed," said Bess, helping Hetta sprinkle the grain amongst the waiting birds. "I am only sorry I didn't know him better. We want to ask you about the day he died."

"Aye, I mind it well, young mistress," he replied.

"Is it true, Jonas, you were the only person left here on the feast of Corpus Christi?" asked Justin.

Jonas replied, with an air of good fellowship. "Aye,

young master, what with one thing and another. Now, I don't hold will this fairing business, I don't. The Devil's tools it be, you mark my words, young master! The Devil's tools!" Suddenly recollecting his company, he amended his words. "At least so they were for those of us ag'in Archbishop Laud and his bishops!"

"But you followed my uncle into battle, surely, Jonas?" asked Bess. "He was for the King! Were you not blinded saving his life at Newbury?"

Jonas was unable, for all his modest words, to keep the pride from his voice as he answered, nodding his old, white head. "I did no more than the next man, Mistress Bess. I saw the need and filled it, so to speak. The Master, he were grateful and good to me. As for being with the King, aye, I rode under my Master's banner, but he no more agreed with that archbishop and his High Church than I did!"

"It is difficult to remember that there were so many differing shades of opinion in the war. One is so used to everyone being either Royalist or Roundhead these days. However, we are more concerned with recent events, so can you tell me for certain who was here on the feast of Corpus Christi?" asked Justin.

"Aye, that I can, young master, and easily, too. First off there were just about everyone who hadn't left for young Master Hal's wedding. Then the fairing party left. The little mistress and Master Ned rode on ponies, the rest of them were walking. Aye and chattering as if they had ten tongues each. There's some as ought to mind their words and think afore they open their foolish mouths!"

"What happened after everyone left, Jonas?" asked Justin patiently, determined not to let him wander from the subject.

The old man's mouth stretched into a toothless grin. "It were a warm morning, sir, if you do remember?"

"Yes, I do," replied Justin. "I marked those from Adamsholme leaving for the fair and remember my father saying they'd find it a thirsty walk."

Jonas grinned again and continued, "Well, I don't greatly recollect the next few hours, young master, but about noon time, I'm sure of that, for I can, on a bright day, mark the course of the sun, and it were high over head. About noon, then, I heard angry voices."

"Angry voices!" cried Justin eagerly.

"Aye, and ones I'd heard time out of mind, in the old days, too! Master Henry and Master Francis, they never could agree."

"Master Francis? My father!" cried Bess, in despair.

"Aye!" Once again Jonas nodded his old head, not

seeming to hear the distress in her voice.

"Mr Francis Westwood was here, on the feast of Corpus Christi?" asked Justin starkly. He was unwilling to hear it, but determined after the truth.

"Aye, he and the Master Henry were going at it hammer and tongs. Damned him to hell he did! But then that were always Master Francis's way! Hasty tempered, up in the air all at once, but down just as quick!" Jonas chuckled at the memory.

"You heard that? You heard them part friends?" asked Justin quickly.

"Well, no. I couldn't hardly hope to hear, for they'd walked off to the house, still shouting at each other. But I don't doubt it were soon over and done with, as usual. Master Francis called out to me cheerily enough later when he were leaving!"

"He did?" asked Justin. "What exactly did he say?"

"He called out that I were an idle old rascal and that when he were master, he'd have me working for my living, not sleeping my days away in the sun. Just like he did back in the spring when he came!" replied the old man laughing again at what was to him a jest.

"He meant it as a jest?" asked Justin, his heart sinking.

"Oh, aye, he were ever the same. He'd abuse me, but under it all he were laughing. He and I, we understand each other,we do," replied the old man loftily.

Justin spoke slowly and carefully, "Jonas, if all this comes to court, will you swear to those words?"

"To what words?" Jonas asked, his white brows contracting in a frown.

"That Mr Francis Westwood was here on the feast of Corpus Christi, that you heard the brothers quarrel, and you heard Mr Francis leave?"

There was a silence as the old man slowly tried to keep pace with all this, and Bess stared at Justin with doubt and dismay on her face.

"What's this you be saying, young master? Why, you be asking me to betray Master Francis?" Jonas cried, his old voice quavering in anger.

"No, I'm asking you to tell the truth!" returned Justin sharply.

"Aye, and damn the consequences! Saving your pardon, young Missy!" He put out a shaking, frail hand and rested it on Hetta's drooping head.

"It is the only way, Jonas, for if you don't tell the truth, then don't you betray your Master, Henry Westwood?" he asked quietly.

The old man looked totally confounded at that and sought refuge in further anger. "You take yourself off, young man! Aye, be off with you, and don't come a-bothering of me with your questions!"

He struggled to get to his feet. "You and your smooth tongue! Why, you be all the same, you lawyers. You trick a man into saying what he ought not! Go on, get away! I've no more to say to you! Go on all o' you! And you, Mistress Bess, you ,too, should be ashamed o' your self for keeping company with the likes of him! Aye, these Johnny-come-lately folk think they are good enough to match with the likes of Westwoods, and none will be the wiser, but bad breeding will always out!"

Justin got hastily to his feet; his angry face much flushed, as he stooped to help Bess up. He turned his back on the old man and walked off stiffly. Bess lingered, begging Jonas to hold his tongue. She had to hurry to catch up with Justin, who had strode off into the garden.

"I do beg pardon for him, Justin," she said breathlessly.

"It's of no consequence," Justin said, in a stately manner.

She caught his arm. "Yes, yes, it is. Please Justin— stop!"

He halted and turned to her, hurt and anger in his eyes. "Yes, Mistress Westwood?"

"Mistress Westwood?" she repeated, turning pale. "What is this? I had thought us friends!"

"Aye, ma'am, so had I, but now I see clearly my mistaken presumption," he replied, with cold formality.

Her heart began to beat fast at her own daring. "I saw no mistake, nor presumption. I see only a friend I will *not* lose because of an old fool's vindictive tongue!"

Some of the anger died from his face and his shoulders became less rigid. "Aye, but I see doubt in your face. And besides which, you are but a child," he added, with the indulgent wisdom of one who was a whole summer the elder. "I dare say your family would see it entirely as Jonas does."

"I do not give a that—" she retorted, snapping her fingers saucily, "for what my family thinks! Nor am I too young. But that I didn't suit, I was to have been married at Michaelmas!"

His eyes flew to her face and then dropped hastily. "To whom?" he asked, his breath coming quickly.

"Philip Eustace, who lives at Dunhill," she replied.

"Oh, a gentleman's son?"

"Yes, but a poor gentleman's son. A gentleman whose father haggled long with mine over the price of the dowry. He is to marry my sister Jane now," she said, her cheeks reddening.

They turned about and began to walk back toward the house. "Was your father pleased with Hal's marriage?" he asked, with the air of one making polite conversation.

"He complained greatly, but that was because it was a match of my uncle's making. I believe secretly he was elated by the size of Libby's dowry!"

Justin nodded. He knew that the dowry had been very handsome. A small smile appeared at the corners of his mouth. "Your father must be found Bess, and quickly," he announced with resolution.

At these words the world crowded back on her, and her pretty castle in the air tumbled into ruins. "Oh Justin, what is the use to make such plans if we are to be disgraced! What shall we tell Hal? It looks more and more as if my father were indeed here and did—"

Calmly he closed his hand over hers as they made their way back to the house. "No, Bess, wait and see; the truth will out!"

Ned, looking particularly grubby, entered the stable yard and hailed his friend of many a bird-nesting spree, the stable lad.

"Hey, Sam, have you seen Will Longstaffe?"

"Mr Longstaffe, why, yes, Master Ned," replied the lad, crossing his eyes in a manner which warned Ned he was close by.

"What would you be wanting with me, Master Ned?" Will came out of a stable, and stood his arms akimbo, whilst Kitty slipped away behind him, running toward the kitchen yard.

Ned grinned up at him. "I was just wondering what had become of you, Will. I've not seen you in days."

"I've been busy, young master, attending to thy uncle's business. Or mayhap I should say thy brother's business, as it seems he is to be master now. But you'll understand that, none better, for I've marked how you've been making up to him these past days!"

"No, I've not!" cried Ned indignantly.

"Aye, well, your nowt but a lad, you'll not understand; no doubt you've been taken in by the famous manners of his!" he sneered viciously.

"No, I've not!" Ned repeated angrily. "I've not at all! I still think he's a Frenchified beau, but he has been worried about my father, so I've been helping him."

Will cast him a sideways look. "Worried with good cause. You know what is being said do you? Aye— and as far away as Oxford?"

Ned nodded, his chubby face concerned. "That my father killed my uncle, yes."

Will watched his young face closely. "And you think he did it, too, don't you?"

Ned frowned and shrugged his shoulders. He felt the strangest desire to weep. "It—it looks like it." Then as he realised he felt as if he had betrayed Hal, he took refuge in anger. "Why shouldn't I? I don't know him that well, so I don't care greatly. He thinks nothing of me, so why should I care what becomes of him?"

"Why indeed?" Will thrust his thumbs into his thick leather belt and began to whistle the refrain of a particular tune under his breath as he frequently did when thinking.

"It all seems to hinge about the feast of Corpus Christi. Do you remember, when we all went to the fair?"

Will nodded, continuing to whistle.

"So, of course, we are all in the clear. We each can say where there other was. You for example, went off with Kitty."

Will winked at him. "Aye, at first I did. But she isn't exactly to my taste lately, so I soon got rid of her and found a prettier wench to spend the afternoon with!"

Ned looked at him with an air of great innocence. "Did you? So that's why Kitty came back in such a pelter! Who is this prettier wench?"

"You'd not know her. She isn't from round here and she's much more accommodating, if you know what I mean!" Will laughed coarsely. "Kitty has got matrimony in her eye. That's why I am staying clear of her as much as possible!"

"So I should think," said Ned, with a shudder of distaste. "Why it must be awful to have to dance attendance and kiss a girl, as Hal does. Though Libby is quite a good sort of a girl in her way!"

"Plainly she is not the one for you. They say she dotes on your brother already, so I guess from that he does his duty as a bridegroom well enough!" sneered Will.

"Yes," said Ned distantly and once again he felt a measure of disloyalty to Hal to hear this man sneer at him. "Never mind that now, I've something I must talk to you about. It seems likely my uncle came back here to Westwood, you know."

Will watched him with narrowed eyes; instinctively he knew the lad was no longer with him. "Aye, he must have done. His body being found here."

"Yes, exactly, and it seems most likely he came back here the day we all went to the fair."

The man frowned heavily. "Why do you say so?"

Recollecting Justin's instructions to give away nothing, Ned squirmed. "Well, that was the last possible day he could come and still be in time for Hal's wedding. He was expected and none saw him come on another."

Will shrugged his wide shoulders, but his frown remained and he began to whistle under his breath again thoughtfully.

"Only, if he did come, where is his horse?" Ned asked rather desperately.

"There's your answer then. He didn't come back here," Will's reply came swiftly.

"But he must have done because the body was here!" replied Ned.

Once again Will shrugged. "Then likely he were set upon by footpads?" he suggested.

"Footpads who decided by chance to bring him back here to his own home and hide his body away in the ruined part of the house? No, Justin, Libby's brother, has explained all that. My uncle must have returned and have been in the hall when he was murdered. Justin thinks he was killed by somebody that he knew and trusted!"

"Aye—thy father," Will nodded decidedly.

"Yes, perhaps," Ned sighed at the thought, "but it doesn't solve the problem of the missing horse. I was wondering, have you seen aught of it?"

"Me? Why should I have seen it?" Will turned on the boy angrily.

"You went to the Gloucester horse fair last week,

didn't you?" Ned was puzzled by his vehemence. "If my uncle was killed here, and we have the body to say he was, then the horse may have been disposed of locally. I thought you might have seen the horse when you were at the fair."

"I saw naught that looked like the master's horse. If you ask my opinion, the master's horse must have been ridden away by his murderer, your father, and probably sold in London!"

Ned sighed. He didn't seem to be making much progress. "No, my father hasn't been back to London."

"At a port then; sold there on his way to France," Will snapped.

"Aye, like as not," agreed Ned rather depressed by the thought. Then, as another thought occurred to him, he asked Will: "What did you buy then?"

"Buy?" repeated Will blankly.

"At the fair. You said you went to the horse fair last week, didn't you? What did you go for?" he asked.

The agent opened and closed his mouth a few times. "I, er, I were looking for—a new mount for you— for your birthday. Master Henry had told me to look out for a likely new pony for you, but there were nothing—nothing suitable!"

"Oh," said Ned, as the first rush of pleasure faded he

became aware the man was lying. "Oh, hello, who is this? It's Mr Hughes, the sheriff, and his man again."

Chapter Sixteen

Libby enjoyed her walk to the rectory with Aunt Kate. It was thoughtful of her to accompany Libby, as she did whenever Libby was confronted by a task that her new position required. Her kindness was such that Libby had been emboldened to ask the questions she been told to. They were still discussing it as she and Aunt Kate walked back together across the park from the rectory, where they had been engaged on the melancholy task of deciding, with the help of Mrs Broxtowe, which of the needy villagers should benefit from certain bequests in her husband's will.

"I must confess I was rather surprised at Hal's impertinence," Aunt Kate was saying, looking as severe as a pretty kitten.

"Impertinence, ma'am? I am so very sorry, but Hal felt he had to ask Aunt Margery," Libby faltered, feeling as absurdly guilty as if she, herself, had been the culprit accused.

"Yes, I understand, my dear. I only wish I could have helped you more. Poor dear Hal; one can see how this is preying so dreadfully on his mind."

Libby swallowed the lump in her throat and blinked away tears at the thought of how Hal suffered. "I cannot deny that it is, ma'am, or I should never have dreamed of bothering you with such impertinent questions at such a time."

"Usually he is such a well-mannered boy," continued Aunt Kate. "Indeed, both Margery and I have often remarked upon it, and thanked heaven for it. Francis, his father, was not known for his gentle manners; indeed, he is more like Ned."

"I'm sure Hal meant no insult, ma'am, but Will Longstaffe said that," stammered Libby.

"Will Longstaffe! There! I told Margery there was some mischief afoot. I've never liked the fellow no matter that she says he is very capable. To my mind he flatters her and so she is taken in by him," Kate nodded her head decidedly.

"I think Hal finds him difficult," Libby suggested tentatively.

"Yes, poor Hal, I understand Will has baited him. I think it is time Will Longstaffe is taken down a peg or two. Henry trusted him, you see, and now he's got above himself, especially if he has dared to rake up the scandal about Margery. The audacity of it! She must have been mortified."

"Hal said she was rather put out."

Aunt Kate sighed, "It was such a pity. What Henry's father could have been about I don't know. I mean, Robin Fenton had run tame through the house with both brothers. They were the best of friends; all of the children. Of course, the Fentons had no money. I suppose that was what was behind it all. The Kingscotts, you understand, are very wealthy. Henry's first wife was a Kingscott and they, and the Westwoods, have been connected for generations. Then Tom's first wife died from the ague. I think they saw the marriage as a means of getting Margery, who had been all but ruined by the elopement with Robin Fenton, settled."

"Did Mr Westwood and Mr Fenton truly fight a duel, ma'am?" asked Libby.

"A duel? Nothing so formal from what Henry said. More like a brawl in the yard of the inn when they caught up with Robin and Margery. 'Tis true, there was a coldness between them, so Henry said, for some years until they met up again in the war. Henry helped Robin in some way. He shot a fellow, who was about to cut Robin down, or something. Henry wouldn't talk of it, but Robin used to call him 'My Saviour.' in jest you understand;"

"Was Aunt Margery unhappy? Hal said she didn't appear to be very disturbed by it all. He said she called it a spring madness, a folly."

Aunt Kate lowered her voice. "My dear, never underestimate Margery. She tries to make out that it was all foolishness and that she's never given it a second thought, but Henry said she was heartbroken. He thought that his father was a brute to force her into marriage with Tom Kingscott so quickly."

"Was he not a good man?" asked Libby in dismay.

"Oh, Tom Kingscott was a fine man. No, I mean more that he was so much older than Margery."

"Mr Westwood was considerably older than you, ma'am, yet you loved him dearly," Libby said, then as she saw tears fill her companion's eyes, she was sorry for her clumsiness. "I am sorry, Aunt Kate. I should not have spoken of him."

"No, no child. I like to talk of my dear Henry, if you can bear with my grief. So few dare to mention him for fear of distressing me. He was a dear, good man, and when we were to be wed, he talked to me of Margery's unhappiness. He asked if I was quite happy to marry one so much my senior in age. I told him at the time the difference was that I wasn't in love with anyone else, as poor Margery was. I had fallen in love with Henry almost immediately, rather like you did with Hal," said Kate, brushing away a few tears.

Libby blushed, "I think there must have been a great likeness, ma'am. I am sorry I never met Hal's uncle."

"Hal is by far more handsome," said Aunt Kate, "but in character they are very like. Did you want to know anything more, dear?"

Libby's blush deepened, "I don't mean to pry, Aunt Kate. Hal just needs to know as much as possible to help find the murderer."

"Yes, my dear, I know. That's why I'm telling you all I this."

"Was Aunt Margery very unhappy married to Mr Kingscott?" asked Libby remembering Hal's instructions.

"I don't think she was greatly dismayed by his death, although she'll never hear a word against him. Rather an autocratic sort, I gathered, with little charm, but he was a good man, who knew his duty."

Libby nodded thinking to herself that a good man who knew his duty could cover a multitude of sins and a magnitude of misery for his wife.

"Certainly she was not unhappy enough to consider

murdering her brother, who had in fact tried his best to ensure her happiness. I know revenge is a dish best served cold, my dear, but not so cold it is spoiled. All this happened many years ago. Margery might have been angry at the loss of her lover when she was a girl, but that anger burned out long ago. She and Robin Fenton have little to say to each other these days. But there, you know that; My Henry always wanted what was best for everyone."

Libby swallowed and asked the question she was dreading, "Who was Uncle Henry's heir, ma'am?"

"Henry's heir? Why 'tis Hal!" Kate was surprised at the question.

"No, ma'am, before Hal. Who was his heir before Hal returned from France?"

"Before the King came again you mean? Oh, my dear, I fear I must fail you in this, for I do not know. If only I had asked Henry, I know he would have told me, but I didn't like to enquire. You see, it was about the time my last baby died, in the spring of '50, poor little lamb. He was so very frail, I knew he couldn't possibly live!" Her voice quavered and she struggled to speak clearly, "He was the fourth in as many years, all of them dead. Henry should never have married me, I was too old for childbirth. I told him so at the time. He needed a younger wife after his first wife died, but he'd not hear of it. It was me, or no one, he insisted. Twenty years they'd been wed, and no child at all. Then, of course, just after she died, Elizabeth Barten, Francis's first wife, gave birth to dear Hal, dying herself in the process. Francis did the only sensible thing; he married Catherine, a wife half his age. They produced half a dozen children in the next few years of which Bess, her sisters and Ned survived. Poor Francis; so many daughters for all his efforts; We knew their mother well, of course, which is why we offered a home to the children. Catherine was so like young Hetta. How you do let me rattle on, dear!"

"I like to hear you talk, ma'am. It helps me to understand things a little better," replied Libby quietly. She felt guilty for stirring up old memories.

"Poor child, you must find everything so very confusing. Now, who is this come visiting at this hour? Oh dear, it's that tiresome Sheriff Hughes and his henchman. Try as one does, one seems to be forever falling over them. I don't know how Hal bears with it! I really don't, but then he is such a patient, dear, boy."

Libby, for her part, could have groaned aloud to see the sheriff and the man he employed, Jack Dutton, a most unpleasant piece of humanity. They crossed from the stables to the house accompanied by the usual cloud of pigeons and a very sulky-looking Ned.

The two women swiftly followed them into the hall to find Ned ranged rebelliously with his sisters, and Justin looking grave.

"Oh, I beg pardon, Mistress Westwood, ma'am," the Sheriff touched his hat. After Kate glanced sharply at it, he removed it, signalling for his man to uncover also. "I was told you were yet abroad. It is Mr Westwood we seek; Mr Henry Westwood."

"Hal has ridden out to see his guardian," said Libby shortly. She could see how Aunt Kate's pallor increased at this formal use of the name Hal shared with his uncle.

The sheriff looked disconcerted, as if he had hardly expected this. "Yet it is imperative I speak with him at once. Can he not be summoned?"

"It's about the dagger, Libby! Some sneak has told him we found a dagger and he insists on seeing it!" Ned was angry.

Libby opened her eyes wide in dismay, knowing Hal would never allow this. Her frightened glance went to her brother.

The sheriff intercepted the look and spoke with due emphasis: "I am given to understand, ma'am, that what is most probably the weapon which killed Mr Westwood has been discovered. Furthermore, I understand that your husband has identified it as a possession of his father and is now concealing it. If this is the case, Mistress Westwood, I have no choice but to warn you that tampering with what is legally termed evidence is itself an offence and carries a penalty!"

Libby looked so terrified that Justin came to her rescue. "It is true, sir, that in looking about the ruined wing of the house a dagger was discovered. But, as this dagger was found amid a pile of weapons and armour, which had been abandoned there since the war, there is no way in which the previous owner can be identified."

"That is not what I've heard," returned the sheriff sharply. "*I* heard it was positively identified as a possession of Mr Francis Westwood!"

Justin frowned over this and asked with equal sharpness, "Who would be your informant in this case, sir?"

"I am not obliged to reveal my sources of information to you, sir. Unless, of course, you are representing the Westwood family in a legal capacity?"

"Sheriff Hughes, this is my brother, Justin Danvers," said Libby softly.

"Well, Mr Danvers, if you are, indeed, a lawyer you will know—" Once again he stopped speaking as he was interrupted, this time by Hal entering the hall.

"Ah, Mr Henry Westwood, the very man I seek! Sir, it has come to my ears that a dagger, positively identified as belonging to your father, has been discovered and that you are concealing this vital piece of evidence from me. I must give you fair warning, sir, that this constitutes an offence and carries with it, as penalty, a period of restraint!"

"The Devil it does!" cried Hal, as events finally took the toll of his scrupulously fine manners. "By what right do you enter my home and threaten me and my family?"

The sheriff was surprised, but unbowed, by this display of temper. "By the right of law, Mr Westwood. A murder most foul has been committed within this house. All rights of you and yours are suspended until the murderer is tracked down and brought to justice. All those who stand in the path of justice deserve punishment!"

Hal glared at the man, hating him for being right. Justin hastily intervened before more damage could be done. "I have just been explaining to the sheriff, Hal, that we did, indeed, find a dagger, but that it was found among other weapons and armour, all of it old, so who could say when any was last used?"

The sheriff guessed, from the expressions of fear on their faces, he was on to something. "This only goes to show the fiendish cunning of the man we seek. Everyone knows there is no better hiding place than in with similar things!"

Hal cast his hat and gloves on the table and stalked to stand before the hearth, his hands tightly clasped behind his back. He'd had time for thought on his ride home and had reluctantly come to the conclusion that the opinions of those as diverse as Justin and Mr Fenton were more to be relied upon than his own confusion and blind panic. He was weary of the struggle, of the endless battle in his head. He could hold back the evidence no longer. "Ned, fetch the dagger!" he commanded.

Ned paused to gaze imploringly at his brother, his own horror clouded by a sense of guilt. It had been his chatter to Will Longstaffe that had reached the ears of the sheriff. Then, as Hal grimly shook his head, he ran noisily from the room. Those remaining stood in awed silence. Aunt Kate looked from one to the other in bewilderment, as if she could no longer grasp what was afoot. Bess shed a few hot tears, which wrung Justin's heart.

Ned soon returned, bearing a grubby handkerchief,

which he laid in state on the table. He stepped back with the air of one who washes his hands of the consequences and went to stand close to his brother. Hal rested a hand on his shoulder in comfort.

Sheriff Hughes pounced upon the handkerchief eagerly, tipping out the contents and snatching up the dagger in triumph. "Mr Westwood, can you deny this is your father's dagger?"

Hal's face was pale. He was determined he'd not sacrifice the truth he held so dear, but neither would he help condemn his father. "I don't deny he once had one similar in design. You must understand, I have not been in my father's company in some weeks. I can have no knowledge if he does, or does not, still posses a similar dagger."

"I'll warrant he does not!" cried Sheriff Hughes. "I am willing to wager he lost this very dagger on the feast of Corpus Christi!"

"As to that—" Hal broke off as footsteps were heard approaching the hall. The screens door was suddenly flung back in a dramatic way, to reveal an middle-aged man of short stature, dressed in the very height of fashion. He looked about with a quizzical, slightly theatrical air and merrily cried, "Good Morrow! I see I have quite a party drawn up to meet me. Am I expected?"

"Father!" cried Bess in disbelief.

"Father!" echoed Hal in despair.

"Mr Francis Westwood?" cried Sheriff Hughes. "Mr Francis Westwood, I arrest you for the murder of your brother, Henry Westwood on or about the day of the feast of Corpus Christi, and I warn you anything you say may be taken and given in evidence against you!"

Chapter Seventeen

The hall exploded in uproar: Hal shouting; Ned swearing; Francis Westwood laughing and Bess sobbing. In the confusion, Aunt Kate slipped away and presently returned bearing a flagon of wine and supported by Aunt Margery, whose voice cut through the hubbub demanding, "What is going on here?"

Everyone fell silent and Francis abruptly stopped laughing to glower at her. "Oh, it's you Margery. I should have known I'd not have to look far for the author of this piece of folly!"

"Folly, sir?" cried Sheriff Hughes, incensed by the dismissive attitude exhibited by Francis Westwood. "I can assure you this is no laughing matter! You stand accused of the murder of your brother!"

"Fool!" Francis Westwood cast him a look of scorn. "I have only just heard of the murder! I haven't set eyes on my brother in weeks!"

"So you say, sir, yet we have a sworn testimony that

you were seen passing through the village of Westwood on the feast of Corpus Christi!"

"Corpus Christi? When is that? Mid-June?" Francis removed his gauntlets and swaggered across the hall to pick up the glass of wine Kate poured. "Thanks, Kate, you at least have an appreciation of a fellow's wants! I'm sorry about Henry, by the way. He and I never did agree, but you must miss him sorely." He turned back to survey his anxious children, then turned to meet the eyes of the sheriff. A smile of amused tolerance swept across his face as he realised the sheriff was watching him narrowly. "Yes, I was here on or about that date. Wasn't that the day you were wed, Hal?"

"Yes, sir," he replied quietly.

"Is it true, sir, that you and your brother quarrelled on that day?" demanded the sheriff.

Francis drank off the remainder of his wine with a flourish. "Most probably, we quarrelled every time we met. Oh aye, I recollect it now! Yes, we damn well did quarrel! I called here to change my horse, intent on riding to join the celebrations for Hal's wedding, and had the misfortune to run into Henry, whom I imagined would already be at the ceremony. The parsimonious old niggard—sorry Kate! My brother told me he was cutting me out of the inheritance! It was just for pure spite, too! He said he was going to leave it all, lock, stock and barrel to young Hal. Did he do so, lad?" He swung round to look at his son.

Libby could only marvel at the man; either he was a consummate actor or completely innocent.

"Yes, sir. Uncle Henry was here at Westwood because he'd just returned from a visit to his man of law in London," replied Hal.

"Aye, so he told me, but I thought perhaps he was just saying that to anger me. Well, I wish you joy of it lad," he added quickly. "I'll not pretend I am not sick at heart. You know how I always dreamed of the old place! Henry was nothing but a mean, old skinflint, who begrudged me my success at court. I'm sorry, Kate, I know I shouldn't speak ill of the dead, but cutting me out of his will was his way of getting even with a more brilliant, younger brother. Still, I'll not fret. In view of this latest news perhaps it would have been inconvenient! You'll not deny me my own place, and I dare say I'll be able to do something with it, however ramshackle it may be."

"I doubt you'll find the opportunity, sir. Will you be so good as to tell me if you recognise this dagger?" the sheriff asked in a satisfied tone.

Francis put down the second glass of wine he'd just

poured and advanced on the man. "Now, where had you that? By Heaven, that's mine! I mislaid it—now when? Oh, sometime back now! Look, don't you see Hal? It is most definitely mine, for here's the missing bit of the blade, you broke off when your horse went lame on the road to Calais. Don't you remember?" Francis chuckled. He seemed unaware of the electric atmosphere his words created. "Mind, I don't see how you can forget. Didn't I cuff your ear soundly for it?"

"Yes, sir, you did," said Hal, hollowly.

"This confirms my suspicions, sir, and means I must ask you to come with me," said the sheriff, laying a hand on Francis's arm.

"Unhand me, you churl!" Francis's temper snapped and he turned on the man irritably. "Be off with you. Can you not see, you dolt, I have but this moment arrived!"

Margery crossed the hall majestically to stand at her brother's side. "Francis, you cannot surely still be unaware of the gravity of the situation! This man accuses you of the murder of your brother! Now is the time to think of your immortal soul!"

"Damn you and your sermons, Margery! Will you never have done with your endless lectures?" He threw off the sheriff's restraining hand and turned as his wife entered the hall in a flurry of rustling silk and expensive perfume.

"Ah, Jacqueline, my love! Here I am at last! Now, why did you disobey my instructions and leave London? I would have been saved all this trouble if you'd remained there!"

"Francis!" Jacqueline hurried to cast herself in his arms. "I wanted to stay as you bid me, but Hal's letter came and Bess said we must come here!" She glanced from one tense face to another. "But what is all this? What is wrong?"

"This fool thinks I've killed Henry and wants to take me off and incarcerate me in a damned prison!" Francis replied imperturbably. "I tell you this, my fine fellow, there never was a cell which could hold me in the war, and there isn't one now!"

Jacqueline broke into voluble French, which soon rose to a crescendo of hysteria.

As both aunts joined in with the argument, Hal took the sheriff to one side. "Surely you need not detain my father, Sheriff? He is a gentleman, and will be glad to attend court to answer any charges you may care to bring against him."

The sheriff's face was harsh and unyielding. "It has taken us a good while to track this gentleman down sir, with precious little help from his family," he replied sarcastically. "How am I to tell if he has just arrived as he claims? Or has he been safely hidden here in this house all the time I've been searching for him? I know that if I allow him to escape me now I'd be failing in my duty."

"You have my word that, not only has he just this moment arrived here, but, he will attend on your bidding." Hal was angry at the man's insolence.

"I thank you for your assurance, Mr Westwood, but in view of the situation, I prefer to take the more regular course!" Once again he caught at Francis Westwood's arm, pulling him from the huddle of women, which surrounded him. "Sir, I must insist you come with me, and I'd be obliged if you did it quietly. We don't want to upset the ladies dragging you off by force!"

Francis Westwood laughed contemptuously. "The mere two of you couldn't hope to hold me! Tell me, my good fellow, why are you arresting me?"

"I have reason to believe you killed your brother, sir," returned the man patiently.

"Does it not occur to you, my fine fellow, that had I done so, I would have been better advised to stay away from this place?" Francis asked, with a lordly air.

"Aye, sir, you would, but like most wicked men of

your ilk, you just could not resist coming back to see the result of your crime. Had you been innocent as you try to suggest, you'd have come here at once, as soon as it was known your brother was dead!"

For the first time, the seriousness of the situation seemed to dawn on Francis. He drew himself up to his full height, and eyed the man coldly. "My dear fellow, I've been detained on important business, I have only just learned of my brother's death through the agency of my son's letters. The death of one's elder brother, however lamentable, is hardly the occasion for abandoning all other concerns!"

"You say important business, sir; Just what important business would that be?" demanded the sheriff.

Francis Westwood hesitated, glanced at the man for a few seconds, then he shrugged his shoulders, "I decline to state," he replied coolly.

"In that case, sir, I decline to believe. You will come with me now," retorted the sheriff, resentful of the distain he saw in the other man's eyes.

Midst the screams of Jacqueline, the tears of Bess and the heated arguments of Hal and Ned, Francis Westwood was borne away by the sheriff and his man. He seemed resigned to the inevitable, for he turned and call back laconically to his son: "Hal, come to me in whatever place they intend keeping me, and if you please, have a care of your step-mother!"

Chapter Eighteen

By the time all the tears and recriminations were over Hal had ridden off in pursuit. He was determined first to seek the counsel of Mr Fenton, then to continue on to Maucester to discover exactly where his father was being held.

So it was that the day was considerably advanced and a very depressed and silent company assembled for supper. Notwithstanding Margery's frequently expressed conviction that Francis had been responsible for his brother's death, the revelation that the authorities also considered him culpable astonished her considerably. She sat in a state of shock.

Jacqueline, however, soon appeared to recover from her fears for her husband's safety. Whether this was the result of a soothing draught thoughtfully brewed for her by Aunt Kate to quench her hysterics, or, as Libby privately considered, the hysterics served no real purpose once Hal wasn't there to be edified by them. She sat down to supper with fewer complaints than usual about the fare provided. She made efforts to chat amicably to them all, only pausing to answer, with an air of injured innocence, when Margery demanded angrily, "Are you totally unconcerned for the fate of your unfortunate husband, Jacqueline?"

"*Non*," she replied. "*Naturellement* I am concerned for Francis, but Hal is with him. Hal will soon arrange something. Hal says I am to keep the cheerful face, so I do. I have faith in Hal."

"I cannot but feel, sister, you have failed to perceive the full gravity of the situation," Margery replied sharply.

Jacqueline turned a look of blank bewilderment on her. "Grav—ity of the situation? Bah! You, I do not understand! You speak the English like no other! This only I know: Francis did not kill his brother! It is not possible! I, Jacqueline, tell you so!"

"Unfortunately, Jacqueline, your word will count for very little in a court of law. I am given to understand from Sheriff Hughes's discourse that evidence is mounting up against poor Francis at an alarming rate!"

"Even if that is so, Margery, I cannot believe Francis, for all his faults, would kill Henry," said Kate quietly. Her anxious eyes travelled down the table to Justin.

She had formed a very favourable opinion of him in the last few hours. She had been impressed by the many points he had raised and his calm comments. "I believe you are a student of the law, Mr Danvers. How does the matter strike you?"

Justin looked uncomfortable, as all eyes turned upon him. "Well, ma'am, I've been assisting Hal in his search for the murderer, as indeed we all have, and I must reluctantly admit, from what we have found so far, it looks as if Mr Francis Westwood is in a most uncomfortable position. However, that is not to say we must despair," he added quickly, as Bess's much-reddened eyes filled with tears again. "We have more questions which must yet be answered and I am sure in my mind we will eventually uncover the truth."

"But will the truth prove Francis innocent?" asked Aunt Margery. Her voice echoed her approval of one who spoke with such fluency and erudition. "Or will it serve merely to confirm his guilt?"

"I pray with all my heart the truth may do so, ma'am. For I fear I know of no other way," Justin replied gravely.

"*Naturellement* it will prove Francis innocent!" cried Jacqueline, weary of this discussion. "Hal, and this young man, Libby's brother, they are both of the cleverness. They *will* get my Francis freed from—from this prison!"

"Getting Francis freed is not the issue!" snapped Margery. She was shocked and frightened by the turn of events. Jacqueline's exuberant words and gestures served only to irritate her. "Clearing the honoured name of Westwood must be our priority at this point in time!"

Jacqueline, unable or unwilling to completely understand her words, cast her a look of deepest scorn and addressed Libby with a cheerfully determined air. "*Ma, chérie,* come you to *ma chambre* once the supper is done. I have there for you the lotion for the skin. Also, Marie, *ma femme,* will trim your hair into the more fashionable *mode!*"

Libby stared at her blankly for a few seconds unable to believe she was serious. She could not think Jacqueline meant to undertake such frivolous tasks at this moment in time. Not when they had decided to all get together to confer, even if Hal had not returned by then.

"But I have never had my hair cut, ma'am," Libby was aware, even as she resisted, a storm of protest must surely follow.

Jacqueline ignored Margery's sigh of exasperation. "*Mais oui, chérie,* that is plain! Only look how it hangs about your face! But it is thick also, and if cut may curl a little, so there is hope. With Bess I have no hope, there is not one bit of shape to her hair, and she will not attend to what I say!"

"Bess looks like a gentlewoman!" announced Margery indignantly. "A woman need ask for nothing more!"

"Pooh!" returned Jacqueline rudely. She noticed with interest the smile Justin flashed at Bess.

Aunt Kate quickly joined the conversation before Margery could explode. "I don't think it would hurt, Libby, to have just a little trimmed off your hair. Jacqueline is right. It is probably the thickness of your hair, which makes it look so severe. A few curls about your face might frame it rather becomingly. A woman can be pretty and still be a gentlewoman, don't you agree, Margery?" She smiled in a manner she hoped might placate her sister-in-law.

"I don't agree with altering the way the good Lord intended us to look," replied Margery flatly. "I make no mention of the suitability of such an occasion as this to even think of such things. All I say is, if a woman's hair were meant to frizz up at the sides of their faces, it would do so of it's own accord! All this talk of beauty is vain and sinful. You'll all be better employed at your prayers!"

There was an uncomfortable silence at this. Immediately everyone around the table felt like a reprobate. All but Jacqueline, who shrugged and addressing no one in particular said, "Me, I do as Hal, who is master here, tells me. Have the cheerful face, he says and keep every one from the brooding."

Justin felt that his sister needed all the help she could get in the awkward position she found herself. He decided to brave Margery's further displeasure by saying in a coaxing tone, "Why not try cutting your hair just a little, Libby? You have ever bemoaned the fact that it didn't curl, and if you decide it isn't quite what you should like, why, then that is a matter soon remedied in time."

As Libby wavered, plainly drawn by the idea of looking prettier for Hal, but frightened of annoying Aunt Margery, Aunt Kate said warmly, "What a very sensible young man you are, Mr Danvers. As you say, nothing grows as quickly as hair, and if the style should make Libby look anything less than a gentlewoman, I for one, shall be surprised!"

Margery was thrown on the defensive. "I wasn't suggesting she was anything like the minx Bess appears to be. I'm sure Libby knows my high opinion of her character. It must be for her to decide. I just give her fair warning not to be taken in by the lure of Satan! Powder and paint, ribbons and laces are temptations of the devil. Take heed what you are about, girl, before you trifle with that wicked fellow. For once you drop into his clutches, he'll never let you go!" With these Cassandra-like words of warning Margery got up and stalked from the table leaving her supper unfinished.

Justin broke the stunned silence. " Phew! Now that is a warning, Libby!"

"Yes, and I think it probably best, ma'am, in view of Aunt Margery's words if I don't have my hair cut!" Libby said addressing Jacqueline.

Jacqueline sat totally unmoved through out the performance. "Margery—bah! That one, she should have been the nun, I am thinking! Either that or put to a husband when yet a child! So, for her, it is now too late, but for you, *ma chérie,* I can do much! You will come with me now—and you also, Bess, for I can see you are the one who needs the chaperone! Once again I must make the effort if I am not to fail."

Libby could see Jacqueline would not be put off. She also had a real desire to see if she could be made to look prettier. It would be something if she could attract Hal's notice she felt. If only she could make him see her as a desirable woman and not just the bride who had mended his fortune. She also felt she should try to distract Bess's mind from worries of her father.

With a token show of reluctance Libby and Bess followed Jacqueline from the supper table. Both were still defensive; Bess almost openly rebellious.

On reaching Jacqueline's comfortable chamber, all this fled and natural curiosity took over. Both girls watched fascinated as Libby, set before a mirror, saw locks of her hair snipped off by Marie, the sallow-skinned Frenchwoman, who attended her mistress with such fierce devotion she was universally disliked by all the other servants. She was a competent hairdresser, and soon the floor was strewn with discarded hair. Jacqueline, meanwhile, moved about the room, mixing various pastes and lotions together in small dishes.

"Why, what is that?" cried Libby, drawing back in dismay, as Marie caught up a length of hair and took from a small brazier in the hearth what looked like an instrument of torture.

"The tongs," replied Jacqueline. "They curl the hair." She watched complacently as the maid tested the heat. "*Oui*, that is hot enough, Marie! This side first, I think." She lifted the shorter hair, whilst Libby gazed into the glass thinking in dismay what an odd appearance she presented. Then she froze in fear of her ears, wrinkling her nose a little at the pungent smell of hot hair.

"*Oui*, that is good! So, here and here, and then just a few little curls at the temple!"

Jacqueline jealously watched the woman's skill. "*Bon! Parfait!* Now the other side." She sat in silence whilst the woman repeated the performance, and then came to her taking the comb from the servant. "Now then, what think you, *ma chérie?*" She pulled out the little curls and ran her fingers through those curls over her ears, pulling here, patting there, whilst Libby gazed in awe at the picture reflected in the mirror.

All at once a fashionable rather pale young lady looked back at her gravely, it is true, but she didn't feel that she had lost any of her dignity with the shedding of a few locks.

"So, *chérie?*" Jacqueline's face joined her at shoulder level in the glass. "You are pleased, no?"

"Yes!" Libby turned her head a little, her face flushed with delight. "Yes, I am! I mean, is that truly me?"

Jacqueline laughed a deep, throaty laugh and turned to Bess with a challenging look in her eyes. "So, Bess, what do you say?"

"It looks very pretty," said Bess in surprise. "It truly does, Libby! I don't know why, but it seems to alter your whole face."

"But of course," sighed Jacqueline, "because Libby's face is so thin, we give her the width here and here! So, will you now put yourself in my hands, Bess?"

"Yes, I suppose so," said Bess reluctantly, and she watched with misgiving as Marie thrust the tongs back into the brazier.

"Come, then, Libby, I have for you the lotion I promised. And this is herbal draught, the one *Maman* gave me the secret of. The one which will make you take quicker with the child!"

Libby blushed hotly as she rose from the glass and cast an embarrassed look at Bess. "I do not think, ma'am—" she began.

Jacqueline interrupted with a hint of impatience. "*Chérie*, you wish to please this husband of yours, *oui*?"

"Yes," agreed Libby, her cheeks aflame.

"And Hal, he wants the heir, no?" she continued mercilessly.

"Well, yes, I—think so!" stammered Libby.

Jacqueline raised her shoulders. "So, we give nature the helping hand! Come, 'tis herbs, Libby. No more— to make you—how you say? Conceive? Where is the harm in that?"

"None, I suppose," replied Libby, looking at Bess to see if she had comprehended this exchange.

Bess was too intent on watching Marie snip her hair to have any attention to spare. Libby took the cup the older woman offered and sipped at it reluctantly.

"*Non!* Drink it down! Do not take the little here and the little there! The taste is not good; be rid of it in one swallow!" she commanded, watching her narrowly. Then as Libby did so, shuddering over the bitter taste, she relaxed smiling. "*Bon!* Now, you come to me each day, and I make the potion for you. I tell you before summer wanes you will have the little one in here!" She patted Libby's stomach and laughed again softly. "Now, the lotion for the face." She produced a crock of thick, creamy paste tinted with a faint yellow hue, which she began to rub into Libby cheeks. "This is the marigold and camomile paste and it must be anointed on the cheeks twice a day to make the skin soft and smooth."

"It stings!" Libby cried, opening her eyes wide.

"Stings? There then, you must have already been walking in the hot sun. You have the burned face! It is well you use this before the damage is done. Now Marie, what have you decided for this one?" Jacqueline turned dismissively from Libby and stood considering Bess's head in the mirror, as the maid outlined her plans in French. Then she nodded, "*Oui,* I agree with what you say, to dress the hair high on the head will only serve to make her look taller and longer! It must be gathered so, into the nape of the neck, and the curls at the side, *oui*, a little longer to rest on her shoulders! *Mais oui! That is it, exactement!*" She nodded pleased, as Marie let the first curl fall in a long ringlet to Bess's shoulder. She stood for a few moments watching the work then said, "Your brother, Libby, he is the wealthy man, no?"

Libby, who had been trying to catch a further glimpse of herself in the mirror, looked surprised. "Justin? No, he has nearly finished his studies."

Jacqueline nodded impatiently. "*Oui*, he is the student, but later, when he is older, he will inherit from your *père*?"

"Oh, yes, when my father dies, yes, then he'll inherit."

"And your *père*, he is the rich man, no?" she continued, still watching Bess, who was now trying to look unconcerned at these questions.

Libby looked uncomfortable. "I don't know that he is exactly rich."

"But what else could he be, Libby? Did he not buy Hal as an husband for you?" Jacqueline asked unkindly. "Do you not think it took much gold to get Hal?"

"I know nothing of these matters," replied Libby, unhappily.

"Bah! You English! Your mothers, they have no sense! They tell you nothing of the money and expect you to understand! I tell you both this. Money is most important. Money, it makes everything happen!"

"I thought that was love," murmured Bess, with a dreamy smile.

"Love? Love, oh, you are still very much the child, Bess!" She laughed once again her scornful eyes dwelling first on Libby's face flushed with excitement, so that she looked very pretty indeed, to Bess, pale and solemn in the candle light, as by magic her face took on a different shape; the light casting an ethereal look on her young beauty.

All at once Jacqueline felt jaded and tired. These two young women stood on the verge of life with all its promise still before them, their innocence there for all to see. She felt a sharp twinge of envy for that lost world, which made her angry. "Have you not done yet, Marie!" she cried sharply. "Well, hurry! Can you not see how weary I am?"

Then as the maid hastened to put the last touches to Bess's hair she turned from them irritably, "*Bon!* If you are finished you may go, both of you!"

Bewildered by her lightening change of mood, Bess stumbled to her feet. She was still half-amazed by the skillful transformation of her hair.

"Oh, you do look nice, Bess!" said Libby quickly. "Jacqueline is so clever. She was exactly right, you don't look half so tall now!"

"Don't I?" asked Bess innocently.

Jacqueline turned on them, her eyes flashing, her voice shrill. "Do you not hear me? Go I say! I will listen no more to your silly chatter! Get out! Go I say!"

Astounded by this sudden display of temper, they hastened to the door, where Libby mindful of her manners, dropped a childish curtsey before they fled. "We beg pardon, ma'am, for annoying you. And I—I thank you very much!"

Chapter Nineteen

"What happened? Why did she change so?" Libby was astonished as they hurried to her chamber where they had previously agreed to meet.

"I don't know. She is often so when she no longer has need of one. One moment so pleasant, almost affectionate, the next quite horrid!" Bess replied.

"Was it something we said, do you think?" Libby reviewed the conversation anxiously.

"I don't know, possibly, but don't think on it. I tell you, she is often so!" Bess, who had long borne with her step-mother's moods, was inclined to be dismissive. "Oh, I wonder if Justin and Ned will have bothered to wait for us or gone off on their own affairs."

"I do hope not—" began Libby and then broke off as they turned the corridor to find Justin and Ned sitting glumly side-by-side on the window seat close to her chamber.

"You've been an age!" grumbled Ned. He jumped to

his feet impatiently and directed a searching look at them both. "What have you done to your hair? It looks foolish!"

"It looks most becoming!" said Justin. He got to his feet also and administered a sharp kick in the shins to his outspoken companion. "Are you pleased, Libby?"

"I don't know. I think so. It feels so very strange! Do you truly think it becoming, Justin?" she asked anxiously as she led the way into her chamber. "Only I dread to think what Aunt Margery will say! Do you think Hal will like it?"

"I don't see how he can fail to do so," sighed Justin.

"If he even notices," added Ned slyly.

Libby looked crestfallen at this and sighed as she and Bess went to sit at the foot of the bed. Justin took the chair by the window and Ned began to rock back and forth on a joint-legged stool. "Don't you think Bess looks pretty?" she asked Justin.

"Very much so. I must confess I'd not thought it possible to improve upon the perfection of nature, but I see I am proved wrong, and am glad of it!" Justin replied gratefully. He was pleased his sister had given him the opportunity to express his admiration of Bess, who gazed back at him, her lips parted in wonderment, her eyes aglow. Then Ned made a derisive noise, and she blushed hotly and quickly looked away.

Justin wished he could reach to tip over Ned's stool. "So, to work. We'd best begin I think and not wait upon Hal. He could be long delayed. So Ned, tell us what you have discovered."

"Nothing at all." He kicked the leg of the stool disconsolately. "Will was in an odd sort of a temper. He did nothing but sneer at Hal. He even asked what sort of a bridegroom he was making! He wasn't at all like he used to be, but rude and angry! Oh, there was one thing of interest he did say; it seems he wasn't with Kitty all afternoon."

"But we knew that. Did he say whom he was with?" asked Justin, restraining his impatience.

Ned shrugged his shoulders. "Another wench, one more accommodating." Noticing Justin's frown he hastily adjusted his words. "A prettier one, I mean."

"I did not think it would be an easy task to get the truth from him. You say, Ned, that Will has a great dislike of Hal?"

"He always has disliked Hal. Right from before we knew for certain he was to come here. Of course, it got worse once Hal arrived and my uncle was so pleased with him. I think Will hated Hal for being so tall and handsome and well-mannered."

Bess wrinkled her brow. "Will Longstaffe isn't un-handsome himself. Certainly the maids all go into a twitter of confusion if he speaks to them. He is considered a fine figure of a man. I cannot think why he should be so jealous of Hal."

Justin felt a faint stirring of jealousy in his heart to hear her warm praise of the man's looks. He was tall himself, but he had not the steward's broadness, nor his look of strength. "Perhaps he knew who was to have inherited before Hal came along. He might have a partisan feeling for this person. After all, he was greatly in your uncle's confidence, was he not?"

"Oh, yes," said Ned. "He was a great favourite with my uncle. That's how he came to be his agent so young."

"How old is he?" Justin was making notes.

Ned looked blank. He had merely repeated what he heard others say. " I don't know. He was already grown when I came here. He might be as much as thirty, I suppose? Oh, as for the matter of my uncle's horse, he said he knew nothing of it. He hadn't seen anything like it for sale at Gloucester Fair. Indeed, he says there is nothing to say the horse had ever been here at Westwood at all. He thinks the murderer most probably rode off on it."

"Very probably the murderer did, but he would still

have to sell the horse somewhere," said Justin trying not to sound depressed.

"Will is convinced the murderer is my father and that we'll find the horse at the nearest port," Ned replied, as if he thought the suggestion was helpful.

Justin duly made another note. "Yes, that is possible. We can look into it. There is nothing to stop us trying another horse fair either. I expect some of the same traders will travel to, say, Stow?"

A silence fell as he read through his notes. Then he sighed and said, "I regret to say Bess and I discovered nothing more than what her father confessed to Sheriff Hughes. He *was* here on the feast of Corpus Christi and he and Mr Henry Westwood *did* quarrel. Old Jonas heard them, but he also heard your father leave, in a cheerful manner. Surely if your father had just killed his brother he would have slipped away without a word to anyone?"

"Yes, surely," cried Bess. She brightened at the thought and then fell silent as she recollected her father imprisoned.

"Libby, did you have any success?" Justin turned hopefully to his sister.

"I fear not," said Libby. "It seems Aunt Kate never asked Uncle Henry who was his heir. It was a difficult subject because she felt she had failed in her duty to provide the son Westwood needed."

The door opened abruptly and Hal walked in. He halted in surprise, looking just a little displeased to see them all gathered there. Justin guessed from his face their presence was unwelcome. "Hal, we beg pardon for this intrusion, and for going ahead without you, but we thought it best to continue with the review of our progress."

Hal nodded wearily and Libby was struck by the change in him. He was no longer the bright-faced, debonair young man she'd married a few short weeks ago. He looked older, careworn, heart-sick and curiously vulnerable. She desired nothing more than to take him in her arms and soothe away the trouble in his dark eyes.

"How did you leave our father, Hal?" asked Bess anxiously.

Hal sank to the stool Ned thoughtfully vacated for him. "As well as we could hope. Mr Fenton was kind enough to accompany me to Maucester. He insisted on father being well-housed in the gatehouse with the warden of the prison. He may receive visitors at any time and also has access to paper and books. We made provision for his meals to be carried to him from the inn." He covered his face with his hand in a gesture, which showed all too plainly the toll the day had taken of him. "I am to ride to London tomorrow."

"To London?" Libby cried in dismay.

He dropped his hand glancing to her face. A tiny frown appeared between his brows at the sight of her hair, but he made no remark, merely holding out his shapely hand to display a heavy signet ring. "Yes, London. I am to take this ring to the King at Whitehall. I am to beg an audience of him and explain what has gone forward here. My father is confident of a letter, I do believe."

"A free pardon?" Justin asked frowning.

Hal shook his head. "More a letter explaining perhaps? I know not."

"You are weary Hal and need rest," said Justin. He could see how exhausted his brother-in-law was. "We'll take ourselves off so you can seek your bed, but first, did you discover aught from Mr Fenton concerning your uncle's other heir?"

"Do not worry, I cannot sleep yet. I must first take a message to Jacqueline. Mr Fenton could tell me nothing. It would seem all my uncle ever said was that his earlier choice of heir would set tongues wagging and upset Aunt Margery!"

"No more than that? Then we are no further forwards. In fact, we are in a worse state than before!" cried Ned disappointed.

"Not entirely," said Justin. He'd been looking at his notes. "I think we must seek out Will Longstaffe's other companion. Would Kitty not know something of her? Bess, perhaps you or Libby could talk to her? We can talk to local horse copers, Ned, and then, if all else fails, well, Hal is to see the King!"

Bess nodded as Justin got to his feet. "Well, I'll leave you to get some rest, Hal. You look as if it will be welcome."

Both Bess and Ned took this hint, and filed silently from the chamber. Libby slid from the bed and came to stand before her husband, asking gently. "Would you like me to fetch you something to eat or drink, Hal?"

He did not lift his head, but replied quietly, "No, I thank you; Mr Fenton insisted we took supper at the inn."

She hesitated, then as he neither moved nor spoke she said tentatively, "Must you see Jacqueline tonight, Hal? Won't tomorrow do just as well?"

"Not take a woman whose husband is imprisoned on a murder charge news of him? Even if I were dying on my feet I do not think I could be so discourteous!" He looked up, irritated by the suggestion, which was exactly in accord with his own inclinations. He was fully aware in his heart that to seek out Jacqueline now would be folly. Yet, perversely, because of this fact, he was determined to do it, to prove she had no power over him.

She turned from him; tears welling in her eyes at the anger in his voice. She knew she was being foolish, that he was beset by enormous worries and problems, but she did think he might have mentioned her hair. "I'll not further detain you then, if I can do nothing for you," she said, with an edge to her voice.

He heard it and was spurred into action. He stood up, dropping his sword to the floor with a clatter. Later, once this coming ordeal was done with, he'd make it right with her again. First, he must use all his resources to withstand Jacqueline.

He crossed to the bowl, bathing his face and hands in the cool water. He then ran a comb through his wind-swept hair. The night was hot and sticky. He still felt dusty and travel weary. On impulse, he cast aside his heavy silk doublet. He pulled his shirt from his back where it clung damply, outlining his muscled shoulders, and went to the door. Jacqueline could complain all she wanted, he'd make no more effort for her.

"No doubt you'll be asleep on my return?" he asked

as he glanced at Libby's stony face.

"No doubt," she replied curtly.

Her coldness smote him, sparking a flicker of anger. He knew he wasn't giving her the attention he should, but surely she should make an attempt to understand some of the problems he had to endure. "Then I'll bid you good night," he said as he left.

He hurried through the silent house, his mind on the events of the evening. It was essential he was prepared for this meeting with his step-mother, and yet he found himself at Jacqueline's chamber still in a state of confusion.

"Are you here, Jacqueline?" he asked sharply, as he entered.

She turned from her mirror and advanced a few steps toward him. "*Oui*, Hal, I am here. You bring me news of Francis?"

"Yes, he is as well-lodged as I and my guardian, Mr Fenton, could manage," he replied. He turned his eyes away from her lovely face and mentally cursed himself for not just sending her a note excusing his attendance on the score of weariness, rather than subject himself to the torment of being near.

"Mr Robert Fenton, the magistrate? The man who was friend to your uncle, no?" she asked quickly.

Hal consciously turned his eyes to the window, where a sliver of a moon was rising, so that he didn't have to look at her. He didn't want to notice how enticingly her gown was caught together at her slender waist and how it fell open at neck to reveal her pearly breasts beneath the tissue of lawn that was her nightgown. "Yes, he has been most kind. You know I went to his house at once begging he might advise me. He is all that is good and kind. He insisted on riding with me to Maucester. Once there he kindly took control of the situation, demanding my father be housed as befits his station in life."

"So, he is not in a loathsome cell, my husband?" she asked softly. Her eyes dwelt on his face as she willed him to look at her, to fall under her spell. She might no longer have youth and innocence on her side, but she was certain she could steal plain, good, little Libby's husband away from her very easily, and was determined to do it so.

"No, he is decently lodged with the warden in his house, much like a guest. I have given the warden's daughter monies to provide him with clean linen. She will arrange for food to be brought to him from the inn. At Mr Fenton's insistence, we are also allowed to visit him at will, and may take him books and writing implements to help while away the time."

"*Bon!* You have done well, Hal, but you look so weary! Come, sit you down, I have ordered food, for you must be a hungered and thirsty!" She indicated with a sweep of her hand the table set for two with a supper.

"No, I thank you. I ate with Mr Fenton at the inn," he replied awkwardly. He was suddenly very glad he had done so.

"A little wine then?" she coaxed, pouring it into a goblet. "Come, Hal do not look at me as if you see a demon! Can we not take a cup of wine together as friends?"

He held himself rigidly for a few seconds and then reluctantly took the cup she held out with a taunting air. He need have no fear, he recognised the danger and was in complete control. He'd drink it down and go. It was as simple as that.

"You have seen Libby?" she asked.

"Yes," he replied,pausing the cup half way to his mouth.

"And? What do you think? *Le Bon Dieu,* Hal, never tell me you did not see!" she cried, as he looked blank.

"Not see what?" he asked, taken completely off his guard.

"Her hair! Oh Hal, did you not notice we had cut

and curled her hair! *Mon Dieu!* All the time I try to make her more beautiful for you, and you do not see!" she cried in mock exasperation.

He realised suddenly what had puzzled him and how he had plainly offended Libby. "Oh, her hair! I knew there was something different about her!" He frowned as he thought. "I do not think I like it."

"Not like it? You ingrate! It was the vast improvement. It made her look quite pretty! But you don't drink Hal! Come, drink with me!" She laughed magnanimously; thrilled to hear him speak in a disparaging way about Libby.

He drank from the goblet as he was bid and brought the picture of Libby to his mind with some difficulty, distracted as he was by the presence of Jacqueline. He closed his eyes, the better to see Libby's innocent face, and clung desperately to this vision. "Yes, yes she does look pretty—but she doesn't look like Libby anymore."

"*Non*, she doesn't," she agreed. She came closer and gazed up into his face. "I thought it gave her the look of me!"

He opened his eyes and the vision of Libby turned, in spite of his desperate attempt to hold onto it, into that of Jacqueline. All at once, the power she had over him came flooding back, making him protest weakly,

"Jacqueline, I don't think it is wise for us to be together alone like this anymore."

She gave a tinkling laugh. "Alone together? Pooh! Finish your wine! I would that you don't disgrace me Hal, by talking of my foolishness! Francis, he is come now. You shall get him free for me and I shan't be troubled by the dreams again!"

"You are troubled by dreams?" he asked. His head felt muzzy and he was trembling. He drank off the last of the wine in his cup, hoping to clear his head, and walked to the window longing for the coolness outside.

She lifted her hands to her head dramatically. "*Mais oui* Hal, such wicked dreams! I dream of lying in your arms, of your lips hot on mine! I dream of the passionate love I know you have within you. A passion which that little mouse of yours will never unlock!"

"Don't Jacqueline!" he cried. Then as she moved even closer to him, he turned to place his cup on the table, determined to leave. He was uncomfortably aware of a buzzing in his head and a trembling in his limbs, which he sought desperately to control. He found that he was swaying as he tried to walk, so that she caught at him, pulling him into her arms.

She held him close, whispering huskily, "*Don't*, you

say? Yet how can I help myself when you are here before me! When I see your face filled with the longing I have in my heart. Your eyes full of the same wanting I have. Your arms longing to hold me as much as I long to hold you! Oh, Hal I can help myself no longer!"

He struggled against what seemed to be a tide of great weariness, as she embraced him fiercely, and kissed him with such passion, that against his will it seemed she fired the latent embers of his own desire.

"Hold me, Hal, hold me tight and swear you'll never let me go!"

Chapter Twenty

Hal did not come back until rosy tendrils of dawn were lightening the sky. He made no pretence of getting into bed, but sat for some while silently considering the events of the night. He was angry and ashamed. He felt he had betrayed the trust of everyone by his foolishness. Finally, he set about making his preparations for the journey with grim determination.

Libby, who had been awake for most of the night and merely feigned sleep on his arrival, watched through half-closed eyes. It was only as she glimpsed him struggling into his best boots, that she could pretend no more. Abruptly she sat up.

"Where are you going?" she asked.

He turned a pale, heavy-eyed face upon her. "To London. I told you so last night."

"But you look so weary," she cried in dismay as she saw the dark smudges beneath his eyes.

"I slept ill," he answered avoiding her glance. Then

as she looked at him with shocked reproach in her eyes, he turned away. "I cannot linger here," he muttered. "Every moment I waste is another hour in prison for my father!"

"Then do not stay," she replied. Her lips felt wooden as she spoke and her throat ached with the desire to weep.

He advanced to the bed, looking the very picture of guilt. He raised his hand to his head, which was rocking with pain. "I am sorry! I know I should stay to try to explain. I am aware I am treating you infamously! I have no defence. I can only beg you will bear with me and try to forgive me! Adieu, we'll talk on my return!"

He hurried away, leaving her to weep further tears into her pillow. Where had he been the whole night long? She wondered in despair, unfortunately, the answer was all too obvious to her.

For the sake of her sanity she pushed such wicked thoughts away. She could never think of doubting Hal. She must remain loyal to her vows and cast all such doubts away. It was this knowledge that made her later go down to breakfast with a very subdued air.

Aunt Margery, observing Libby's demeanour and thinking her penitent for not having heeded her advice, made strenuous efforts to be civil to all. Indeed, she went so far as to remark loudly, that contrary to her expectations, both Libby and Bess looked neat and lady-like.

Knowing this to be praise of the highest order, Aunt Kate viewed Libby's face with some misgiving. She knew it wouldn't be long before Margery would be making, what she would term, delicate questions as to the likelihood of the early expectation of an heir. In order to avert the catastrophe, Kate suggested Libby and Bess take alms to an old woman who lived in a remote area near the village.

They set off in good accord, Bess still speculating on all that had happened. Libby made an effort to appear interested and would not to let her mind wander. She felt mentally exhausted and was vaguely aware that a period of calm reflection could only be of benefit. Then, perhaps she might be able to understand why Hal was so fascinated by his step-mother and plan how to make herself more interesting to Hal.

They paused for breath at the top of the hill and stopped to look back at the vista of the house set in the valley. "Oh, look there," said Bess, "that man on horseback. Isn't that Will Longstaffe?"

Libby squinted her eyes against the sun. "Is it? I'm afraid I don't know him well enough to say, but it would appear whoever it is has seen us and is riding this way."

The girls stood waiting until the man on the roan came closer. It was, as they thought, Will Longstaffe. At first, as he recognised them, he seemed surprised and then made haste to bow awkwardly in the saddle. "Mistress Bess and Mistress Westwood, too! What are you doing this far from home?"

"We're going to visit Goody Stokes, and we thought we'd take a short cut through the wood. It will be cool and shady there away from this hot sun."

"True enough. It is cool and shady. No sunlight ever dares penetrate that wood and precious few folk, either!" he replied. His voice was odd.

Libby turned her eyes upon his face. She was aware at once he was in some way angry with them and yet also frightened. "Why?"

"'Tis haunted, Mistress," he replied roughly. "And has been, I don't know how many years!"

Bess turned to eye the innocent-looking glade, with its tall slender birches and magnificent beeches, which looked so very inviting after the heat of the sun. "Haunted? Why, I've never heard that said before!"

He shrugged his broad shoulders. "Happen not, Mistress Bess, you being but lately come. You should ask thy brother Ned if it is not so."

"Who haunts it?" asked Libby, as Bess looked alarmed.

"Evil spirits, ma'am. Witches and their familiars and such like!"

"I don't believe it," said Libby. She was certain in her mind he was, for some reason, lying to frighten them away.

"Many like you, Mistress, have scoffed," he warned, "and lived to rue the day! Some entered that wood as strong and brave as any man, only to come out a broken wretch!"

"We'll go back!" announced Bess.

Libby thought she detected a glimmer of satisfaction in his eyes. "No," she said firmly. "We'll go round the wood and onto the road. It will take longer, but never mind!"

"It will be hotter and dustier. Oh, Libby, let us go back!" wailed Bess.

"No," she repeated firmly. "There is nothing to be afraid of, Bess. We'll go on!"

"Mistress Westwood is town-bred," said Will, with an attempt at jocular politeness. "She doesn't understand our country ways or how she defies local tradition. Why, in the village they even mutter that your destination is the home of a witch!"

"Now that can be nothing but wicked gossip, or your aunt would never have sent us there, Bess!" said Libby. She was annoyed by the man's odious, patronising manner. "Come, we cannot linger here all morning. You, too, must have work to do, Master Longstaffe."

A dull, red, colour flooded his face at these words. It sounded like a rebuke for time wasting from his master's wife. He snatched at the bit, and the nervous filly he was riding started, half-rearing, and nearly unseating him. He cursed under his breath, struggling to get control of the animal, and then, with a vicious kick, cantered back down the slope. "You've been warned. Good day to you both!"

"I really do think we should go back Libby," said Bess. Her eyes followed the man as he struggled still with the half-broken horse.

"Can't you see he was out to frighten us off?" asked Libby impatiently.

"Yes, and he has succeeded. I'm frightened!" replied Bess honestly.

Libby gritted her teeth. "Well, he's not going to frighten me! I shall visit Goody Stokes, even if I have to do so alone."

Bess, seeing she would not be turned from her decision, capitulated. "Oh, very well, but I tell you, nothing would make me set foot in that wood!"

"Yes, we'll skirt it," agreed Libby, with relief.

It was half-an-hour later that they arrived at Goody Stokes's cottage. This was a ruinous affair of broken walls and sagging thatch. It was distanced far enough from the village to make the occupant rather unused to visitors and nervous enough in their presence to be thought a little odd. Libby and Bess both knew it needed only oddness, poverty and a solitary life for any old woman to be branded a witch, but even so, both were on tenterhooks for the first few minutes, especially when she said, "So, you had words with Master Longstaffe this morn? How is that fine gentleman these days?"

"How—how—did you know?" stammered Bess. She threw Libby a frightened look; for the ability to see far distant events was a known sign of witchcraft.

The old woman replied, looking surprised. "Why, I saw you, Mistress. I was out gathering campion and feverfew in Westwood and saw him join you. I thought at the time happen you were acoming here to visit me. Sweet Mistress Westwood sent word someone would come soon, if she could not. But then, when you turned away, I thought you must be bound elsewhere."

"You aren't afraid of the wood?" whispered Bess.

"Lord-a-mercy, no, Mistress! Whyever should I be?" she asked in amazement. She glanced from Bess's frightened face to Libby's in amazement.

"We were told it's haunted," said Libby baldly.

The old woman laughed. She didn't cackle or simper ominously, Libby noted; she just laughed. "Stuff and nonsense! Who has been filling your pretty heads with such tales?"

"Will Longstaffe!" said Bess indignantly. "Isn't it true?"

A fleeting shade of anxiety showed in Goody's old eyes for a second. "No truer than the wicked rumour that I am a witch. But I don't understand. That Will Longstaffe is no fool, like the village wenches. Why should he tell you such a foolish thing?"

"Because he wanted to frighten us," said Libby slowly.

The old woman dragged a stool up to the table and sat down with them, looking bewildered. "Now why should Will want to do such a thing? He's not a bad boy, he never was. A little strong-willed mayhap. Of course he's resentful, because of his position, but he's not bad."

"I wonder if it was something that happened when we were here, back in the Spring?" Bess blushed and looked embarrassed as both turned to look at her in surprise. "Only Father, Hal and I came to Westwood at that time. Jane stayed in London with Jacqueline, who hates the country. Everyone was very kind and pleased to see us returned home, except Will. He ignored father, and hated Hal, I could tell, but strangely enough he was very attentive to me. He would find an excuse to talk to me everyday and was forever smiling and waving to me. One day he had followed me into the garden and we were talking, when my father came upon us. He sent Will about his business pretty sharply, and not very kindly, either. He declared Will wasn't fit to match with a true-born Westwood and he'd better put the idea from his head. Will was furiously angry; he said not a word in reply to father, but I saw his face. It was a slight he would never forgive."

The old woman nodded wisely. "Ah, happen it were that, Mistress. It has the ring of truth. For make no mistake, that would have cut him on the raw, it would! Likely saying that were his way of frightening you."

"Why should he want to frighten Bess?" asked Libby. "It wasn't her fault. Bess didn't insult him." She paused suddenly and turned thoughtfully to the old woman again. "Why should it particularly cut Will Longstaffe on the raw? And why should he be resentful of his position? I'd have thought he'd be proud of it. Everyone says he is young to take so great a responsibility."

"Oh, he's proud of being the Westwood agent, right and true, but 'pride goeth before destruction and vanity before a fall!'" quoted Goody Stokes, nodding her old head again.

She glanced from one bright, enquiring face to the other. "I shouldn't rightly say a word," she announced. "I swore to Mary I never would. She were the closest friend I ever had, for all that I were old enough to have been her mother. Aye, not that it did her any good either, for she were no more than five and twenty when she were took. The cough it were," she added, by way of explanation.

"I nursed her myself. We had Longman's Farm then. My Jack farmed it right up until he were took, the same year as Noll Cromwell. I always said to him we should have taken the boy ourselves when Mary died. He weren't no more than a mite at the time and we had no chick of our own. He were a good, biddable lad in those days. Aye well, too good for the like of we, he be now. Him, with all his book learning and such. Lessons with the Rector he had, whilst he was still here. Then the master took him to help on the estate along about the time that silly ranting preacher fellow came; he that used to stand in the rain and preach hell-fire to us."

Libby nodded. She could recollect from her child-hood the itinerant preachers, who replaced the estab-lished clergy, at the time of the Lord Protector.

"He has no family then?" asked Libby politely. "No father to follow into trade?"

The old dame tapped the side of her nose and chuck-led "Kin is it? Aye, well, least said, soonest mended."

Both girls were bewildered. They exchanged glances and Bess gave a hint of a shrug as the old woman con-tinued.

"The lad has kin you might say, and the finest in the county I'll swear, but none that own him."

"Oh he's a love-child!" said Bess as her brow cleared, "but of course!"

"Not that they didn't stand by him; No, he couldn't say that, whatever else he claims. He couldn't say he had no help."

"I'm sure he couldn't," said Libby as an answer seemed called for. "It is well known then, his parentage?"

"Least said—"

"Soonest mended," agreed Bess as she began to un-pack her basket. "My Aunt Kingscott has sent this blan-ket. She said she hopes you'll feel the benefit come the winter."

"Mistress Kingscott, now there's a fine lady. One who

knows how to act pretty, so to speak. She and I were of an age you know. I were born on Lady Day and she around Lammas. You'd not think to look at us now, we were both as young and lovely as you pretty creatures, would you?"

Bess privately agreed. The years had not dealt easily with Goody Stokes, her proportions were as ample as her wrinkles.

"Life, it don't seem but a moment," sighed the old woman. "One minute you're a pretty young wench, with all the lads eager to dance with you at sheep shearing, the next you're an old woman none wants to think of." She seemed to recollect herself for she sighed again and smoothed the blanket. "Mistress Margery, I mind how she were sent off in disgrace the spring I wed my Jack."

"Aunt Margery sent off in disgrace?" Bess was incredulous.

"Aye, it were a serious thing, mark you," she replied. "All on account of that there Robin Fenton. Him that be the Justice now, set up over all of us. Aye, and him no better than he ought to be."

"Mr Fenton!" Libby remembered in dismay that Hal did not want it talked about.

"Ah, but she loved him," said the old woman. "I were

fond of my Jack, well, he were a merry lad, and we dealt well together, but Mistress Margery, she fell head over heels for that Robin Fenton. I remember Mary telling me all about it."

"Mary?" Bess wrinkled her nose. The old woman's rambling story was hard to follow.

"Aye, Mary, she were maid to Mistress Margery. She went off with her to kin in Devon, which be a goodly way from these parts and from Robin Fenton."

"I had thought she had been married," said Libby frowning, "That is to say, I thought Hal told us they married her off to Mr Kingscott."

"Aye, that were later in that autumn. But in that spring and it were a lovely spring; warm and gentle like the kiss of an angel; in that spring she were in love with Robin Fenton. Oh, how she wept when they sent her away, as if her heart would break. Not that they do, my dear." She smiled up at Bess revealing but a few blackened teeth and knobbly gums. "No, not break. They twist and tear a little, but not break."

"And in the autumn she came back to marry Mr Kingscott?" asked Libby.

This was a part of the story they had not been told. She couldn't help seeing Aunt Margery, the stern-faced matriarch, in a totally different light.

"No, Mary came back with the little babe, Will, but Mistress Margery, we never set eyes on her in many a year. The old Master and Master Henry, they took her up to the Kingscott home and she were wed to that gentleman and much good did it do her. No babe of her own for all the years and Master Kingscott dead now and his son in his place. No, it wasn't until the old Master died that Mistress Margery—Kingscott I should call her, come a-visiting and my, hadn't she changed. Sharp where she used to be gentle and all her prettiness gone. Rubbed away by the dour looks of her husband mostlike!"

Libby's brain was racing. Surely it couldn't be. Surely, no! She glanced at Bess, who was merely putting out the various comforts and talking about them.

"Whose child was it?" asked Libby.

The old dame looked at her from under her brows. "Ah, whose? I don't know, and Mary, well she died a few years back now, so she won't tell. All I say is that Master Henry and Mistress Margery used to visit Mary and the lad regular."

"Aunt Margery did say she had a high regard for Will Longstaffe," Libby was following her own train of thought.

Bess looked startled, "What are you thinking, Libby?

You cannot possibly mean—"

"Can I not?" she replied, "Goody Stokes, is Will Longstaffe Aunt Margery's son?"

The old lady looked scandalised, "Well now, I never said that," she cried in a panic. "I never said any such thing! I only know she and Mary went away to Devon and Mary came back with a babe! And none can deny that the family have ever looked after Will. I don't say whose lad he be!"

"That's what she was hiding!" cried Libby, "Hal said he didn't think she was telling the truth, but if this is the truth, who could blame her?"

"Aunt Margery? Have you taken leave of your senses? Aunt Margery to bear a child out of wedlock! It just couldn't happen!" cried Bess, horrified.

"I don't see why not. It happens again and again, you know it does! Very often maidens have to be wed in haste," Libby replied.

"Maidens mayhap, village lasses, farmer's daughters, even tradesmen's—" Bess broke off, blushing and looking appalled. "Oh, I'm sorry, I didn't mean to say that! It just slipped out."

"Yes, even lawyer's daughters, and gentlemen's daughters, too," Libby nodded.

"No," said Goody Stokes.

"No?" both girls turned to her.

The old woman nodded darkly. "They be worth too much in marriage portions. They are kept close, and if they should go astray, well, there's an escape route."

"I don't believe it. It doesn't make sense," said Bess.

"I do. I'm sure I've found the answer," Libby was certain.

Bess was impatient. "The answer to what? What if you are right? What if the unbelievable is true? How does that solve anything?"

Libby's face crumpled as she realised what Bess was saying. "Oh no, I don't suppose it does, does it? Perhaps Will thinks he should be acknowledged or some such thing?"

"Some such thing? I can hardly see that happening!" scoffed Bess.

"Well, I shall tell Hal anyway," said Libby defiantly.

"Do, but it'll make no difference! You are chasing after windmills and if Aunt Margery should hear of this, there'll be no end to the trouble. Oh, dear heaven, just think of the rumpus she'll make, and I can't say as I'd blame her," Bess cried.

"Now, don't either of you ever mention it. I beg of you. I only told you all this now that's he's dead and can't be harmed by any scandal, but that sweet lady of his can! And that were his biggest concern after he married her, that she should never find out."

"What do you mean his biggest concern? Are you talking of my husband's uncle?" Libby was amazed by the old woman's words.

"Aye, that's right. Master Henry, who was so cruelly murdered," Goody Stokes nodded.

"*That* was what my father meant," said Bess, whilst Libby tried to marshal order out of her thoughts.

"Aye, Mistress, happen Will thought married to you he might become more of a Westwood," agreed the old woman sagely.

"And my father would have none of it," said Bess slowly.

Both girls looked at each other, wondering if they had not stumbled on vital evidence, then reason took over. "No, it's just all too fantastic," said Libby, having second thoughts, and Bess made haste to agree.

"Yes,too fantastic. Will's a surly fellow, but he's not bad at heart," she said, as if anxious to convince them both.

"No man is bad at heart, Mistress, until he sees his heart's desire snatched out of reach. Then there's no saying what a man might do!" said Goody Stokes.

Chapter Twenty One

As Justin rode back into the stables at Westwood Hall, he wondered just how he should occupy himself for the next few hours. Time hung heavily on his hands he noticed when Bess was absent. He had been to the prison in the town of Maucester on a visit to Francis Westwood. Justin had carried messages of support, fresh linen and other necessities to lighten Hal's father's confinement, but now that was accomplished he was not sure what to do. He could, of course, write another letter to his father, telling him how matters were progressing, even perhaps mentioning something of his own hopes with regard to Bess. But in truth, he'd not been so well received by Francis Westwood as to be sanguine of these.

Bess's father had been grateful for the visit, there was no doubt of that. He had indeed been both easy and affable in his manner to his guest, in spite of its unusual circumstances, but there had been steel behind the glove. Justin couldn't fail to be conscious of it, nor that the self-important little man was shrewder than he'd given him credit for.

No, he thought as he handed his horse over to the stable lad. There had been something about his smile. Something faintly patronising in his eyes, which had told Justin the older man had been well aware of his motives in visiting him, and had not been taken in by them. Francis Westwood was well aware that he loved his daughter, and however agreeable it might be to have a companion prepared to while away a morning of captivity with a game of chess, he wasn't going to succumb to any feelings of obligation.

Filled with sudden gloom, he made his way from the stables. He might as well write to his father, he supposed; he had nothing better to do. Suddenly he heard the familiar tune of *Summer is A-Coming In*. Abruptly he turned right under the arch to avoid the meeting. He was in no mood for Will Longstaffe, he decided. He found himself in a small courtyard, with the pungent smell of soap assailing his nostrils. He was wondering if there was some way into the house from there or if he'd have to wait until Will passed by, when Kitty appeared in an open doorway with a basket of washing under her arm.

"Kitty, isn't it?" he said. He knew Bess had not yet had time to talk to her and realized it would be good do so now. "I appear to be lost. Can you direct me into the house?"

"You can go through that door there, Master Danvers, if you be wishing," she replied dully.

He eyed her thoughtfully, noting her red-rimmed eyes and weary expression. "Thank you. I would like to talk to you, Kitty— if I may," he added tentatively.

"Me?" she replied. "I can't think why; none want to talk to me! Besides which, I'm too busy. I've this washing to lay out in the orchard."

"Well, I do want to talk to you, so I'll come with you and carry that heavy basket, if I may. We can talk as we walk."

Kitty stared at him for a moment and then shrugged her shoulders relinquishing the basket. "Don't you go getting the smell of horses on my clean linen, mind!" she admonished. Without further ado, she led the way between two buildings and out into the drying ground, which ran behind the stables. Justin followed mindful of his hands.

"What do you want to ask me?" she asked, glancing back over her shoulder.

He caught her up, falling into step beside her. "I want

to talk about the day you went to the fair."

"Well, I don't. A pox on that fair! 'Twas nothing but bad luck for all, I say!"

"Bad luck for your master, certainly. How so for you?" Justin asked.

"'Tain't none of your business," she snapped, adding a reluctant, "Sir."

Justin was irked at her hesitation, but he agreed peaceably, "Indeed, no, it isn't any of my business, but I know you have been badly used Kitty, and I am sorry for it."

Her face puckered. "Badly used! You don't know the half of it! Ruined, that's what I am. Ruined!"

To his horror, she gave vent to a bout of hearty tears, leaning her head on the gatepost and weeping fit to burst.

Justin carefully balanced the basket on the gate and patted her shoulder ineffectually. "There, there, Kitty, don't weep," he begged. "Only tell me what is wrong and I'll do my best to help you."

She looked up at him through her tears; her face red and swollen. "Oh, aye? Marry me will you, to give a name to the brat Will Longstaffe got on me?"

Justin was so astounded he let go of the basket and it tipped over, scattering its contents on the lush grass.

"Look what you're at, you great lumpkin!" she cried

angrily. "Why, if you got mud on that I'll—"

He caught her hands, forcing her to look at him. "Never mind that now! Do you tell me you are with child by Will Longstaffe?"

"Nay, 'twere Robin Goodfellow!" she cried angrily, shaking off his hand. "Will Longstaffe bother with the likes of me? I must have dreamed it!"

"You are angry," he observed, as she bent gathering up the linen, muttering under her breath. "And I don't blame you."

"Why, that's good of you," she snapped as she gathered up the last of the washing, and pushed open the gate.

"I mean, I understand why you are angry," he said. He took the basket from her again and followed her as she began to spread out petticoats and shifts on the hedges and bushes. "And does Will refuse to marry you?"

She made no reply to him, but vented her feelings on the washing, shaking it so hard as to make it snap. "He does now," she replied. "At first, when I told him, he said we should be wed. 'Meet me in the church at Chipping Barbury,' he said, 'the one just across the fields from the fair.' Two hours I sat in that porch like a fool, and him off with some other wench!" Tears filled her eyes and trickled down her cheeks again. "I hope she leads him a merry dance, I do. I hope she breaks his heart. Not that he's got a heart, but I hope he suffers!" She wiped the tears from her face with the back of her hand and sniffed loudly.

Justin was moved to pity by her plight. "If you can prove he is the father of your child, Kitty, I am sure Mr Westwood will make him marry you."

"Master's dead, ain't he? There ain't none to make Will Longstaffe do aught now," she replied miserably.

"Master Hal will speak up for you if you can show him proof."

"Master Hal? He's naught but a boy himself, so who is going to listen to him?" Kitty sighed wearily.

"He is the Master of Westwood now. All, even Will Longstaffe, must listen to him," replied Justin firmly.

"He denies it all now anyway," she said tears falling again. "He says he ain't never lain with me and that it's his word agin mine. He says none will believe me agin him."

"I believe you, Kitty," said Justin gently, "and I can convince Master Hal. He'll see you are not ruined Kitty, if only you'll help us a little."

"I can't help no one," she said sniffing. "Hold the basket nearer, do!"

"Yes, you can. You can tell me who Will's new wench is. I know you'll know," he added quickly, as she turned on him, her face furious again. "You are no fool, Kitty. If you don't know who it is now, you'll find out soon enough."

"No fool, ain't I? Well then, why am I ruined like this? Don't you see? If you tell Master Hal I'm in the family way, I'll be sent off?" she wailed.

"No, I promise you, he'll not do that. He'll make sure Will marries you."

She turned to face him, looking him over suspiciously, "You don't think he'd make me do penance, do you, like in the old days? I can remember when I was a lass, one of the wenches from the village got caught in the hay with a field hand. They were both made to walk to church barefoot in their shifts. I couldn't do that, I couldn't! Why, I'd sooner do away with myself."

Justin covered her fluttering hands gently. "No, don't even say so! I give you my word, you'll suffer no more if you will but help me. I'll do all in my power to see Will Longstaffe marries you."

"I don't see that you've got much power, not even enough to settle your own wooing," she replied flatly. Then, as he flushed with embarrassment and looked nettled, she smiled sourly. "What, did you think we none of us have eyes in our heads? I reckon you've as much chance of wedding Mistress Bess as I have of getting Will Longstaffe to husband!"

Justin wondered why he endured her impertinence, and couldn't help but reply stiffly, "Be that as it may, I'll engage to speak to my brother-in-law about you. I know that he will not suffer you to be treated unjustly."

She sniffed again, impressed in spite of herself by his calm air of competence. "So you say."

"I can do no more for you, you'll have to trust me, Kitty," he replied wearily.

"Well, the wench's name in Nancy Spicer, for all the good it will do you, which ain't much, for she's the sort who'd never tell the truth to save her life," said Kitty grudgingly.

"Is that so? You think then she'd back Will up in any lies he cares to tell?" he asked, trying not to sound disappointed.

"'Tis more than likely! Unless it were to her disadvantage, of course," replied the girl. She spread out the last piece of linen and took the basket from him. They turned their steps back toward the house.

Justin walked silently thinking things over until they returned to the yard. There, as they parted, he said firmly. "As soon as your master is returned from London I shall acquaint him of this problem of yours. Please do not distress yourself further, in the meantime."

Kitty cast him a doubtful look, not entirely sure of him. Half of her longed to believe him, but more recent experience taught her she was a fool to trust in any man. "Aye," she said with a marked lack of enthusiasm. "If you go through that door over there, you'll find yourself in the passage at the back of the hall."

Justin retired in good order, wondering why the servant's opinion should be worth so much trouble to him. He made his way to his chamber and spent sometime in the composition of the letter to his father, a task that did little to improve his spirits.

Once Libby and Bess returned, the afternoon seemed brighter. They spent it with young Hetta and Ned in the nearby hay field, watching the last of the hay being cut. There was much laughter and joking at the men as they, with Ned's help, tried to catch the rabbits, which had taken refuge in there. There was little further discussion of the problem once Justin had spoken of his interview with Kitty. On Ned's return they decided both he and Justin should ride to Chawcester the day after tomorrow, as the market there was known for its horse traders. Other than that, it was generally agreed between them little more could be done until Hal's return.

Justin noticed Libby was preoccupied and silent for the most of the time they spent together. Under different circumstances he would, if he hadn't been taken up with thoughts of Bess, most surely have enquired into it. As it was, any pity he had to spare was for his own plight.

The next day passed in the similar vein of outward quiet contentment and inner turmoil, but the following day saw Justin and Ned at a fair in the nearby town of Chawcester. The market was well under way by the time they got to the town. They sauntered slowly through the crowded street, past traders selling all manner of wares. There was fresh butter and eggs brought in by stout farmer's wives from the countryside, cattle and pigs, sheep and hens all jostling down side alleys, waiting to be sold. There was the tinker mending old bent pots and the barber extracting teeth from a poor fellow in pain, whilst the crowd looked on in merriment. Justin hauled Ned away from a tray of hot pies and continued the search for the horse-coper.

They finally found him down a back alley close to the abbey. It smelled of stale ale and was strewn liberally with cabbage stalks. Justin glanced at Ned and nodded as they approached the wizened man with the string of broken down nags and half-tamed ponies.

"That's a neat grey. Suitable for a lady, is she?" asked Ned, patting the nose of the only respectable horse.

The man sniffed and admitted reluctantly, "She's a mite too nervous for a lady. She shies at every loud noise. This bay would be ideal; he's a grand chap. Just give him a mouthful of oats and he'll ride his heart out for you!"

"I don't doubt it. He's been worked hard in his time, poor fellow." Ned reached out to pat one of the hacks. "He's too big for my sister; she only reaches my shoulder."

The man eyed him for a few seconds acknowledging the boy, though young, wasn't a green lad in the matter of horseflesh. "I seen you here afore, I reckon. Don't you live over by Bolden Hill?"

"That way, aye," agreed Ned. "I live at Westwood."

"Aye?" The man recognising quality folk, ducked under the rail and led the way down the row of horses. "Now what about this pony? Ideal size for your sister, I'd say."

Justin joined Ned as he opened the animal's mouth. "Westwood, hey? There's an odd thing. That's where the murder were, ain't it? Henry Westwood, him that were murdered by his brother. Aye, and that's another thing," he continued as Justin looked over Ned's shoulder whilst Ned examined all four of the beast's hooves. "I saw that fellow of his, over at Gloucester a few weeks back!"

"Aye? At the Mid-Summer fair?" asked Ned.

"Thereabouts. Tall he is, this fellow. Wears a leather jerkin, I've seen him with you, I reckon."

"Happen," said Ned laconically. "Pretty mare. Wrong colour."

"Wrong colour?" cried the man crestfallen.

"She won't have anything but a grey. You know what females are!" said Ned with a shrug.

"None better," said the man, gloom settling across his face.

"So, what was he buying at Gloucester, this fellow wearing a leather jerkin, that I should know?" asked Ned affably.

"Oh, he weren't buying; he were selling. A beautiful beast it were. Aye, that were a grey, too! Not a pony though, a real thoroughbred; a gentleman's horse I thought." He sighed, "Way beyond my means, of course."

"What was the name of the fellow? Happen I do know him," said Ned. Justin clutched at his shoulder anxious that he shouldn't say too much.

"I don't know as I remember ever hearing his name." The man frowned. "I've seen him about often these last few years. He's a tall sort of man, big shoulders, lightish hair. Will? Will somebody?"

"Will, you say? I know a good few Wills. He was not buying a horse, you say, but selling?" Ned was well aware of Justin's barely restrained impatience.

"Aye, selling. Horse, saddle, the lot. Won it in a game of dice, he told me, at the Chipping Barbury fair," said the horse-coper sourly.

"The fair at Chipping Barbury? The one in mid-June?" said Ned, doubt entering his voice.

The man shrugged. "I reckon so."

"If you didn't buy the horse yourself, do you know who did?" asked Justin.

The man's eyes flickered to his face suspiciously. "Maybe," he agreed reluctantly.

"Not many would deal in so fine a beast," Ned remarked hastily. He could see the man knew Justin wasn't used to attending horse fairs. "I guess it would be Jan Larby from Upton, or perhaps Wat Brewer from Gloucester!"

"You'd be wrong then. 'Twere a fellow from Ross that took him. And he weren't a dealer at all."

"You are sure?" asked Ned quickly.

"Well now, I didn't see nothing, but 'tis common knowledge it were taken by a man from Ross."

"Is his name equally common knowledge?" asked Justin.

"Nay, I tell you, I don't know him. He just weren't a dealer. I'd never heard of him."

"Nor know any who have?" Ned was hopeful but wasn't really surprised when the man shrugged.

Justin, however, for all that he may have been a novice with horseflesh, had the better understanding of human nature. He took two coins from the pouch at his belt and handed them over. "It would greatly assist us if you could find out. Thank you for your help."

They hadn't gone more than a dozen paces down the street when the man caught them up. "I never heard tell of his name," he said, "but the gossip is that he owns the inn a mile out of Ross on the Monmouth road. The Bull. Only don't tell anybody I told you so!"

Justin hastily gave him the last of his coins, and Ned called out his thanks as he retreated. In discussion on the journey home, they decided that much as they wanted to rush off to Ross as soon as possible, they should wait a little longer for Hal to return before following up this interesting information.

❧

Ned sat in the hayloft with his great friend Sam, silently concealed from view. As usual his lessons had been left undone and the Rector was searching for him. Occasionally he looked out wanting to see the plump figure of Mr Broxbourne on his pony trotting back to the village, but the yard remained deserted. He picked up another of the pies he and Sam had taken from the kitchen earlier and began to chew at the pastry.

As he leaned forward he got a good view of his sister Bess as she entered the yard via the gate from the meadow in company with Justin.

"What do you think of they then?" asked Sam with a chuckle, following his glance.

"My sister and this clerk fellow, Danvers? My father will be angry," he replied promptly.

The stable lad grinned, "He ain't the only one. Master Longstaffe has been like a bear with a sore head ever since he saw how she gazes up at the lawyer like he were a hero."

Ned chewed at his mouthful of pie. "Wenches!" he said, with the contempt of a brother. "Nothing in their heads at all. Look at him! Built like a beanpole. He doesn't hunt or wrestle. He can't handle a musket or a bow. He has no eye at all and as for the way he sits a horse—"

The young groom grinned, "He gets by as long as he don't go no faster than a gentle canter."

"Yet she looks at him as if he were the sun, the moon, and the stars rolled into one," groaned Ned, "I don't think I'll ever understand females!"

Sam suddenly craned forward, "Hey up! Now we'll see some sport! 'Tis Master Longstaffe!"

"Where?" hissed Ned, "Oh, I see; Justin Danvers has waylaid him. Oh, here's trouble!"

"Aye, Master Longstaffe's had the black dog all day!" The lad felt his ear, which still sang from the agent's blow not an hour since.

"Oh, he doesn't like that." Ned couldn't quite catch their words, but could see from their postures the meeting wasn't going well. "Look! Look! Now Bess is intervening! Foolish girl! Can't she see she is but fuel to the flames? No, don't put your hand on Danvers's arm as if he is so— Oh! Too late! Now Will *is* in a black rage! Yes, look! He's squaring up to him! Oh, I can't watch! Danvers doesn't stand a chance!"

"He's going to have a go though!" The young groom was full of admiration. "You can't fault him for courage! Now, why do wenches do that? What good can it do to flutter about weeping when fellows get down to a good tussle? Oh, there he goes! Master Longstaffe caught him a good blow!"

"He's getting up though," Ned's admiration was reluctant. "By God, he's furious! Will you look at that! I'd have sworn he hadn't got it in him! Will is a least twice his weight!"

"They're both as tall as houses," said Sam. "Come on Master Danvers, give the mean sod one for me!"

"Oh no! There he goes! Will's laid him out cold, I think! I'd better go and stop it before it's murder! Oh no, now Bess is going for him! Dear God, look at that, she's hitting Will with both fists! I'm gone! I'll see you at first light at the brook, Sam!"

Suddenly Ned could see how serious the situation was. He swung down from his perch and hastened from the stable and across the yard at a run. He got to them in time to see Will Longstaffe catch both of Bess's wrists in his huge hands and use them to pull her uncomfortably close to him. His face was a mask of anger and desire, so naked, even Ned recognised it and felt uncomfortable.

"Let her go Will!" he said, and in that moment command came to his voice and he was no longer a child.

Will turned, his eyes blazing. He expected to see Hal and he was amazed to see Ned before him, a challenge in his young face. Abruptly, he released Bess, who was white with fear. She staggered and almost fell across the yard to where Justin was sitting with his head between his hands.

"You'd best say sorry, Will," said Ned slowly. He was unsure quite how to handle the situation.

"Sorry? To that jumped up lawyer's clerk?"

"To my sister! She's not one of your drabs to be manhandled," snapped Ned. He heard his words in growing amazement. Even to his own ears he sounded like Hal.

The agent glared at him as some of the fury died down in his breast. His eyes, unclouded by a red mist of rage, took in the scene. The belligerent boy standing with clenched fists, the weeping girl and the guest of the house, with a bloodied nose and what promised to be a black eye of huge proportions. Realisation of the enormity of his actions came to him. "If I've distressed Mistress Bess, I'm sorry!" he snapped.

Ned blinked as Will stalked out of the yard and he walked over to Justin asking, "Can you walk?"

Justin struggled to his feet, and found himself supported on either side.

"I am *so* sorry!" whispered Bess through her tears, as she gazed up into his bloodied face.

"Let's tidy you up at the well before we go back into the house," said Ned practically.

Then, as Sam came running with a cloth and obligingly raised the pail, Ned plunged the cloth into the chilly water and laid it over Justin's wounds.

"Let the cold take out the heat. Then we'll seek our Aunt Kate; she'll have a salve and she doesn't lecture."

"I don't know what to say," sobbed Bess through her tears. "I don't know what possessed him!"

Ned glanced keenly at her and filled a mug from the pail, "Drink this, and stop weeping! Otherwise, they'll put you to bed with a tisane."

Chapter Twenty Two

"I don't understand," said Libby, applying a cold compress to her brother's forehead. "What has happened?"

"Nothing of any great significance," replied Justin. His voice sounded rather odd due to the swelling of his nose.

"Nothing of significance?" Libby returned to the mixture she was stirring in a cup, glancing to the book beside it, and hesitating over the size of the required leaf. "I'm sure I don't understand you, Justin. You arrive here looking as if you have been in a riot, accompanied by Bess in hysterics, yet you say nothing of significance has occurred!"

"He's fallen foul of Will Longstaffe, that's all," said Ned, who was rummaging through the jars in the still room hoping to find something pleasant to eat. "Ugh, that's horrible!"

"Ned! For heaven's sake!" Only further exasperated, Libby removed a jar from his grasp. "Have a care, if you spill or drop anything Aunt Margery will have something to say!"

Libby finished off her mixture and poured its contents into a little water, watching in dismay as it all turned muddy. "Why should Will Longstaffe, who only a few days ago insisted he wanted to help, suddenly attack you? Drink this, Justin. It will ease the pain." Justin eyed the dose doubtfully.

"I wouldn't, if it tastes as bad as it looks," said Ned helpfully.

"I hope it works!" said Justin. He tipped back his head and swallowed it in one gulp, although he couldn't stop his shudder in spite of his bravery.

"Because he's a hankering for Bess," said Ned, who seemed to have a habit for answering the question before last.

"Justin?" she said sharply, "Justin has an interest in Bess?"

"No, well, yes," said Ned, as Justin made an inarticulate protest, "but I was speaking of Will."

"Good heavens!" said Libby faintly. She replaced the compress with another and watched her brother's closed eyes with dismay as by the minute they became blacker. "You look terrible Justin! You'll have to keep from sight until your appearance improves."

He opened one swollen, blood-shot eye. "I'm not overly concerned at my appearance," he muttered, "more with getting my hands on that bastard!"

"Justin!" Libby looked amazed.

"You'd best leave it," advised Ned with a weary man-of-the-world sigh. "He is twice your weight and a bit of a devil in a fight. None round here would take him on."

"*What* is going on?" asked Hal.

"Oh, Hal," Libby fell back looking dismayed.

Hal looked round in astonishment as his eyes took in the scene and Justin's face.

"You are hurt," he observed.

"Yes," agreed Justin, "I am."

"What has happened?" asked Hal again.

"Justin and Will had a fight." Ned's eyes were alight with interest.

"A fight?" repeated Hal incredulously, "Why?"

"He doesn't appear to like my face," Justin said.

"Nor mine, but he has never attempted to alter it!" replied Hal.

"Perhaps he thought I wouldn't mind." Justin tried to laugh it all off.

"What does Will look like?" asked Hal.

"Much the same," said Ned. "We stopped a massacre!"

"I was getting my second wind!" snapped Justin.

"You were nearly out on your feet," retorted Ned, "If Bess hadn't intervened, you'd have been in serious trouble."

"Bess?" said Hal with a sinking feeling in his stomach. "Why was Bess involved? Where did this take place?"

"In the stable yard," Ned said, as Justin lost interest, shutting his eyes against the headache.

"The stable yard," Hal compressed his lips firmly as he comprehended the situation. "What were you about, Libby, to allow my sister to witness a brawl in the stable yard?"

Libby was taken aback by the suddenness of his attack. "I—I did not know she was—"

Justin grew irritated by Hal's peremptory tone. "Why must Libby have your sister in charge? Surely Bess is in the care of your aunts, not your wife?"

"Bess is in the care of my family," Hal responded tartly. "Or so I thought. In practice she was running wild it would seem! My father will not be best pleased. As for you, Justin, I am mortified that you should have received such discourtesy from my agent. I apologise most wholeheartedly on his behalf and shall seek him out to call him to book for this intolerable conduct."

"Best let it go, Hal. Will Longstaffe is in one of his black moods," Ned said tentatively.

"I am sorry for that, but the ups and downs of Will's temper are of little interest to me. The comfort of my family and the safety of my guests are."

Justin could see that Hal was seriously displeased and realised that if things weren't to get worse, his ruffled feathers must be soothed. In spite of feeling rather ill he made light of it asking mildly, "There is no disputing that. How went your visit to the King?"

"It went very well," Hal replied.

"Indeed, what can we be thinking of?" cried Libby, "Did you get to see the King? Will he help your father?"

"So much so, that I am happy to say he was released when I arrived in Maucester with the King's warrant." Hal was glad to talk of happier things. "I was never more relieved! As luck would have it, Mr Fenton was at the prison, visiting my father. Thank you, too, Justin. I understand you have been most kind in giving up your time to keep my father company. We are most grateful."

"Yes, Ned and I went as often as we could, but your father wouldn't let Bess or Libby go," Justin replied feeling awkward, wondering if anything had been discussed between father and son about his love of Bess.

"We did want to go, Hal, but Justin said your father forbade it," Libby agreed.

Ned was his usual blunt self. "Yes, Father said he wouldn't have the girls subjected to such indignity as to visit a place where felons are kept, but I think it was more because Jacqueline never went."

"Yes, hardly a devoted wife; I mean, if I had been in that cell, I can't imagine, for all my faults, anyone keeping Libby away," Hal said thoughtfully.

"Indeed no, I would have come, and stayed nearby and visited you everyday. Yet Jacqueline never once even asked to go, but busied herself with our hair and my gowns." Libby hesitated and then said fairly, "She said your father had told her to stop us all moping, Hal."

"I don't doubt by the time he comes he will have thought of some reason to excuse her absence," Hal replied austerely.

There was a small silence, which Ned broke quickly, "So, you saw the King, Hal?"

Hal smiled at the wonderment in their voices. "Yes, but recollect, I knew the King already from our years in exile. I must admit, he was most kind to me. He said Father is one of his most able servants. I knew often he went to other countries for the King, but I had not known my father worked in secret matters for him. That was where he was of course, when we were so desperately seeking him! That information must not be known generally; it must be a secret among us. The King has bidden me to take you to court to be presented Libby. He says he wants to know if my bride is as pretty as the ladies of his court! He also commended me on the sense of our marriage. He thinks that if only there could be many more like it we would soon heal the breach in our country!"

"I am to be presented to the King!" Libby cried, her eyes wide in a combination of wonder and disbelief.

"Yes, will you greatly dislike that?" he asked hesitantly.

"Dislike it? Why, it will be splendid! Oh Hal, what will my father say? He'll be beside himself with delight! His daughter to be presented to the King!"

Hal laughed, all his doubts and unease on the subject fleeing, "And I thought I'd have to persuade you to it and bribe you into good behaviour!"

"Libby never needs bribing into good behaviour; she is naturally good," said Justin. He tried to keep the disapproval from his voice, but found it increasingly difficult to talk as the strong potion Libby had brewed began to take effect.

Hal agreed with a brief smile. "Well, I must go and

pass on the information to my aunts, and then perhaps change from these dusty clothes."

"I'll come with you Hal, and find your clean clothes," said Libby. "Justin, you'd better change your shirt, too, before someone sees you."

❧

Once Hal had accomplished these tasks, he went in search of his agent. He was concerned by the tale he had heard and determined to get to the bottom of it all. He found the agent as ever in the stable yard and realised at once that it was a great effort for the man to even speak civilly to him.

"You must understand my concerns, Will," he said keeping his voice carefully neutral.

"Aye, Master Hal, I do," he agreed shortly.

"Not only is Mr Danvers my wife's brother, but a guest in the house. A guest must always be treated with consideration."

"Even when he's pawing a daughter of the house?" snapped the agent explosively.

"I cannot think my brother-in-law has violated any cannon of trust," Hal said mildly.

"Then you're a bloody fool! Begging your pardon Master Hal," he added roughly. "Don't you see, that's his slippery lawyer way around it! Has he begged permission to pay court to Mistress Bess like an honest man? No! He's gone behind thy back whilst you were attending thy father's wants."

Part of Hal was forced to acknowledge the truth of this, which irritated him. "There is much in what you say, Will," he agreed, still carefully, "but I think we can leave it to Justin's sense of fair play, rather than plunging headlong into abuse and physical retribution."

"I don't want to offend you, Master Hal, but you are yet young in the ways of the world. There ain't much fair play when it comes to men and women! Him there," he nodded his head in the direction of the house where Justin was still nursing his bruised face. "He's seen his sister climb high and reckons to scramble after her by bedding thy sister! Fair play? Phew! There's no fair play in love or war!"

Hal refrained from making the sharp reply that was hovering on his lips. "Thank you for the warning Will. I'll bear it in mind when I discuss the matter with my brother-in-law. In the meantime, I am forearmed, he has been warned off, for which I give admittedly limited thanks. But the fact remains, I require an apology of you, for your injury both to Mr Danvers's face and reputation."

The agent cast him a disgusted look. "An apology?"

"I am aware, Will, you hold my sister in affectionate regard," said Hal. "I am also aware my father has abused you and—"

"Your father don't give a damn who his daughters wed so long as they've got plenty o' brass! There weren't no call for him to talk to me as if I were nothing but a —" The man stopped short and began again. "There were no call for him to talk to me as he did, in front of all the lads in the yard and to threaten to take his whip to me!"

"It was very tactless," agreed Hal, who was doggedly determined not to get into a quarrel with the agent. "And whilst I cannot always applaud the marriages my father proposes for his daughters, they are *his* daughters and as such it is not for you or I to agree or disagree. Say what we will, Bess will marry the fellow my father chooses for her."

Will cast him a dark look, but said no more.

"It is for us however," continued Hal, glad he'd taken the point, "to decide what must be done for the best. You, I am certain, would not want any odium to reflect upon Westwood. So you must see that some explanation is due to Mr Danvers. It is fortunate he has sustained no permanent injury from your meeting. Indeed, in some small way, he seems to have gained favour, at least in the eyes of the females of the house, for his valour." Hal's voice unconsciously echoed his puzzlement and discontent over this.

"Master." Will contented himself with a nod by way of a limited assent, and Hal, relieved he'd achieved that much, made good his escape.

Chapter Twenty Three

Hal returned to his own chamber. With the intolerable burden of his father's release lifted from his shoulders and the immediate problem of Will Longstaffe settled, he felt he could finally turn his mind to other things. The most important of these things was to reestablish his relationship with Libby.

He entered without ceremony and pulled up short at the sight of Jacqueline's French maid handing Libby a goblet.

"Don't drink that!" he commanded. His thoughts flew back to his last encounter with Jacqueline, and as they did so a flush rose to his cheek and much of the joy of his father's release drained away, as his soul writhed at the thought of what he had done.

"Hal! What a fright you gave me!" cried Libby, slopping the liquid in surprise.

"What are you doing here?" Hal demanded of the maid, who was gaping at him in astonishment.

"Madame sent me here! She says I am to dress the Mistress Libby's hair and give her the tisane," said the maid in offended tones.

Hal advanced swiftly on them, taking the cup from Libby's hand and sniffing at it suspiciously. He glanced to her face and noting its sickly hue and dark-ringed eyes. Was that his fault or had more evil work been going on here? "What is that?" he said, addressing them both.

The maid shrugged her shoulders. "Herbs in wine. Madame makes it. It is to help Mistress Libby conceive of the child."

Libby blushed hotly. She could remember only too well how they had parted with enmity as he had left for London. If he thought she had been plotting with his step-mother he would think her more foolish than ever.

Hal felt a cold prickling of his spine. He could recollect very little of what had occurred the night before he left for London and what he did remember filled him with shame. But one thing stood out clear from the mists of confusion and that had been the passionate words Jacqueline had whispered as she'd clung to him. 'Libby—she is but a sickly child. Who can say how long she might live?'

His thoughts shied away from the capacity of Jacqueline's wickedness. He didn't care to wager on whether she would be prepared to harm a good and trusting soul like Libby if she stood in the way of something she wanted. Libby was altogether too trusting and he'd been a vain and arrogant fool to be flattered by Jacqueline's attentions.

He handed the cup to Marie. "My complements to your Mistress. Pray tell her Libby needs no help but mine in the conception of her child! Thank you, you may go."

The maid departed with a dark, sullen look.

"Hal!" protested Libby. She was scandalised and yet half-laughing, "She'll repeat that to Jacqueline!"

"So I intend," he answered. He smiled at her look of horror and embarrassment then, as she looked at him shyly, he held out his hand. "Libby," he said slowly, "I've been all sorts of a fool. I said we must talk on my return, and we will. But first, I must tell you how sorry I am for my behaviour lately. I've been difficult and preoccupied with all manner of things, but I can learn from my mistakes. It can't be undone, Libby, but it can be forgotten if you will forgive me."

"I think I could forgive you anything, Hal, if you'll but ask it of me," she replied quietly.

"Do you forgive so easily, with no reproach?" He was incredulous.

"What good do reproaches do? You say you have learnt, I hope so, for I can't deny I have been unhappy."

"I would make you happy, if I could. It is my duty, and my inclination, to make surely the best of wives as happy as possible. I am yours to command, Libby. What would make you happy?" he asked.

She smiled realising he was in earnest and thought how impossible it was for her to say what would indeed make her the happiest of women. How could she demand his undying love? Love couldn't be demanded, but must come of its own accord. "I don't know; we have so little knowledge of each other. You could admire my hair perhaps?" she replied, laughing, a little embarrassed.

"Admire your hair?" He, too, laughed suddenly recollecting he never had said a word of it. "Indeed I do! It was very wrong of me to never say I think you look very pretty."

"Pretty! Do I truly look pretty, Hal?" she asked artlessly.

"Very pretty," he replied firmly, "but rather pale." He frowned as he scanned her face and remembered how wan and defenceless she looked when he'd first entered. "How long had you been drinking that potion of Jacqueline's?"

"Four days; only since you went to London. Why do you ask? Do you think it might disagree with me?"

"I think it might very well do so, if you continued to take it. Is that all she gave you to take?" Hal had grim look on his face as he realised Jacqueline was a problem he would have to discuss with his father.

"All but this pot of marigold paste for my complexion," She showed him the pot.

"There is nothing wrong with your complexion, so don't use it. Don't use anything Jacqueline gives you. Neither you, nor Bess."

"Do you think I should allow my hair to grow then?" she asked, confused by the wholesale condemnation.

"No, I like it well enough now I am used to it, but get your woman to learn how to do it, so that you can be fashionable, if that is what you want," he replied with a smile.

"Is it not what you want? Jacqueline said it would be. She said my gowns were hopelessly old-fashioned and that you required your wife to be fashionable like the ladies of the King's court!" She spread wide her skirts. "Marie re-trimmed my gowns for me. She has been kind and I do think they are prettier, don't you?"

He nodded his agreement, "Yes, I can't deny that Jacqueline has very good taste and her maid is skilful. As for that other nonsense, I don't want a fashionable wife to parade at Court, but a good and sensible woman, to help me in our life here. Pay no heed to Jacqueline; she has only her own interests at heart. She may seem to want to help but—"

"But what, Hal?" she asked, looking up anxiously.

"Don't trust her, Libby," he said gravely. "I can prove nothing, but I have the darkest suspicions. Never trust her, or that woman of hers."

Libby gaped in astonishment. "What suspicions?"

He turned from her, "I cannot even name them, Libby, they are too despicable. I have no proof, but she is treachery itself. Do not ask more of me, I beg!"

She stared at his broad back in dismay. She half-guessed what he meant, but drew back from the horror of it. She had no desire to tread such muddy waters. A change of subject was needed. "What am I thinking of with all this discussion of me? We must meet with Justin; he is waiting for us!"

They left the house and walked in the garden more in accord than at any time since their marriage. Hal relaxed and was content to listen to her chatter of what had occurred in the last few days.

They found Ned who was eager for more news. "Where is Father then?" he asked, as they all began to walk where the sunshine beckoned.

"He has some business with a man of law," Hal said, "and like me, was full weary, I do believe. He admitted his imprisonment had been something of a strain. He and Mr Fenton, who has been so stalwart in this matter, went to see the lawyer together. I rode on ahead, leaving father to follow when he is ready."

Ned frowned over this. "So it is all over, then?"

"Hardly that Ned. There still must be some sort of investiga—" He stopped abruptly as they turned into the yew walk. At the far end of the line of trees, Bess leaned forward to bashfully kiss Justin's blackened eye.

"They've been like that for the past two days. I vow, it is enough to turn a fellow's stomach!" Ned's tone was gloomy.

Libby glanced uneasily at Hal's stern face. "Do you think your father will disapprove, Hal? Indeed, do you dislike it?" she asked anxiously.

"I think it could be difficult," he replied in a tone, which conveyed his feelings more than any words could.

"Jacqueline appears to approve. She says Justin will inherit a good fortune in due course," Ned remarked.

"Jacqueline just wishes to be rid of the trouble of

finding Bess a husband," Hal replied austerely. "Anyway, my father's fortunes are on the increase. He says he can see no further need to sacrifice his children to expediency. He would rather match them to well connected families."

As soon as the words had passed his lips, he wished them unsaid. For he had unthinkingly quoted verbatim from his father's lament of the previous evening. Now, confronted with Libby's stricken eyes, Hal hurried to repeat his own words. "I told Father, that for my part, I was glad of expediency as it had brought me a wife, who suited me very well indeed."

Ned couldn't control his exclamation of disgust at this sign of a courtship. But luckily Justin and Bess, having caught sight of them now, came hurrying red-faced to meet them.

"Hal!" said Justin quickly. "There you are! We've been looking for you."

"Not very diligently, I observe." Hal's tone was sharp.

"When will father be here, Hal?" cried Bess.

"He should be on his way here at this very moment."

"The King gave him a free pardon?" asked Justin, with a frown.

"No, not a free pardon, for he has committed no crime. The King has commanded my father be released from imprisonment. Furthermore, it is stated that at the time in question he was about the King's business."

Bess exclaimed in delight at such an outcome, but Justin interrupted, "But that doesn't exonerate him! Oh, I grant he'll not be tried for murder with such a letter, but to my mind, it makes him look as if he is definitely the murderer. And because he is the King's servant, the King lets him off. Everyone will say so!"

Hal glared at him arrogantly. "Only petty minded fools!"

"The world is, for most part, composed of petty minded fools, who like to gossip about their betters!" Justin retorted. "This is no answer. True your father is released, but we still have to prove him innocent!"

"We have been trying to do so from the first," snapped Hal. "You keep saying we must do this and ask that, but to my mind, you've been no more successful than I, for all your cleverness!"

There was an abrupt silence at this, as Hal's jealousy was laid bare. Libby made haste to say quickly, "You are both right for different reasons. Hal, your first need was to find your father, and then get him released. You have done so successfully. Now, as Justin says, for the good of all, we must try to prove him innocent, or we all remain tainted by suspicion.

"Not so easily done. Although we have made one discovery, Hal," said Ned.

"Yes, it is," interrupted Justin. His temper was rather ruffled as he realised that, far from finding an ally to his suit in Hal, he was more likely to find bitter opposition. "We find the one who *is* guilty."

"We've tried that," said Hal, in a voice of weary impatience. "Don't you remember? All your clues pointed to my father, whom we now know, on the King's authority, to be innocent."

Justin glanced irritably at him. his head ached; his plans in ruins. He opened his mouth to dispute that they knew any thing of the sort, but Libby shook her head. He thought better of it, saying instead, quietly, "I think we have discovered just who the murderer is."

All stared at him. Libby and Bess in admiration; Hal and Ned in annoyed disbelief;

"Who is it then?" demanded Ned.

"I've had him in my mind for sometime. In fact if we thought it through properly, he is the obvious choice, because of his opportunities. I have said nothing, because there is no proof. Indeed, I've still no proof, and what is worse, can't think of a way to get any. But the latest evidence points strongly to it. I had the good fortune to fall in with Kitty the day before yesterday and managed, with some difficulty, to get rather a sorry tale from her. You'll remember how Ned said she went off the moment she got to the fair on the feast of Corpus Christi? Well, it seems she'd gone to meet a man to be wed that day, in the church across the fields from the fair. He had seduced her in the Spring and she is now with child by him. He had promised to meet her there, but she said she waited for hours in the porch but Will Longstaffe never came."

"Will Longstaffe!" cried Hal, in astonishment. "And she with child by him?"

"Yes," said Justin. "Or so she claims, and I don't think, for all her faults, she would lie. She is plainly distraught by the situation she finds herself in, for it seems now he denies all knowledge of the meeting, the wedding, or her and her child."

Justin hesitated eyeing his volatile brother-in-law, and then added slowly, "I promised her I would speak to you for her, Hal. She has a fear she'll either be sent off if Will refuses to marry her, or worse still to her mind, be made to do penance. I told her, if she helped us by giving us the name of Will's new wench, I would see that you protected her."

There was a short silence whilst Hal digested this news, then he said firmly. "Naturally, if her story is true and Will Longstaffe has fathered a child on Kitty, he shall be made to marry her, or leave my employment."

"Thank you," said Justin. "I was certain you'd stand for justice in this matter. As for her information, I fear it did us little good. Apparently Will's latest love is a flighty young woman renowned for her light ways. She is reputed to back any man in a lie for the price of a bunch of ribbons! However Ned and I discovered that a man called Will sold a grey horse, a thoroughbred, gentleman's horse, at Gloucester Horse Fair not long after Mid-Summer."

"Indeed?" Hal frowned. "A man called Will, you say? I think we'll need a little more proof than that! As for the matter of the wench, Kitty, I shall look into it, but I fail to see what this unsavoury tale has to do with my uncle's murderer."

"Wait, there is more. Firstly, Will Longstaffe can no longer prove where he was. He wasn't with Kitty, as we all thought. The only proof he could bring in a court of law is this other wench's testimony and that is not likely to hold up, if she is well known. Therefore, there is none to say that he was in Chipping Barbury, and he could easily have come back here."

"Yes, but we still can't prove that he was here," interrupted Hal. "He could have been anywhere! Even if we could prove Will Longstaffe was here, why should he, of all people, want to kill my uncle? He was devoted to him!"

"Indeed, so everyone has told me," replied Justin. "And it seems, with good cause. Libby, tell Hal what Goody Stokes told you and Bess."

Libby blinked, for she had given little thought to the matter since telling her brother of it. "Do you think it matters, Justin? We did promise to Goody Stokes we'd not repeat it."

"I think it very important, as will Hal when you've told him."

"Goody Stokes, do you know her, Hal? Well, she lives on the edge of the village," she added as he shook his head. "She has plainly been a dependant of the Westwoods. Her husband was a tenant farmer. On the day you left for London, Bess and I took a basket of alms to her, and during the conversation she told us she'd known Will Longstaffe all his life. That he and his mother, a maidservant to Aunt Margery, had lived on her farm and that after his mother died, Goody and her husband had thoughts of bring him up as their own son. The Westwoods, that is, your Uncle Henry and Aunt Margery always had an interest in the lad. On

his mother's death he was put to school and later became your uncle's agent."

"You mean Will Longstaffe? Yes, I knew he was ille-
gitimate, but what has this to do with anything?"

"Libby thinks he is Aunt Margery's love-child," said
Bess.

Hal's mouth dropped open, as Libby blushed hotly.
"Aunt Margery's? Are you mad?" he demanded.

"Hal, you know of her love affair with Mr Fenton,"
said Libby, "but none said how she was sent away in
disgrace and how Mary her maid came back with a
baby and that baby is Will!"

Hal cast her an offended look, "My aunt has explained the circumstances in full, Libby. I don't think
we need to delve further into such an unsavoury tale.
Plainly, her maid had a falling from grace; such things
occur. The matter seems to have been dealt with com-
petently. I see no call to rake over old sores in pursuit
of what Justin calls the truth."

"Well, I do," Justin was adamant. "Yes, I know, and
I'm sorry if you or your aunt are offended, Hal, but
unless we delve into everything, unless we *do* rake over
old sores, we'll never get to the truth."

Hal's face mirrored his distaste. "Delve into everything? I'm sorry Justin, but you don't seem to under-

stand. Everything is settled now. There is no further need to cause all this upset of accusations and counter claims. You cannot, in all honesty, expect my aunt to consent to listen to such infamy."

"If we don't at least try to—" Justin stopped as a voice rang out in a lordly manner from the direction of the stables.

"It is father!" cried Bess. All three of his children ran in that direction, leaving Libby and Justin to follow at a more leisurely pace as the doves rose up in a cloud of wings.

Chapter Twenty Four

"Well, Jonas, how are you, you idle, good-for-nothing rascal?" a hearty voice was saying as Libby and Justin entered the square of garden, close by the dovecote. "I tell my boy here to have you off that bench and back to hard work, but the lad says he thinks the task fitting for one so stricken in years and honour!"

The old man cackled in delight. "I am well enough, Master Francis, well enough. Praise be to God that you are returned, for we've had some dark days, Master, dark days!"

"Ah, and here is my new daughter, of whom I must make proper acquaintance. In the confusion of my arrival and arrest some days ago, it was overlooked! Welcome, Daughter, to my family, doubly welcome, for I understand from Hal that he would not be parted from his wife for all the gold in Christendom!"

Libby blushed at this tribute, murmuring, "This is my brother, Justin, sir."

"Why, Mistress, Mr Danvers and I are right good companions! Many an hour he has spent with me, sharing my detention. Such hours as I guess he could spare from my daughter." His sharp glance went to Bess, who was trying to hide behind Hal.

Francis's glance travelled from there to Ned, who stood rather truculently just outside the circle. "Well met, Ned. Come, give me your hand, lad! Hal tells me none have worked more diligently in searching for my brother's murderer!" He ruffled the boy's red locks as he came to a shake his hand, and caught him to his side, hugging him. "Not so good at books, eh, Ned? But then neither was I! Perhaps then a more active life would appeal? We shall see."

He glanced up from the boy's flushed face and his bright eyes swept swift about the circle. "What, no Madame Wife come to greet the returned prisoner? No sweet sisters?"

"None know you are here, sir. Shall I not run and fetch them?" said Libby, feeling sorry for him.

"Stay, Mistress, time enough for all things. We might yet linger here and enjoy the sunshine! 'Tis wondrous good to a man, who has not seen it in days!" he replied. Then as a familiar tune came to their ears he said, "Ah, it would seem Will Longstaffe approaches!"

Jonas, who sat silent throughout, reached up suddenly, clutching his master's velvet-clad arm. "Master Francis! Did we not both hear that very self-same whistle the day thy brother were killed? As you left, you stopped to speak to me, as you ever do, and did that tune not drift over to us on the breeze?"

Francis Westwood nodded his head. "Aye, I recollect hearing it, but when I got to the stables, none were there! I recollect it well, for I cursed at having to saddle my own horse!"

He broke off as Will Longstaffe, still whistling *Summer is A-Coming In*, came through the arch. He halted when he saw them all staring at him, the whistle dying on his lips. "Is something amiss?" he asked, looking warily from one to the other.

Justin stepped forward. "We fear so, Mr Longstaffe. I do believe when asked you said you attended the fair on the feast of Corpus Christi, is that not so?"

Will directed a compelling look at Ned. "Aye, for did I not travel there in the company of young Master Ned?"

"Ned says he lost sight of you there," said Justin.

"A fair is a busy place, young sir. And I must confess I had—" he paused, making a wry face, "if the young ladies will forgive me—an assignation!"

"We know all about poor Kitty, waiting for you at the church to be wed," said Hal sharply.

Will turned his eyes on Hal, and Libby saw the hatred in them for him. "I know nothing of maidservant's gossip, Master," he replied insolently. He had a way of making the title sound like an insult. "My meeting was with a widowed lady of some property!"

"Yet," continued Justin, while Hal turned red in anger and began to say hotly that if Will had taken Kitty he would have to wed her, widow or no. "Yet two witnesses can swear to you being in this very stable that afternoon."

"What witnesses?" Will asked scornfully. "Not more tales from a slut of a wench with a brat to hide!"

"Why, Jonas here for one," said Justin.

Will threw back his head and laughed. "A blind man! He saw me, did he?"

"No, he heard you. He heard you whistle *Summer is A-Coming In*! and Mr Francis Westwood heard it, too, as he took his leave of his brother!"

"Leaving him dead, no doubt!" snapped Will. "Maybe I was here, maybe I wasn't! I don't call that proof!" His laughter was all gone now, leaving naked venom in his face as he turned to Justin. "You think you're so fine, don't you? Such a clever, upstanding, young gentleman! But don't think for one moment they'll let the likes of you wed their daughter! Your birth is little better than mine. You're nothing but the son of a tradesman, for all your cleverness and money! I am at least the son of a gentleman, and if I had my rights I'd be master of you all!"

"Fortunately, right has something to do with it!" said Francis Westwood contemptuously. "Right means that for all that your father was a gentleman, you still are, and will always be, nothing but a bastard!"

Will Longstaffe's face began to work as he roared, "Bastard am I? Aye, that's as maybe, but I've ruined you, haven't I? I may not have got Westwood, but then no more have you! And as for your precious sons, they'll never lift their heads up again, when everyone knows their father is a murderer!"

Justin interrupted his ranting calmly. "None shall even think to believe it when we have done telling our tale. Mr Westwood is in possession of the King's pardon and we'll do our very best to prove you guilty."

"You'll never succeed! I've covered my tracks too well for that!" snarled Will.

"I think the dagger will prove our case," returned Justin, with a solemn air of finality.

"The dagger? There is nothing in the dagger to connect it with me! The dagger is his!" Will incensed by wrath, pointed dramatically at Francis Westwood. "Ned found it in a pile of old armour and he identified it as his father's own!"

Justin struggled to keep a triumphant ring from his voice. "You have condemned yourself out of your own mouth! For we had told none where we found the dagger! Only the man who had hidden it there would have known!"

If Will Longstaffe had not been so beside himself with rage, he might have noticed the puzzled frowns on the faces of those ringed about him. As it was, all he saw was the noose close. Without another word, he suddenly took to his heels and ran back through the archway to the stables.

"Stop him! He's getting away!" Hal shouted.

Galvanised into action, he, Justin and Ned leapt to the chase, scattering the cloud of doves.

Will Longstaffe snatched the roan filly from the hand of a bemused stable lad, hauled himself into the saddle, and kicked out viciously, turning the animal's head for the cloud of whirling pigeons. The horse, terrified by his violence and the flapping of many wings, which the shouts only increased, started, reared, plunged and galloped, in a panic, toward the gate.

Hal, who was first through the arch shouted, "You, boy, hold the gate! Stop that man! Someone, get me a horse!"

Even as the last words left his lips, Will Longstaffe set the horse at the gate. The filly leapt it, sailing over, stumbled on the far side, and threw her rider into a ditch beside the lane.

"He's down! Catch him, Hal, don't let him get away now!" Ned raced across the yard after Hal, who had abandoned the idea of a horse, with Justin in pursuit. Those remaining all crowded into the archway.

Hal cleared the gate in one vault and landed in the soft mud of the lane. He leapt the ditch as Ned clambered over the gate and Justin paused to lift the latch before passing through. Hal bent over, grasping Will Longstaffe's shoulder to pull him from his position face-down in the ditch. Will's head lolled back, revealing sightless eyes.

"My God!" breathed Justin, joining, them in time to see. "He's dead!"

"His neck is broken, just as if he'd been hanged!" said Hal quietly.

"That's justice," Ned said in pleased tones.

Chapter Twenty Five

It was very late in the day, and long after all the fuss had died down, that Sheriff Hughes had finally consented to believe the evidence of his eyes. Mr Fenton had done marvelling over the inequity of Will Longstaffe and both had declined to take supper with them. A weary group of people sat in the soft twilight. They did not talk so much now, but seemed to reflect on the drama of the day.

There was a long pause and they'd all declared they'd talk no more of it that evening when Aunt Margery asked, "Tell me, Justin, how was it you said none knew where the dagger had been found? I knew, so did Kate."

"I think almost everybody knew, ma'am," replied Justin ruefully. "I was merely hoping and praying Will might not know that we knew! You see, we had absolutely nothing against him that we could prove. I was trying desperately to trick him into admitting he had killed Mr Henry Westwood."

"None of it would have stood up in a court of law, young man," remarked Francis, who sat by his wife, lazily drinking a cup of wine.

"No sir, I am very aware of that. I was trying to get him to confess. A confession was the only hope we had! That or the end we did get." He hesitated, his eyes going past Margery to the soft evening beyond. "Perhaps the way it ended was better for all concerned."

"Certainly neater for us, although I'm not sure Sheriff Hughes will ever be convinced we didn't have a hand in it somewhere. He would have sooner found me guilty," said Francis, reflectively.

Margery sighed. "I cannot think why we did not see it earlier. After all we knew Will Longstaffe was Uncle Henry's—"

"Bastard," Ned supplied the word as she hesitated. Then as Hal stared, he added, "Oh, did you not know?"

Justin closed his eyes in disbelief. "Are you saying, Ned, you knew all along?"

"Yes, didn't all of you? I thought everyone knew."

Justin was forced to resist the impulse to smack Ned's head and Hal sat looking stunned. "That was why he hated me so! Do you think it was he my uncle had named as heir in his earlier will?"

"I think it likely. Did Mr Fenton not tell you your

Uncle Henry said he'd never leave this land for his brother to ruin? And that his will would set the cat amongst the pigeons?" Justin asked quietly.

"Or even set up a flutter in the dovecote," Hal smiled sadly at the aptness of it. "So all Will's love for my uncle turned to hate and he killed his own father."

Justin nodded. "So it would seem. Alas, we have no proof of this, and so it must remain idle speculation, as Sheriff Hughes took great pains to point out. Like him, I doubt the horse coper's testimony, if he could be persuaded to give it, would stand up. And that was if we could track down the man from Ross. I imagine the gentleman's horse is long gone. I think Will was hoping Hal would prove unsuitable. Had he not said Hal would be little better than a fop or a fool? Perhaps he was hoping you'd refuse to marry the heiress your uncle had chosen. Who can say? Then, when you proved neither a fool nor difficult, he was set to teach you. It must have seemed an insult."

"I can well understand his hatred of me," agreed Hal.

"Never forget he killed his father, your uncle, in cold blood. He then did his best to make it look as if your father was guilty, and would, but for the King's Grace, have seen him hanged for murder. I don't think he would have stopped there either. I think you'd have been the next target, and finally as you'd wavered in your allegiance, Ned, you would have followed."

"This is foolish!" cried Hal, "Mayhap it all happened as you say, but to kill Ned and I? No, it cannot be! Did he think none would suspect?"

"Once a murderer has killed successfully his confidence grows and begins to know no bounds," Justin replied. "I don't suppose you'd have suffered a dagger in the heart, Hal. No, yours most likely would have been an accident—out riding perhaps? Then the tale would go round that the Westwoods were cursed, to prepare the way for Ned's end. Don't you see? He was close to you all, so his opportunities were endless."

"It is as well you've thought it all out, Mr Danvers, for that Sheriff Hughes had little idea. He seemed very confused I thought," said Aunt Kate with a look of admiration for Justin.

"As well he may," agreed Francis.

"Bah! That odious man! I do not know why he is allowed to come here! If I were mistress of Westwood, I would have never let him set foot in the place again!" cried Jacqueline.

"I very much doubt he ever will, Jacqueline, so Libby need not consider it," Hal's words came sharply.

"*Bon!*" she replied, ignoring this barb. "Me, I am relieved in my mind by this assurance, now we may all sleep sounder in our beds!"

"Not you and I, my lovely," said Francis. He had subjected his son's shadowed face to a thoughtful stare for some time, now he spoke out. "At least only for this one night. Tomorrow we are off on our travels again."

"Travels? What is this?" she demanded, turning to stare at him.

"I have a little business to transact in Holland and then we shall travel on to Paris for a while. Perhaps we shall stay all the summer, perhaps longer, who can say?"

"*Paris! Bon!*" Jacqueline cried with delight as she clapped her hands. "Now you tell me something I like. But how is this, Francis? First you say I must come to England to make the home for your daughters, now you say we must go to France!"

"Yes, you'll be better there, where I can keep an eye on you," Francis murmured, his eyes veiled. He hadn't needed the hints Margery had insisted on dropping into his ear not half an hour since. He could tell from the manner in which Jacqueline looked at Hal's wife there was trouble in the air. He was a fool, he supposed, to have brought home so young and lovely a wife. He'd imagined at first it wouldn't matter. A young man often fell in love with his new step-mother, if she was young and pretty enough. Provided that woman was one of character, no harm need be done, but Jacqueline was a different kettle of fish. He'd seen as soon as he arrived Hal was uneasy in her presence. And when he'd spoken to him of it there had been something different in his manner. There was an awkwardness in the way Hal talked, which had never been there before. It was obvious she was up to her usual tricks, and it would be better to remove her from where she could make the sort of mischief she so delighted in. He must leave his son to make his way in peace with his young wife.

Jacqueline had been thinking over his words and had not liked the inherent criticism implied in them. "What of your daughters? Where are they to go?"

"In the batch of letters, which arrived from London the other day, I received a letter from Mr Eustace agreeing terms for Jane's dowry," Francis replied. "There is no reason the wedding can't go forward as planned in the autumn. Hal has said he will attend to all the details. In the meantime, Jane will return here to keep company with Bess." His slightly amused glance travelled to Justin, who, he noted, had been careful to select a seat at some distance from his love. "As to sweet Bess's fate, I cannot say. None has yet made her an offer."

Justin's head came up at this, his eyes flying to the older man's face. "Is one given to understand, sir, that you have abandoned your search for a great match for Bess?"

Francis grinned. "I'll admit I don't think I could find one better that the one staring me in the face. Young man, you've saved what reputation I had left to me. I am weary of the task of finding suitable husbands for my daughters. If you want her, she's yours!"

"Father!" protested Hal as he got to his feet. Libby turned to him in consternation, certain his dislike of Justin would prevent this hoped-for union. "Sir, is that not an offhand way in which to present so lovely a jewel to one to whom you owe your life and honour?"

Hal went to where Bess sat, taking her hand and making her rise, too, as he turned to confront Justin.

"Justin, as a family we owe you much. More than we could ever repay you. We are glad to consent to your betrothal to Bess, secure in the knowledge that she'll find a good and gentle husband in you."

Libby clasped Hal's sleeve as Bess took Justin's hand, her eyes starry. "Oh, Hal, thank you, thank you!" she whispered.

"Tell your father to write to Hal, young man. He'll pass the letter on to my lawyer to settle everything,"

Francis said, as his sisters sighed contentedly. Both Margery and Kate had been loud in praise of Libby's brother and not backward in hinting at his reward.

Francis's eyes travelled to Ned, who was looking in patent disgust from Bess and Justin to Hal standing with his arm about Libby's waist, as she congratulated her brother. "Well, young Ned, have you had enough of these lovers? Will you throw in your lot with me and come adventuring?"

Ned looked to him, his eyes bright, plainly drawn by the prospect. Then as Hal, his attention caught by the question, turned to look, he shook his head decidedly. "No sir," he said simply. "I can't do that! I've to stay here and help Hal. We agreed it earlier. He says now Will Longstaffe is gone, he'll need me more than ever!"

"Is that so?" asked Francis in surprise. "Am I to leave all my children in your care, Hal?"

"Libby and I would be honoured if you would do so, sir. And I can think of no better place for them to be, than here at Westwood Hall."

⚜

Watch for the next Hal Westwood Restoration Mystery:

The Storm in the Wassail Bowl

ISBN 0-9740949-1-9